The Jezebel Letters

The Jezebel Letters

Religion and Politics in Ninth-Century Israel

Eleanor Ferris Beach

Fortress Press / Minneapolis

THE JEZEBEL LETTERS

Copyright © 2005 Augsburg Fortress. All rights reserved. Except for brief quotations in critical articles or reviews, no part of this book may be reproduced in any manner without prior written permission from the publisher. Write: Permissions, Augsburg Fortress, Box 1209, Minneapolis, MN 55440-1209.

Scripture quotations are from the New Revised Standard Version Bible, copyright (c) 1989 by the Division of Christian Education of the National Council of the Churches of Christ in the USA and used by permission.

Excerpts from James Pritchard, *Ancient Near Eastern Texts Relating to the Old Testament,* Third Edition, with Supplement © 1950, 1955, 1969, renewed 1978 by Princeton University Press are reprinted by permission of Princeton University Press.

Anson Rainey's translation of the Tel Dan Incription from his article, "The Suffix Conjugation Pattern in Ancient Hebrew Tense and Modal Functions," *Ancient Near Eastern Studies* 40 (2003), is used by permission.

Drawings are by the author. The source of each drawing is given on pages 193–200.
Photographs are by the author unless otherwise credited.

Cover art: *Seal.* Provenance Unknown, 9th–8th cent. BCE, IAA 65-321. The Israel Museum, Jerusalem. Used by permission. "*Woman at a Window.*" Detail of furniture. Ivory, formerly gilded. From Arslan Tash (Hadatu), Syria. 8th cent. BCE. Inv.: AO 11459, Louvre, Paris, France. Réunion des Musées Nationaux / Art Resource, N.Y. Used by permission.

Author photo: Author is standing in front of a plaster cast of Shalmaneser III's Black Obelisk, showing Jehu bowing (at the Oriental Institute Museum at the University of Chicago). Photo by Robert Haak.

Jacket and book design: Zan Ceeley
Maps: Robert Cronan, Lucidity Information Design

Library of Congress Cataloging-in-Publication Data
Beach, Eleanor Ferris
  The Jezebel letters : religion and politics in ninth-century Israel / Eleanor Ferris Beach.
    p. cm.
  Includes bibliographical references (p.   ) and index.
  ISBN 0-8006-3754-2 (hardcover : alk. paper)
    1. Jezebel, Queen, consort of Ahab, King of Israel. 2. Palestine
—Politics and government. 3. Palestine—History—To 70 A.D.
  I. Title.
BS580.J45B43 2005
222'.5092—dc22
                                    2005020873

The paper used in this publication meets the minimum requirements of American National Standard for Information Sciences—Permanence of Paper for Printed Library Materials, ANSI Z329.48-1984.

Manufactured in the U.S.A.
09   08   07   06   05   1   2   3   4   5   6   7   8   9   10

Contents

Preface ix
Introduction 1
Maps 8
Chronology 12
Genealogy 16

1 Prologues / 17
The Conspirators' Prologue (822 BCE) 17
Jizebul's Prologue (824 BCE) 18

2 Tyre / 20
Omri Becomes King of Israel (text, 885 BCE) 20
Jizebul's Betrothal to Ahab (memoir, 883 BCE) 21
The Covenant Ceremony on Baal's Headland (memoir, 882 BCE) 25
Hymn of Praise to Baal (text) 28

3 Tirzah / 30
Jizebul Writes to Ethbaal: A Letter from Tirzah (letter, 881 BCE) 30
Life at Tirzah (memoir, 881 BCE) 31
Jizebul Writes to Ethbaal: The Birth of Atalyah (letter, 881 BCE) 35
Names and Gods (memoir, 881 BCE) 36

Contents

4 Samaria / 40

King Omri Acquires Samaria (text, 881 BCE) 40
Omri's Vision for Israel (memoir, 879 BCE) 40
Jizebul Writes to Ethbaal: The Move to Samaria (letter, 879 BCE) 44
The View from Samaria (memoir, 879 BCE) 45
Jizebul Writes to Ethbaal: Ashurnasirpal's Threat (letter, 876 BCE) 49
Ashurnasirpal II's Inscription (text, 875 BCE) 50
Sons of the Prophets (memoir, 875 BCE) 52

5 Baal's Headland / 55

Ahab Becomes King of Israel (text, 874 BCE) 55
King Ahab's Beginnings (memoir, 874 BCE) 55
Jizebul Writes to Ethbaal: A Plea for Covenant Renewal (letter, 873 BCE) 60
Eliyahu on Baal's Headland (text, 871 BCE) 61
Covenant Renewal and Rain (memoir, 871 BCE) 64
Hymn of Praise to Baal (text) 66

6 Jezreel / 70

Jehoshaphat Becomes King in Jerusalem (text, 869 BCE) 70
Shalom with Jehoshaphat (memoir, 869 BCE) 71
Naboth's Vineyard (text, 869 BCE) 74
Stopping the Blight at Jezreel (memoir, 869 BCE) 76

7 Beth-hakkherem / 80

Jehoshaphat's Beginnings (text, 869 BCE) 80
A Covenant Hymn (text) 81
Atalyah's Marriage (memoir, 866 BCE) 82
Jehoshaphat's Administration (text, 865 BCE) 85
Jizebul Writes to Atalyah: Concerns in Jerusalem (letter, 865 BCE) 86
The Fruits of *Shalom* (memoir, 858 BCE) 88
Shalmaneser III's First Year (text, 858 BCE) 90

8 Karkar / 92

Jizebul Writes to Baal-azzor: Tyre's Covenant with Israel (letter, 855 BCE) 92
Jizebul Writes to Atalyah: Preparations for War (letter, 853 BCE) 93
Shalmaneser III's Monolith Inscription (text, 853 BCE) 95
The Lessons of Karkar (memoir, 853 BCE) 96
The Death of Ahab (text, 853 BCE) 98
Ahab's *Marzeaḥ* (memoir, 853 BCE) 98

9 Ekron / 103

Ahaziah Becomes King in Israel (text, 853 BCE) 103
Jizebul Writes to Atalyah: Ahaziah's Beginnings (letter, 852 BCE) 103
A Royal Wedding Song from Samaria (text) 105
The Death of Ahaziah (text, 852 BCE) 106
How Ahaziah Died (memoir, 852 BCE) 108

10 Dibon / 111

Joram's Troubles with Moab (text, 850 BCE) 111
The Mesha Inscription (text, 850 BCE) 113
Insurrections (memoir, 845 BCE) 114
Jizebul Writes to Atalyah: Advice about Jehoram (letter, 845 BCE) 116
Jehoram's Administration (text, 845 BCE) 117

11 Damascus / 119

Elisha and Hazael of Aram (text, 843 BCE) 119
Jizebul Writes to Baal-azzor: Concerns about Hazael (letter, 843 BCE) 120
Jizebul Writes to Atalyah: Growing Dangers (letter, 843 BCE) 121
Hazael's Opportunity (memoir, 843–841 BCE) 122
Shalmaneser III's Description of Hazael (text, 845–841 BCE) 125
Ahaziyah Becomes King in Jerusalem (text, 841 BCE) 125

Contents

12 Ramoth-gilead / 127
Hazael's Victories: The Tel Dan Inscription (text, 841 BCE) 127
Jehu's Revolt (text, 841 BCE) 128
What Did Not Happen at Jezreel (memoir, 841 BCE) 132
Jehu's Purges (text, 841 BCE) 133
Jizebul Writes to Atalyah: Jehu's Coup (letter, 841 BCE) 135
Shalmaneser III's Victory (text, 841 BCE) 136
Jehu's Losses (memoir, 840 BCE) 137

13 Jerusalem / 139
Atalyah Becomes Queen in Jerusalem (text, 841 BCE) 139
How Atalyah Became Queen (memoir, 841 BCE) 139
Jizebul Writes to Atalyah: Sad News (letter, 837 BCE) 142
The Death of Atalyah (text, 835 BCE) 144
Who Is King Jehoash? (memoir, 835 BCE) 145
A Psalm for Relief (text) 147

14 Dor / 149
Jizebul Writes to Jehozabad: Advice (letter, 826 BCE) 149
The Death of Jehoiada the Priest (text, 826 BCE) 151
Eclipse (memoir, 824 BCE) 152
The Return of Baal (text) 155

15 Epilogues / 157
Epilogue for Jozacar and Jehozabad (text) 157
Author's Epilogue 158

Notes to the Story 162
Notes to the Illustrations 193
Glossary 201
Works Cited 209
Suggestions for Further Reading 214
Index of Biblical and Other Ancient Texts 217

Preface

She strides into the room, a tall staff in her right hand, hair covered by a long, gauzy scarf with gold threads shimmering through multicolored bands. She pauses, looking intently into the faces staring at her.

"Stand up, stand up I say! Don't you know enough to rise before the queen?"

They stand awkwardly, looking out of the corner of their eyes to see if everyone else obeys. She points the staff at them.

"And say 'Your Majesty' before you ask your questions."

The noble youths are not accustomed to being scolded. This imperious woman is not at all like the seductive one they had heard about. And she obviously is not going to invite them to the women's quarters to share intimate stories over raisin cakes and wine. And yet, there is something about her eyes.

With a disconcerting smile, she approves of their confusion and starts talking politics.

The Jezebel Letters gives readers an extended exposure to what students experience when "Jezebel" visits my classes. What would you want to ask her? What would she be willing to disclose? She has chosen to share certain letters, to augment her political memoirs with documents from others. She knows what you've heard about her. Whoever you are, she wants to change your mind.

My own interest in Jezebel did not begin as a quest for the historical Jezebel or for a feminist Jezebel. She arrived, uninvited, in a flash of intuition shortly after I had completed a research paper on ancient Near Eastern ivory carvings. Reading 2 Kings 9, I was struck by how much her literary death scene resembled the "woman at the window" ivory design I had just studied. How could I prove that a biblical author intended this allusion? How would an early audience have understood the resemblance? These questions have fueled my scholarship on the connection between the visual and literary arts of the biblical world.

But Jezebel kept showing up. In an introductory Bible class where students had only hearsay knowledge of her bad reputation, they looked in vain for anything about her sex life in the texts. In a course on the prophets, students noticed that the Bible doesn't even mention the mighty Assyrians in the ninth century BCE when Assyrian texts do mention her husband Ahab's military prowess. A women's studies class puzzled over why the Bible condemns the foreign Queen Jezebel as manipulative, but it praises the foreign Queen Esther for using her beauty and skill in bed to win a crown while deceiving her husband the king about her identity. Was Jezebel—the literate political wife of one of Israel's most astute kings—really a slut?

The Jezebel Letters invites readers to become detectives, to interrogate multiple witnesses about Jezebel's situation in the ninth century: biblical texts, ancient Near Eastern records and artifacts, and the lady herself. Readers may come to recognize what detectives take for granted: that no single witness has the complete story, that each witness's testimony is shaped by the experiences and perspectives through which their perception of truth is filtered. If any one witness controls the interpretation, the truth will be shortchanged.

While I hope your sleuthing will be both entertaining and enlightening, I need to remind readers that the outcome matters a great deal to real women today. The image of a God-despising, conniving, and seductive Jezebel has been used for two thousand years to demean women, to put them in "their place." Although I do not personally share all the values of the Jezebel in these *Letters*, I take issue more with those who continue to use her name and biblical authority to undermine women's empowerment and well-being.

I wrote this book to dismantle the myth about Jezebel.

My investigation is less about sex and more about religion and politics and who shapes the discourse that justifies or criticizes public policies, then and now. The biblical condemnations of whoring "females"—Israel (Hosea 2) and Jerusalem (Isaiah 1, Jeremiah 2–4, Ezekiel 16 and 23)—were insults aimed by male prophets at the male heads of society: at the rulers, other prophets, and priests (Mic 3:9-12), not at any woman. The critiques were part of larger debates among many parties about national priorities, although the biblical account is often a monologue. For Jezebel to have attracted the rhetoric of harlotry, she must have been a person of considerable public power. Putting Jezebel into historical and cultural context to understand more fully the biblical authors' response to her is a strategy I recommend for studying any biblical reference before applying it to today's issues.

This book about Jezebel, art, religion, and politics has benefited from many friendly conversations, here and in the Middle East, and I regret not being able to acknowledge all my intellectual companions over thirty years in the space of a paragraph. Graduate study, discussions with students and colleagues, talks to adult groups, archaeological experiences, scholarly presentations, and opportunities to publish have helped me to articulate my thoughts. If you are reading this and were part of such an occasion, you have my warmest thanks. I will mention my gratitude to the editorial midwives who helped me deliver the volume: Edgar W. Smith Jr., who was the first reader; K. C. Hanson, who brought the manuscript to Fortress Press, and Michael West, who saw it through; Ann Delgehausen and Zan Ceeley, who transformed it into a book. I especially thank my husband, Robert Haak, for being a contrarian conversation partner and for challenging me to look for the political dynamics behind biblical texts when I only wanted to look at pictures.

Seal of Jizebul

Introduction

One might think that Jezebel needs no introduction. Wasn't she that idolatrous queen in the Bible, the one who painted her eyes to seduce someone and got pushed out of a window?

The biblical storyline goes like this.

Daughter of Ethbaal, the king of Tyre, and wife of the northern Israelite king Ahab, Jezebel is held responsible for Ahab's building a temple to her foreign god Baal in Israel's capital, Samaria (1 Kgs 16:31-33). Ahab appears weak and unable to oppose her killing prophets of Yhwh,○ Israel's national god (1 Kgs 18:3-4). Ahab also benefits directly from her manipulations of the judicial system to acquire Naboth's vineyard by perjury and murder (1 Kings 21). The army commander Jehu meets her son King Ahaziah outside Jezreel, castigates the king for his mother's "whoredoms and sorceries," then kills him and drives a chariot into the city to claim the throne. Jezebel dresses up and calls to Jehu from a palace window, only to be thrown down and trampled by his horses (2 Kings 9). Jehu claims to be fulfilling the prophet Elijah's divinely ordained curses against Ahab and Jezebel. A warrior for Yhwh, Jehu entices the followers of Baal into their temple, then massacres them (2 Kings 10). Jezebel's Baal-worshiping daughter Atalyah seizes the throne of the southern kingdom in Jerusalem after Jehu has also killed that king,

---

○This mark indicates that there is a note on this item at the end of the book. Notes are organized by chapter title, document title, page number, and reference phrase, in this case, Yhwh.

her son. Seven years later, a priestly coup reestablishes worship of Yhwh and a rightful king in Jerusalem by assassinating Atalyah (2 Kings 11).

This cluster of sexual, religious, and political associations is reinforced in Revelation, where a prophetess's claim to Christian leadership is condemned with sexual imagery (Rev 2:18-23). Again, religious differences and women's political power converge under Jezebel's tainted name. Much later, "Jezebel" is the brush opponents use to tar Catholic queens—Isabella of Spain and the Marys of England and Scotland—by casting aspersions on their morality, religion, and politics.○

Because her name entered our common language with certain connotations, a dictionary defines the noun "jezebel" as "an impudent, shameless, or morally unrestricted woman."○ In recent times, Jezebel has been reduced to this purely sexual referent, as in Ann-Margaret's 1970s Las Vegas nightclub act, "Jezebel Desirée" and 1990s Latin singer Ricky Martin's sultry "Jezabel (Kiss and Tell)." A careful reading of the Bible, however, will unearth no mention of Jezebel's sexual conduct, shameless or otherwise. One will find only a taunt about the queen mother's harlotries from the mouth of a usurper, Jehu, who insults the king he is about to murder. This characterization is also typically used symbolically of "going after false gods" in biblical condemnations, rather than being descriptive of someone's behavior. Jezebel's appearance at the window as a "painted lady" loses its sexual undertones when one hears her mocking reproach to Jehu, that he will last no longer than Zimri, a usurper for seven days (1 Kgs 16:8-20). Jezebel's is not the only biblical story in which the components of a foreign woman, idolatry, and deceptive sexuality constitute a literary *topos* in the books of Joshua through 2 Kings. They are literary and ideological conventions, and they do not form an accurate description of the historical Jezebel.

The biblical name Jezebel may be a distorted form of the Phoenician phrase ʾi zᵉbul,○ alluding to her god as zᵉbul, "Prince" Baal. *Zebel*, "dung," transforms the divine title into a derogatory form, much the way Baal-zebul is modified into Baal-zebub (2 Kgs 1:2), which produced the notorious "Lord of the Flies" in the Greek version. In the following texts, the biblical translations retain the denigrating Hebrew version, Jezebel, but the other documents use a reconstructed and Anglicized original, Jizebul.

Introduction

The Jizebul in these letters and memoirs is an astute, well-educated, and well-informed royal woman, who participated with authority in her family's political business during much of the ninth century BCE. Documents from such women were preserved in Mesopotamian archives from as early as fifteen hundred years before Jizebul's time.○ Women's correspondence and journals are now valued as important resources for historical inquiry in many periods. It is only lack of preservation, not lack of their having been composed, that prevents us from using women's letters for the ninth century BCE. The few ancient examples of Hebrew and Phoenician letters from women and women's seals contribute further reminders of women's literacy and correspondence.○ I believe I am re-creating Jizebul's role and the genre of her letters, not inventing them.

What did she have to write about?

The ninth century was a crucial period in Israelite history. Behind the biblical stories lies the turmoil of a transitional era, whose developments included the evolving nature of monarchy, transformation of kinship-based subsistence economies into state-based extractive production, the challenge of military invasions into the small Levantine states by the Assyrian empire, the involvement of priests in economics and governance, and the activity of prophetic figures in political debates. All of these elements were in ferment, and all were at markedly different stages in 800 BCE than they had been in 900 BCE. Jizebul was the political link between three active parties at this time: the commercially prosperous island city of Tyre ruled by her father Ethbaal;○ the agriculturally rich and militarily successful region of Israel,○ governed from Samaria in the central highlands by her husband Ahab's family; and the southern hill country known in the Bible as Judah, ruled from Jerusalem by King David's descendants who married women from Ahab's family.

Statehood in Israel and Judah was not achieved in a linear process but was frequently undermined and eventually thwarted by militarily and economically stronger neighbors or distant empires. The biblical account in I Kings depicts the monarchy of northern Israel as a breakaway endeavor, a rebellious state characterized by religious apostasy and dynastic instability unlike its older Davidic base in Jerusalem. *The Jezebel Letters* adopts and illustrates an alternative premise, held by a growing number of archaeologists and biblical scholars, that a more mature monarchy—

with its accompanying military establishment, administrative infrastructure, economic networks, and public building displays—emerged during the ninth century in Israel, under whose influence the southern kingdom was revived.○ In this view, the earlier "United Monarchy" under David and Solomon may well have existed as a brief strategic, administrative, and economic union of several regions under Jerusalem's control, but it was not a golden age, except in the creative memory of later Jerusalemite kings and priests who used it to validate their own standing. Ironically, Solomon's "achievements" may testify in part to the outreach of King Hiram of Tyre, who supported Davidic rule in Jerusalem a century before Jizebul's father, Ethbaal, stimulated Ahab's success in Samaria.

The documentary evidence for this period is not all contemporaneous with the events.

Document Types in This Collection

The Jezebel Letters includes two kinds of *fictional* documents: **letters**, reflecting events as they would have been perceived at the time, and Jizebul's **memoirs**, written near the end of her long life (yes, contrary to the biblical account). The letters open with formulae modeled after extant Phoenician and Hebrew letters; the memoirs have no ancient counterpart. All are fiction but not fantasy. They are based on recent archaeological investigations, historical texts, cultural history, and environmental and geographic conditions. If written in an expository style, this story could be considered nonfiction—a creative interpretation of historically grounded research.

But, readers, try to imagine that Jizebul's letters and memoirs are preserved on papyrus and parchment scrolls, recently found sealed inside jars in a cave overlooking the Jordan Valley, where they were hidden during the late ninth-century conspiracy of Jozacar and Jehozabad of Judah. The assassination of King Jehoash of Jerusalem (835–796 BCE?) by these two royal servants is a minor episode in 2 Kings 12 and 2 Chronicles 24, given little attention in either popular or scholarly biblical histories. For the purposes of this story, however, it is a pivotal moment in Jerusalem's monarchy and the occasion for gathering these documents.

Introduction

Why the two officials rebelled, and why Jizebul's writings would support their cause, unfolds throughout the whole story. Read the documents as you would a mystery, as clues to understanding the enigmatic prologues, which are full of references you will come to recognize as you get deeper into the story. Some of the clues are highlighted in boldface type in the texts. And defer the question of how Jizebul could have lived long enough to write memoirs when the Bible places her death several decades before the assassination of King Jehoash.

Those who expect titillating accounts of palace "affairs" should keep in mind the protocols restricting ancient women and the intended public use of Jizebul's letters and memoirs. Anything she would have allowed to be included in the conspirators' archives serves a political purpose. There are few candid revelations in the memoirs because she writes with self-protective understatement and innuendo to elicit the reader's agreement and sympathy. There are many murders but no explicit bedroom scenes. Remember that Jizebul's power derived from the status of her royal father, husband, and children. Any known indiscretion on her part could have been used to undermine them and to demote her, a risk I believe she would have been unwilling to take during their active reigns (and so I discount Jehu's reference to her "harlotries" as metaphor).

I have supplemented these "recently discovered" letters and memoirs with ancient accounts long known from the Bible and from ancient Near Eastern texts relevant to the period.○

The **biblical excerpts** are primarily from the Deuteronomistic "history" of 1–2 Kings, written and edited in the seventh to fifth centuries BCE (two to four hundred years after Jizebul!) from a Jerusalem-centered ideology. Notice that the biblical reports are all from the southern perspective, though some may be interpretations of northern annals. I use them to represent the polemic of the priestly Jehoiada clan in late ninth-century Jerusalem, when stories about Ahab's dynasty would have been in a formative stage. Jizebul is not mentioned in the later composition of parallel narratives in 1–2 Chronicles (probably from the fourth century BCE), but their interest in royal administration and priestly privilege adds some useful detail to the story. I have adapted the New Revised Standard Version's (NRSV) translation in some places to highlight the vivid idioms

Introduction

and terse style of a more literal rendering of the Hebrew. Royal names have been edited to avoid the same name being used for more than one king, a sometimes confusing biblical occurrence. The northern names are spelled in a contracted style, following a practice shown on seals to abbreviate the divine Name in them.◯

Several biblical **Psalms** long recognized for their "Canaanite" or northern Israelite origins have been included to show how some factions in Jerusalem absorbed this moving imagery from Baal traditions into Yhwh liturgy, rather than spurning it. I have adapted them by reinstating Baalist forms for the later Hebrew divine Name. Excerpts from **Ugaritic documents** are included to represent Late Bronze Age (1550–1200 BCE) religious literature (both oral and written) that may well have been part of Jizebul's heritage.

Monumental inscriptions from Assyria, Moab, and Aram are the most contemporary records for ninth-century events. They must be read as royal propaganda, uniformly favorable to the ruler whose exploits they report. They are "historical" as artifacts but no less biased than Jizebul's "newly discovered" letters and the later Jerusalem-centered biblical accounts.

All these documents have been arranged in chronological order according to the date of events they describe, not by the date of their (supposed) writing. Dates in the table of contents likewise refer to the events, not the documents.

Readers of the Bible are often discouraged by the many unfamiliar events, people, places, and empires. Several kinds of reference materials are included to help visitors to the biblical world. A **chronology**, adapted from the works of several scholars, tracks the generally agreed-upon dates for historical events (adjusted slightly in some cases to make for a feasible plot◯) and the actions of the story. A **genealogy** charts the marriage relations between the families of Ethbaal, Omri, and David. **Notes** for annotations to the story are indicated by a small moon mark (◯) in the text and are located at the end of the book. I encourage readers to consult the notes because they include things that the ancient authors would have taken for granted and therefore did not bother to explain. A **glossary** provides a brief description of names and terms, with an indication of their origin in the Bible, other document, or my imagination. Only four of

Introduction

the characters are fictional in the sense that they do not appear in ancient documents. The **maps** are extremely important references for understanding the tensions across a small region with open frontiers.

The **illustrations** give substance to Jizebul's perspective. They are included to give today's reader some of the visual cues shared by the ancient authors and audience, without whose connotations much of the biblical text's (and this story's) meaning is lost.º All are photographs and drawings of actual places and artifacts, as documented in the **notes to the illustrations.**

Although this project was begun before September 11, 2001, the writing was done in the aftermath of those events and during the U.S.-led wars in Afghanistan and Iraq. I am aware of having shaped some intentional allusions to recent situations in the Middle East, and others may have crept in. I hope my characters convey a sympathetic depiction of how national aspirations, religion, and international economic systems complicate people's attempts to live with security and material sufficiency amid changing political models of military dictatorships, tribal kinship loyalties, inherited monarchies, and imperial influence from abroad. There is, however, no consistent one-to-one match between any kingdom or person in the story and a modern government or person.

Map 1: Regional Features

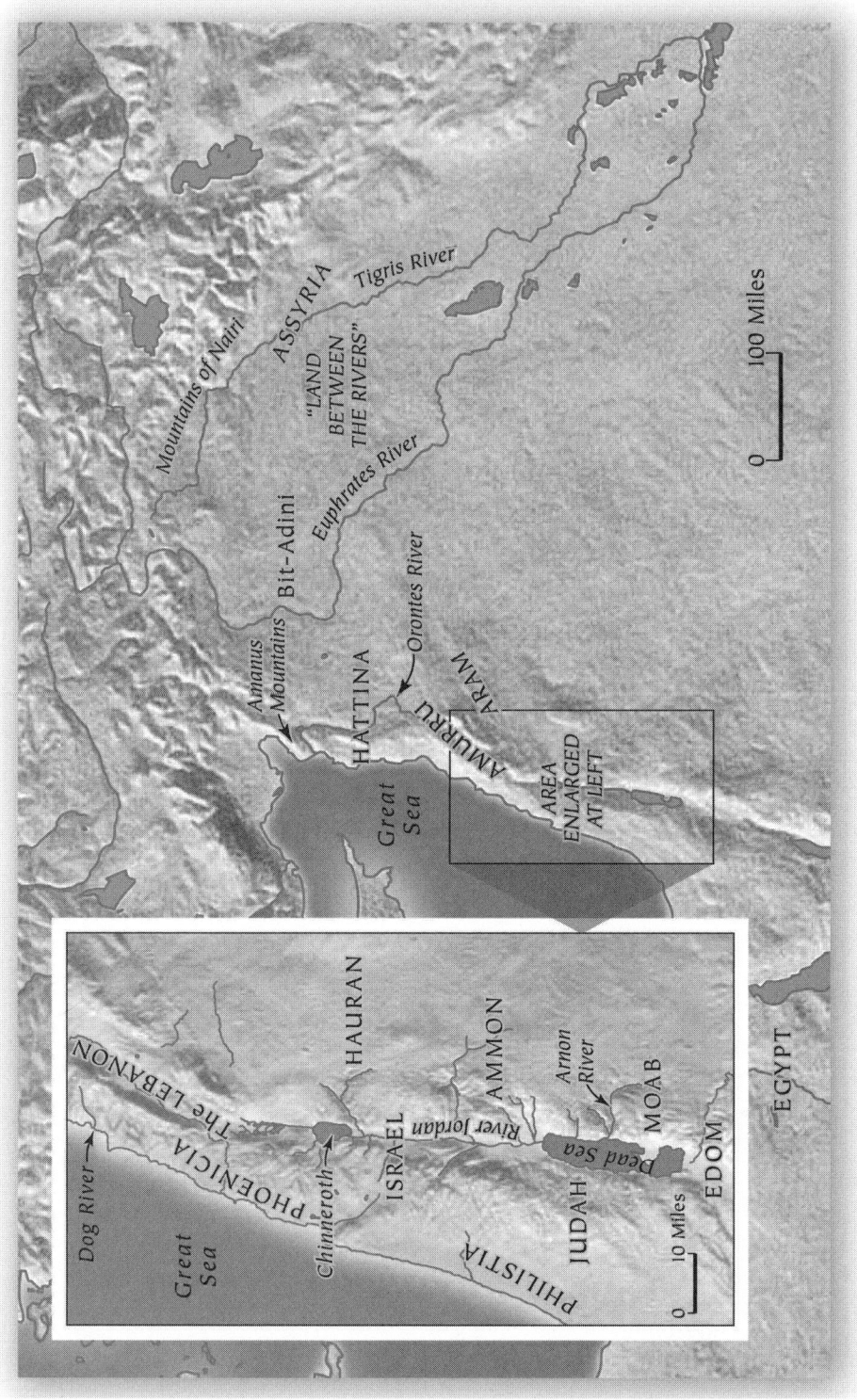

Map 2: Towns outside Israel

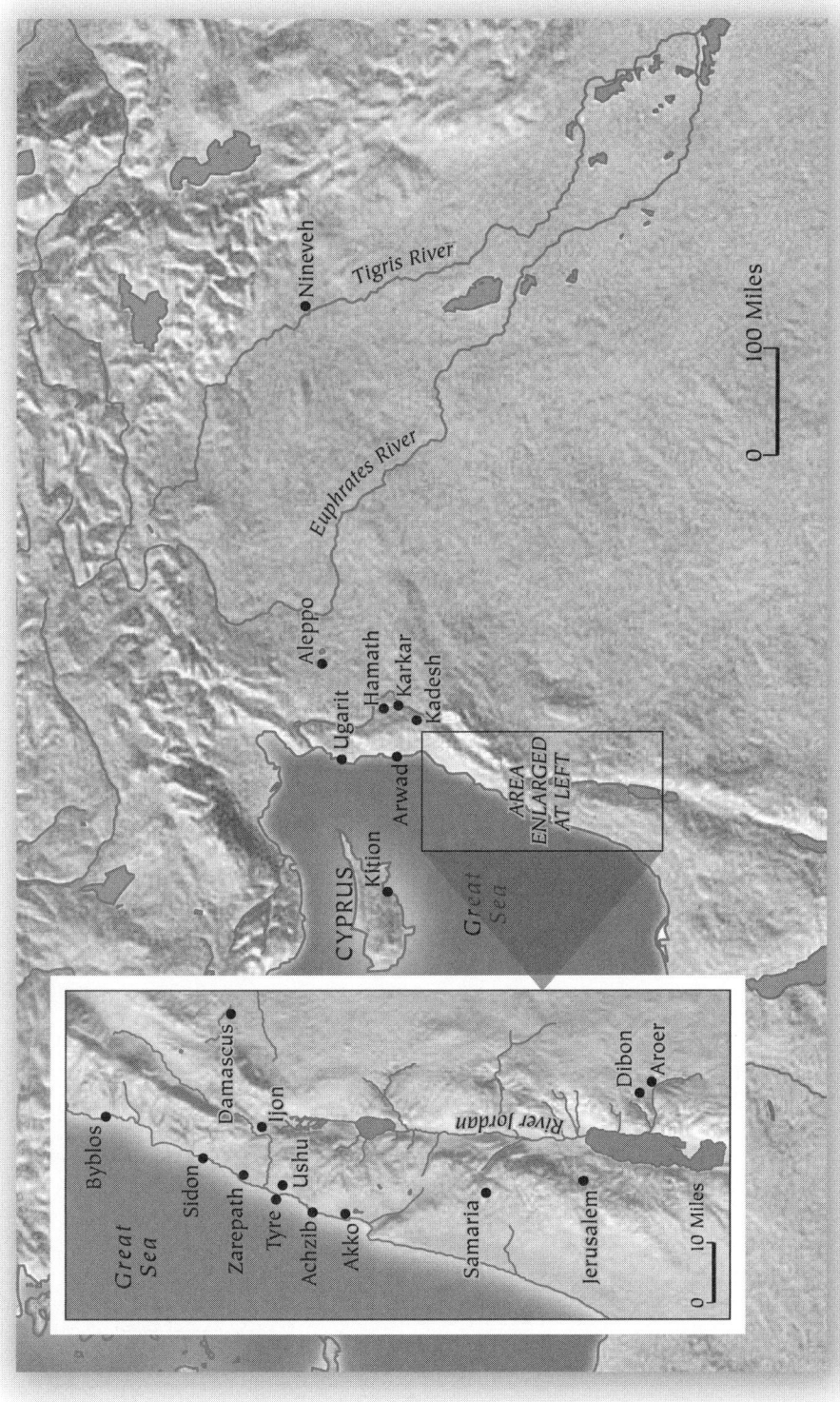

Map 3: Local Geography

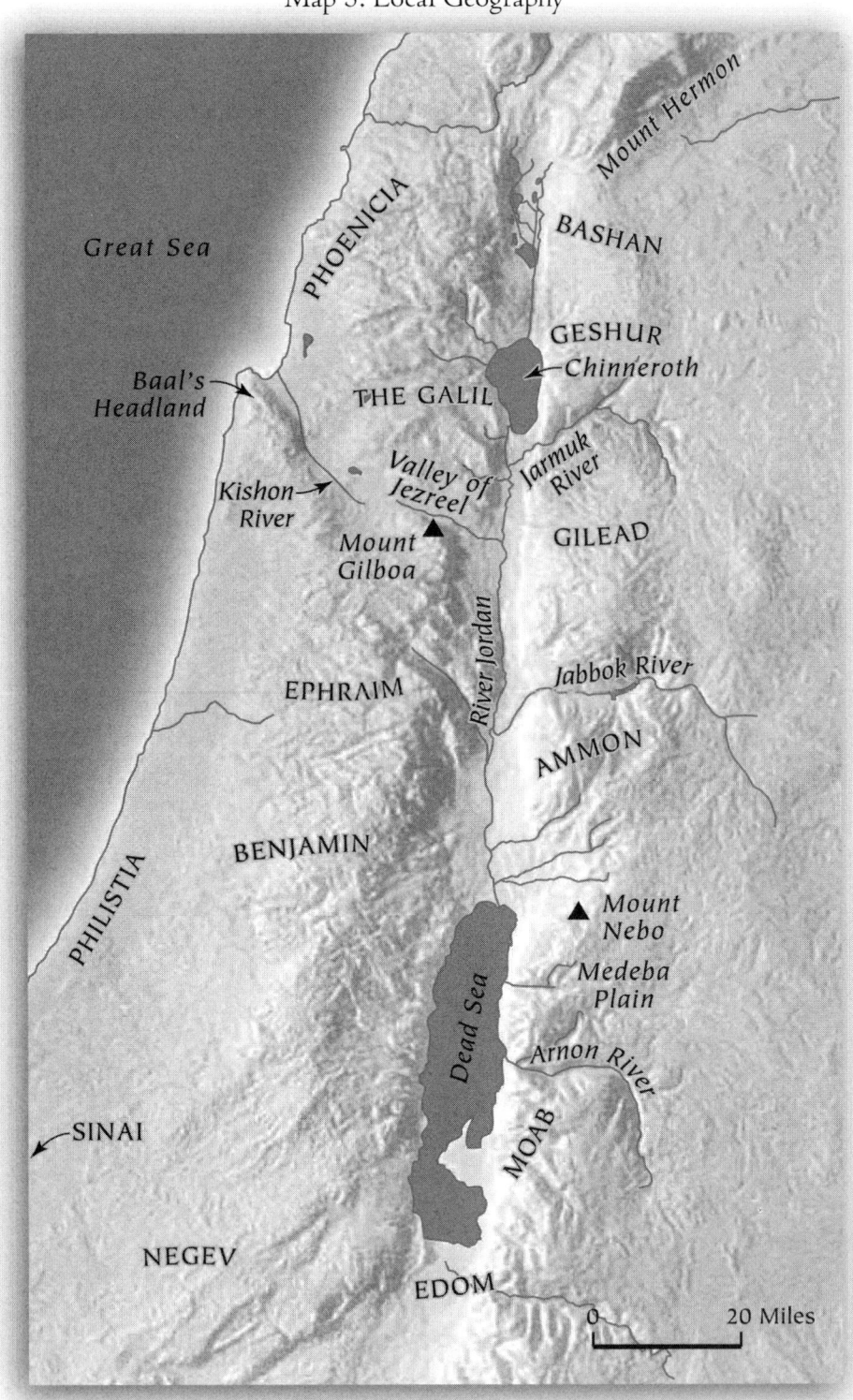

Map 4: Local Cities

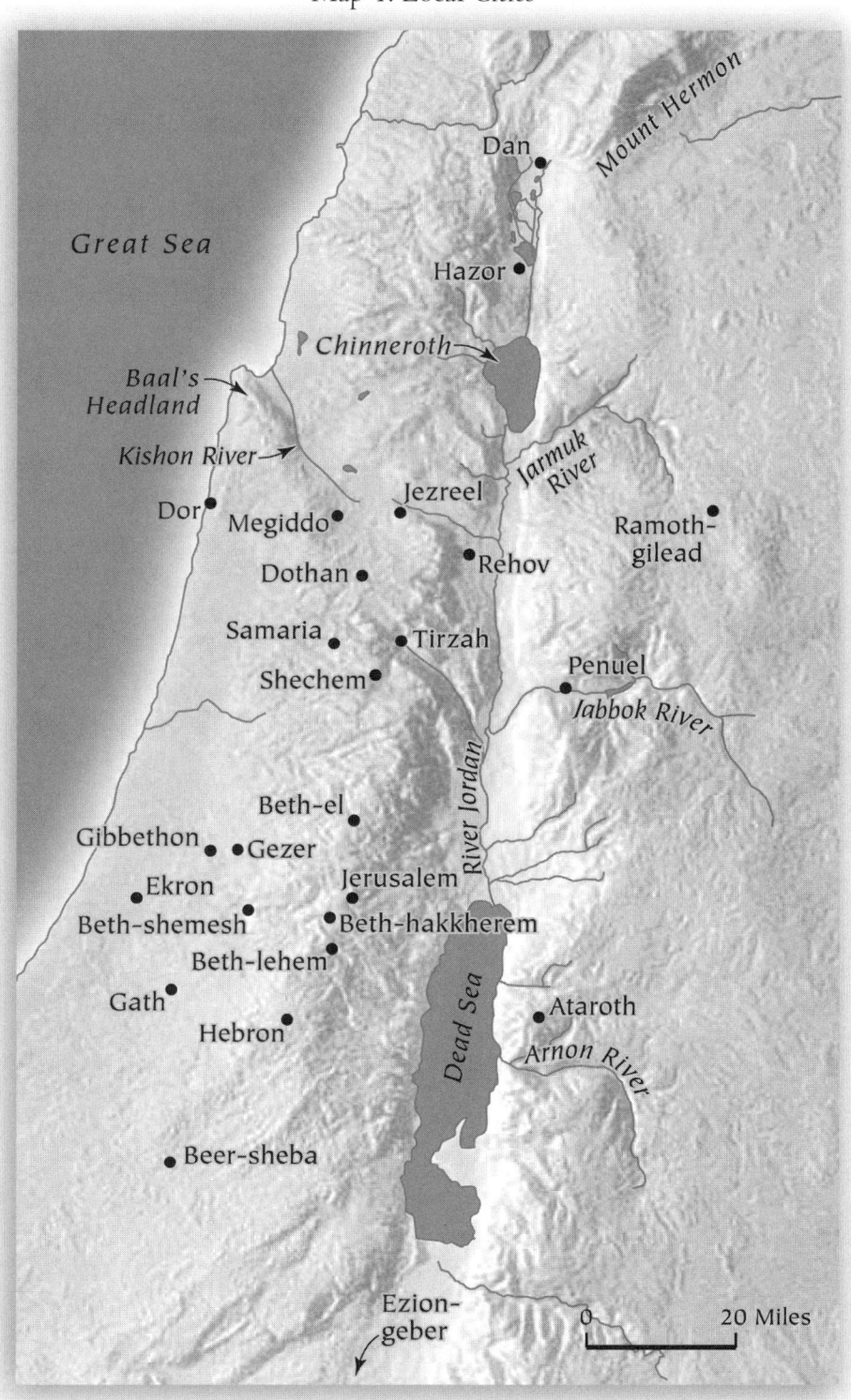

Chronology

Year	Tyre	Israel	Jerusalem	Assyria & Aram
890		Baasha is ruling in Tirzah	Asa is ruling in Jerusalem	
889				
888				
887	Ethbaal becomes king			
886		Baasha dies/son Elah rules		
885		Zimri kills Elah/ Omri kills Zimri		
884				Assyria: Ashurnasirpal II rules
883	Jizebul betrothed to Ahab			
882		Jizebul marries Ahab		
881		Atalyah born to Jizebul		
880				
879		Ahaziah born to Jizebul		Ashurnasirpal's palace dedicated
878				
877				
876	Baal-azzor born to Ethbaal			
875	Tyre pays Ashurbanipal	Joram born to Jizebul		Ashurnasirpal to Great Sea
874		Omri dies/son Ahab rules		Aram: Ben-hadad rules
873				
872			Jehoshaphat coregent	
871	Covenant renewed with Israel			
870				
869		Atalyah betrothed to Jehoram	Asa dies/ son Jehoshaphat rules	

continues on next page

Year	Tyre	Israel	Jerusalem	Assyria & Aram
868				
867				
866			Atalyah marries Jehoram	
865			Ahaziyah born to Atalyah	
864				
863				
862				
861				
860				
859				Ashurnasirpal dies
858				Shalmaneser III rules, to Great Sea
857				
856				
855	Ethbaal dies/son Baal-azzor rules			
854				
853		Ahab dies/son Ahaziah rules	Jehoram coregent	Shalmaneser in west to Karkar
852		Ahaziah dies/brother Joram rules		
851				
850				
849				Shalmaneser in west
848			Jehoshaphat dies/ son Jehoram rules	Shalmaneser in west
847				
846				
845				Shalmaneser in west

continues on next page

Year	Tyre	Israel	Jerusalem	Assyria & Aram
844				
843	Baal-azzor deals with Hazael		Ahaziyah marries Samaria girl	Aram: Hazael usurps
842				
841	Tyre pays, Jizebul to Dor	Joram killed/Jehu rules, pays	Jehoram dies/ Ahaziyah rules, killed/ Atalyah rules	Shalmaneser to Baal's Headland
840				
839				
838	Tyre sends payment			Shalmaneser's last west campaign
837				
836				
835			Atalyah killed/ Jehoash rules	
834				
833				
832				
831	solar eclipse	solar eclipse		
830	Baal-azzor dies/Mattan rules			
829				
828				
827				
826				
825			solar eclipse	
824	Jizebul writes memoirs			Shalmaneser dies/ Shamshi-Adad V rules

continues on next page

Year	Tyre	Israel	Jerusalem	Assyria & Aram
823	Jizebul dies, age 75			
822			Conspirators gather records	
821				
820				
819				
818				
817				
816				
815				
814		Jehu dies/son Jehoahaz rules		
813				
812				
811				Adad-Nirari III rules
810				

Genealogy

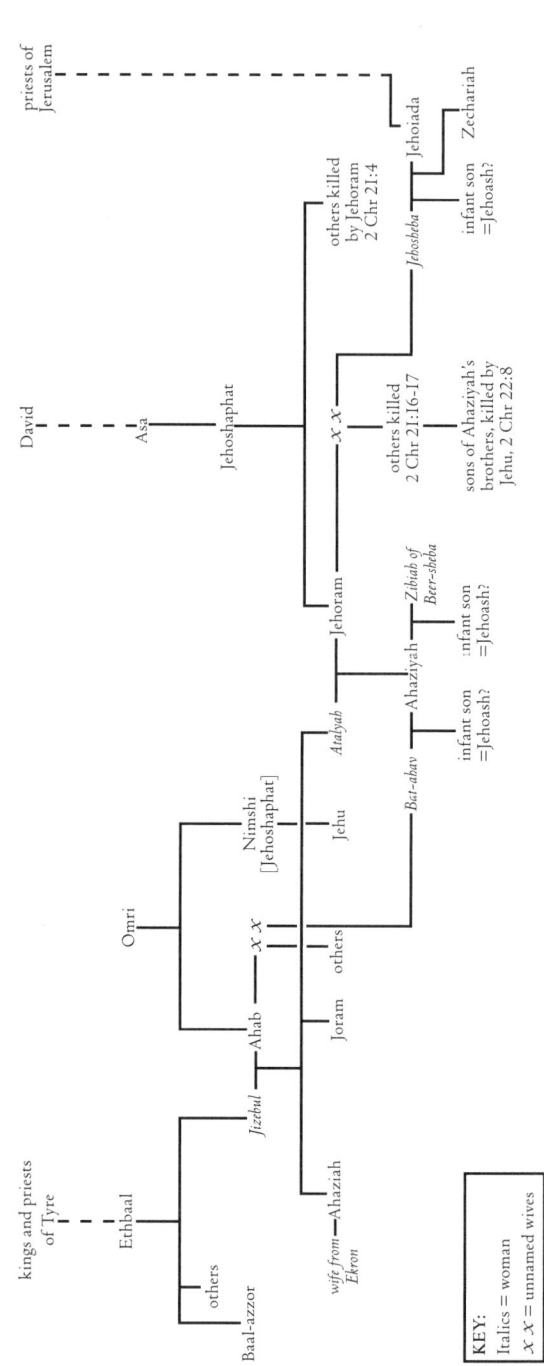

16

I
Prologues

The Conspirators' Prologue

822 BCE, LETTER FROM THE CONSPIRATORS TO THEIR SONS AND ALLIES,
INTRODUCING THE DOCUMENTS

*Jozacar of the Shemeathites, scribe of the king, and Jehozabad, commander of a thousand in the king's army, servants of our lord Jehoash, king of the House of David in Jerusalem, send to greet our sons and those who come after us, seeking truth. We bless you by Y*HWH*.*

In the thirteenth year of our lord Jehoash, many lies justify his bowing down to Hazael of Aram. Scribes of the priest Jehoiada and his son Zechariah spread falsehoods to shield the king from our charge that he is not walking rightly in the path of his fathers of the House of David. We, like others who point the finger, have enduring loyalty to that House. We stand before our lord the king in the offices of our fathers before us, since the days of King Jehoshaphat. Our families served King Jehoram son of Jehoshaphat, and his son Ahaziyah, and the gevirah° *Atalyah, whom Jehoiada killed. May their names be preserved in honor. Our lord King Jehoash has been a weak branch from the root of Jesse, bending to the priests' windy words. Unless he amends his ways, he may be cut off.*

Since the reign of King Jehoshaphat, the shalom of the House of David in Jerusalem has been linked by covenant and kinship to the House of Omri in

Samaria. In that brotherhood, our people were blessed. The priests who led our lord the king away from the path of shalom by seeking the favor of Aram violated their sacred trust, taking the wealth of the land for their own gain. In Samaria, also, wicked counselors speak against our brotherhood, while the House of Omri loses its place among the great kingdoms. We have pledged ourselves to restore this union, and if we are not successful, then may our sons take up the cause for the shalom of their own children.

Fearing that the truth may be lost, we have gathered evidence to prove our claim, should we perish in the endeavors at hand. The scrolls preserved here are true reports, faithfully copied from the archives of the gevirah Atalyah and her mother. That lady, Jizebul, who dictated her recollections at our request, died last year, and her ashes were buried at Dor. May her name be preserved in honor.

May these documents testify to the enduring bonds of covenant between the House of David and the House of Omri, over many generations.

May any man who denies those covenant bonds have his sword turned against him.

And may the two lands now ravaged by Hazael of Aram, rod of YHWH's wrath for these betrayals, live again in the peace and prosperity of brotherhood under their kindred kings.

Jizebul's Prologue

824 BCE, LETTER FROM JIZEBUL TO THE CONSPIRATORS' SONS AND ALLIES

Jizebul, daughter of Ethbaal king of Tyre, wife of Ahab king of Israel, gevirah *of Ahaziah and Joram kings of Israel, and mother of Atalyah* gevirah *of Ahaziyah king in Jerusalem, sends to greet those who seek the* shalom *of the House of Omri and the House of David. I bless you to* YHWH *and his Asherah.*°

Jozacar and Jehozabad, two servants loyal to the House of David, came to me at Dor. They entreated me to record how the House of David in Jerusalem cut a covenant with the House of Omri in Samaria forever, a covenant to which their King Jehoash is heir. They report to me what falsehoods are being sown in Jerusalem and Samaria so I may uproot them.

Prologues

I escaped from Jehu's treacheries at Jezreel, but now I am old and may not outlive him. His prophets and scribes in Samaria will speak cunning words to his advantage, just as priests in Jerusalem plant lies about my daughter Atalyah, the gevirah whom they killed, and the House of David, which they seek to control. So I must set down my testimony.

⁂

"Your mother Jezebel is a witch and a whore." Sheqer! *A lie! Who would judge a woman by a soldier's taunt? Who would turn the name of the Prince to dung?*○

*My lord Ahab and I were cursed by Y*HWH *the god of Israel for honoring Baal Shamem the god of Tyre.*○ Sheqer!

*My lord Ahab and I were cursed by Y*HWH *the god of Israel for taking the vineyard of Naboth the Jezreelite.* Sheqer!

*Jehu was appointed by Y*HWH *the god of Israel to kill my son Joram king of Israel and my grandson Ahaziyah king in Jerusalem.* Sheqer!

My daughter Atalyah, gevirah *of Ahaziyah in Jerusalem, treacherously seized the throne and killed the sons of the king.* Sheqer!

Jehoash, now king in Jerusalem, walked faithfully in the path of his fathers of the House of David when he obeyed the priests and sent tribute to Hazael of Aram. Sheqer!

⁂

May all who beget these deceptive words see their children and grandchildren killed before their eyes.

May the work of Jozacar and Jehozabad prosper. May the reports they gather be preserved. May those who receive these writings have wisdom to discern the truth in them.

May the brothers in the two kingdoms live together again as one. May their union shield them from Hazael of Aram so they may enjoy the fruits of their own land.

Sealed by my own hand.

2

Tyre

Omri Becomes King of Israel

885 BCE, EVENTS IN THE NORTHERN KINGDOM OF ISRAEL, AS DESCRIBED MUCH LATER BY PRIESTLY SCRIBES FROM JERUSALEM○

In the twenty-sixth year of Asa king of Judah, Elah son of Baasha began to reign over Israel in Tirzah; he reigned two years.

But his servant Zimri, commander of half his chariots, conspired against him. When he was at Tirzah, drinking himself drunk in the house of Arza, who was in charge of the palace at Tirzah, Zimri came in and struck him down and killed him . . . and succeeded him.

When he began to reign, as soon as he sat on his throne, he killed all the house of Baasha; he did not leave him anyone who pees against a wall,○ neither of his kindred nor his friends. Thus Zimri destroyed all the house of Baasha. . . . Zimri reigned seven days in Tirzah.

Now the troops were encamped against Gibbethon, which belonged to the Philistines, and the troops who were encamped heard it said, "Zimri has conspired, and he has killed the king"; so all Israel made Omri, the commander of the army, king over Israel on that day in the camp.

And Omri went up, and all Israel with him, from Gibbethon, and they besieged Tirzah. When Zimri saw that the city was captured, he went into the stronghold of the king's house; he burned down the king's house over himself with fire, and he died. . . .

Tyre

Now the rest of the acts of Zimri, and the conspiracy that he conspired, are they not written in the Book of the Daily Affairs of the Kings of Israel?○

Then the people of Israel were divided into two parts; half of the people followed Tibni son of Ginath, to make him king, and half followed Omri. But the people who followed Omri were stronger than the people who followed Tibni son of Ginath; so Tibni died, and Omri reigned.

Jizebul's Betrothal to Ahab

883 BCE○

"Daughter, you will be my eyes and my ears."

The words of my noble father Ethbaal king of Tyre filled me with pride. It was the spring of my fifteenth year, and, for more than a year, ambassadors from several kingdoms had been seeking a marriage alliance. Their real purpose was to acquire most-favored nation status for trade along Tyre's maritime network. I would be merely the seal on an agreement.

But my father was not willing for me to be a diplomatic hostage in a distant palace. Instead, I was to be his insider, his correspondent in a province of Tyre's expanding empire of commerce. Our fleet was a marvel, a better defense than chariot or wall, so strong that any king whose army controlled the land must have our ships for warfare and trade. Better to befriend the island city of Tyre than to destroy her, my father said.

He had started my formal training early, in my eighth year, while he was still priest in the Lady Astarte's temple. Even earlier, I had delighted in the marks that carry one's words to another. Writing takes many forms—the pictures of Egypt, the bird tracks of the Assyrians. I liked ours the best. There were fewer signs to learn because the scribes had reduced them to the simple sounds. Other peoples were even adapting our *alef-bayit* signs for their writing.

When I was very young, I pestered Abdi-Ptah, the Egyptian scribe, to let me help him finish my father's letters. After the ink dried, he would roll the papyrus sheet, wrap it with cords, and add a dab of soft clay to secure them.○ My job, when he let me, was to press the flat side of the seal into the clay and pull it off again, leaving the sculptured image in reverse. He wore the seal on a leather thong around his neck and reached for it often, turning it in his fingers before replying to a question. On the rounded side was the sacred scarab—the Cosmic Beetle that pushes the Sun across the heavens like the dung beetle rolls its eggs in balls across the ground.

Abdi-Ptah taught me to practice the marks myself by copying sayings on wax-coated wooden tablets. The name of each letter corresponded to its shape: *alef* for the head of an ox, *bayit* for the walls of a house, *gimel* for the hump of a camel.

Phoenician A, B, C (read right to left)

Ox, house, camel. Ox, house, camel. And the letters were also numbers: one, two, three. The name of the first letter and number made a pun, *alef,* having the same letters as the word "to learn." And with the names, I learned the stories.

The horned oxhead was first, my father said, because it stood for Bull El, king of the gods. But Father El of the old stories○ did not have a temple at Tyre. The storm god whose stone image wore the bull's horns was Baal Shamem. His temple had once stood on its own islet, but King Hiram, may his name be preserved in honor, had joined that reef to the Sor, the Rock of Tyre, many years ago.○

Abdi-Ptah had a different story for *alef*'s horns. "Look at the other end," he teased, pointing to a carved ivory cow on the banquet couch, who turned to lick the rump of her suckling calf.

A cow with long horns! Egypt's Hathor, the wild cow of the Nile and goddess of the western hills of the dead, had great horns set with a disk. It was she, Abdi-Ptah said, who gives life and rebirth to her calves, to pharaohs and kings. Was his Hathor the same as Tanit, the Lady whose sign was scratched into stones in our cremation cemetery on the shore? Or was she like Anath in the old stories, who mated as a heifer with

Ivory plaque with cow and calf

the stormy Baal—Virgin Anath who killed Baal's enemies and mourned for him as a cow yearns for her calf? Or, was that warrior-goddess our Astarte, whose figure looked out from her temple to the pillars of Baal Shamem's sanctuary across the city? Could not the horned *alef* stand for a cow as well as a bull, for a goddess as well as a god?

The gods were my family. My own mother had died before I could remember her, and Lady Astarte took her place for me. My Lady's sea provided Tyre's safety and prosperity. Her voice sang me to sleep with the sounds of waves and gulls. In the old stories, the white-bearded Father El ruled from a high throne with a footstool, as did my father, who seized the throne of Tyre when I was eleven.

When he became king, my future changed. I was no longer a priest's daughter, a priestess in training for Tyre. A king's daughter must go away, to live in another house. Writing and the reports of messengers would be my only contact with Tyre.

Not that I would have to write my own letters—I thought there would always be a scribe to mark down my words or read to me. But my father insisted that I should read and write well, so I could check a scribe's work. And, he said, I should have a special seal to show I had reviewed what I dictated and sent to him, so he could be sure of its source.

When I showed the first blood of the moons, the women celebrated in our quarters, but I preferred my father's way. He had promised he would not start the marriage talks until I was a true woman. Then, I should choose my seal as a token of my womanhood and of my role as his deputy. After my second moon flow, he had sent Abdi-Ptah to me with a small pouch of softest leather, holding several seals for me to inspect. I knew mine at once—the largest one, the moon-colored stone with all the mighty creatures of Egypt. The seated guardian cherub, winged and with a woman's head, holds the ankh between its long lion paws, balanced by its upraised, almost twitching, tail. The winged Sun rises above the sacred falcon with royal flail, framed by two crowned cobras. The letters of my name would be engraved among the creatures.

My father always looked beyond the present. Before he became king, he sometimes sat with me to play the game of colored stone markers on the ivory board, to be won by those who could see many moves ahead. As king, he saw the Great Sea as such a board. He would outmaneuver our rival city-state, Sidon, and build a Tyrian base beyond Byblos, near the northern river valley leading to the inland routes. He would carve out a second harbor at Tyre, facing Egypt, and make a secure port on the coast west of Egypt, on the way to the silver mines. He would establish an outpost for Tyre near the copper mines of Kition. But all his game pieces—sailors and traders and settlers—must eat, and there was not much land around our sister city Ushu on the mainland, which supplied our island with food and water. The highways of the sea must be served by fields of earth. He looked to the south, inland from Tyre's port at Akko, to the fertile valleys and hills of Israel. King Hiram had once linked Akko's plain to Tyre by grants from the House of David in Jerusalem; now the plain was controlled by an Israelite army commander, Omri.

"Daughter, you will be my eyes and my ears. You are betrothed to Ahab son of Omri the Israelite."

The Covenant Ceremony on Baal's Headland

882 BCE

ON THE MOUNTAIN, the west wind stole most words of the covenant ritual, but I heard part of a hymn from my place at the assembly's side: "Baal will give his people power, Baal will bless his people with peace, as our two Houses will live as one." I was that one, I thought, but at that moment, I had no house.

Seven days earlier, I had bowed to the ground in farewell before my father and my brothers at Tyre's harbor, before boarding a ship to Akko. The same west wind had blown there, flapping and slapping the loose canvas. The gulls and the rumbling carts and the sailors' cries and the creaking ships had raised their familiar music against the rhythm of waves hitting the dock's stone wall. These were the sounds of my house.

But the harbor breeze had also carried smells that were rare at our higher wind-cooled palace on the western ridge. Leeward, in the lower sector built on fill by King Hiram, ships' cargoes fed an industrial district—metal foundries and glass workshops, fish-processing sheds and vats for distilling precious purple dye from sea snails' nauseating glands.

I picked up a smooth sea-washed pebble from the gravel path and walked to the ship.

I had seen our island city from the mainland but not from the sea. I had watched ships glide over the water like great pelicans, double banks of oars on each side raised and lowered like wings, tips dipping into the foam. But the ship I rode was not gliding. To shift my thoughts from my stomach and the unsteady deck, I picked out the buildings on the western ridge—the king's house and the temples of Astarte and of Milkqart, divine king of the city—and I counted the towers on the high enclosure walls. The Rock receded from my view, smaller and smaller, until it vanished against the background of the coastal range like a ship going below the horizon. I busied my mind with the changing shoreline and the marriage ceremony ahead and my father's trust in me and the life to come. Only later did grief catch up on its own wings.

Now, on Baal's Headland,° that promontory south of Akko where Baal Shamem's storms first touch land, there was still the west wind but no familiar sounds. If not for the heavily embroidered veil, I might have looked toward the Great Sea, but I could not hear the waves. I might have looked eastward over the fields of Jezreel's wide valley, but I could not hear its birds. The wind itself moaned around the ceremonial stone pillars and stone altars. It carried cries of animals at the knife and the smell of burning flesh.

When the Israelites looked at me, they saw Tyre's wealth. If they could have seen my face, they would not have thought me any different from one of their own girls—small, dark, active, with long black hair the weight of which lifted my chin, like the bird—"Cormorant," that was my mother's name for me—but the gold claimed their attention. Rows of gold disks hung on chains across my chest over the finely woven stripes of my linen robe, embroidered with gold. Gold rings, some set with carnelian and crystal, covered my fingers, and links of a gold bracelet rang on my right arm as I held my robe to walk.

Phoenician gold bracelet

Tyre

These trappings, like those of a chariot horse on parade, were not the measure of my true worth to these Houses. In the year since the betrothal, I had been instructed in Tyre's commerce and Israel's strategies. By sending me to Ahab, my father signaled two things: his approval of Omri's military advances in Israel's highlands, and his confidence in Omri's plans to control the whole region. The southern foothills toward Philistia, the fertile plain of Jezreel and terraces of the highlands, the passes to the Jordan River and its valleys, even the eastern pastures toward Damascus—all could be to Tyre's advantage. Omri's ambassador had pledged that Tyre would have protected access to the eastern bazaars as well as to Israel's own products and markets. Omri and Ahab were to unite the inland realms with Tyre's coastal network for an unrivaled partnership. As my father's deputy, I was the link in these strategies.

And, the gods willing, I would have sons. No ruler of Israel had passed the throne successfully even to his son, much less his grandson. Ahab was Omri's designated successor. At twenty-five, he was already second-in-command to his father in military operations. But a kingdom cannot be ruled by arms alone. Omri agreed with my father: it is better to build loyalty with reward than to bind it only by force. Small, sea-bound Tyre had learned this lesson from experience; the Israelites were willing pupils. Ahab would win battles with arms but bind Israel's neighbors to the king with prosperity.

My husband—from then on I should call him my lord Ahab—had already fathered sons, but his first wife was of no consequence. I knew she was a booty wife taken by Ahab the soldier before the civil war had put Omri on the throne. If I, the treaty wife, daughter of Tyre, bore sons to Ahab, they would be the princes of Israel and heirs to the kingdom over their older half-brothers. In my son's reign, I would be queen mother, *gevirah*, in the House of Omri.

The men all around me appraised my small shape, robe molded close by the wind. The men of Tyre did not see a woman but trade, moving through the valleys from Damascus to Tyre and back, through Jizebul daughter of Ethbaal. The men of Israel did not see a woman but kingship, moving from Omri to his sons of the third and fourth generations, through Jizebul daughter of Ethbaal.

The visions of far-sighted soldiers and merchant kings did not steady my shaking legs. I clutched Tyre's pebble tightly in my left hand as the ambassador took my jangling right arm. He guided me to the front and gave my hand to Ahab.

Hymn of Praise to Baal○

Ascribe to Baal, O sons of El,
    ascribe to Baal glory and strength.
Ascribe to Baal the glory of his name;
Worship Baal
    in holy splendor.
The voice of Baal
    is over the Waters;
the God of glory
    thunders,
Baal, over Mighty Waters.
The voice of Baal
    is powerful;
the voice of Baal
    is full of majesty.
The voice of Baal
    breaks the cedars;
and Baal
    breaks the cedars of the Lebanon.○

Tyre

He makes Lebanon skip like a calf,
        and Sirion like a young wild ox.
The voice of Baal
        flashes forth flames of fire.
The voice of Baal
        shakes the wilderness;
Baal shakes
        the wilderness of Kadesh.
The voice of Baal
        causes the deer to calve,
and strips the forest bare;
and in his temple
        all say, "Glory!"
Baal sits enthroned
        over the Flood;
Baal sits enthroned
        as king forever.
May Baal give strength to his people!
        May Baal bless his people with peace!

3
Tirzah

**Jizebul Writes to Ethbaal:
A Letter from Tirzah**

881 BCE

 To Ethbaal king of Tyre. Your daughter Jizebul, your servant in the House of Omri at Tirzah, sends to greet my lord and the sons of your house. I bless you to Baal Shamem, the Lady Astarte, and all the gods of Tyre. May they guard you and keep you well.
 I received your letter inquiring about my well-being and why I have not written. For my part, I am with child. The scribes at Tirzah are few, and more attentive to news of war than to my condition.
 The reports you heard of King Omri's success are true. YHWH, the god of Israel's army, has granted many victories. The Philistines are subdued as far south as Gibbethon. Across the Jordan, Omri has humbled Moab, and his forces occupy the entire land of Medeba. Seeing how many cities are delivered into Omri's hand, Ben-hadad king of Aram in Damascus has sent servants to seek the favor of Israel, turning away from the enmity purchased by Asa king in Jerusalem, as you hoped. My lord Ahab has gone to Ramoth-gilead to make peace with the commanders of Aram. He says a king is growing stronger in the Land Between the Rivers,○ whose troops are pushing toward the Great Sea. Our western kingdoms should be

Tirzah

watchful. Only the House of David in Jerusalem remains apart. It sits alone on its hilltop and closes its shutters before a darkening sky.

If you want to receive letters from me, send me a scribe. Send Abdi-Ptah who knows me. His loyalty to you is sure. He can be your eyes at the king's house, because I do not live there.

Written and sealed by my own hand.

Life at Tirzah

881 BCE

I THOUGHT I HAD BEEN GIVEN TO A PRINCE. I thought I would live in the king's house in a royal city. I thought my eyes were deceiving me when the journey from Baal's Headland ended at Tirzah, a ruined town in the hills.

That it had once been a fortified city, I could tell from the top of its steep-sided mound, a sharp contour against the taller, softly rounded hills. At large pools around the spring, children from the households were outnumbered by shepherds, sheep, and a few dark-haired goats.

Spring at Tirzah

At first, I saw more buildings apart from the mound than on it. To the northeast, a small village of poor houses was set into the rocky hillside. As our wagons rolled up the mound's western ramp, I saw another spring and then a large camp, the army's headquarters. Finally, we passed through ruins of a gate—destroyed, I was told, in the civil war, leaving large stones strewn on either side of a cleared path—to the king's house, or rather to a cluster of buildings, still obviously under construction, which tried to seem imposing. My memory of Tyre was too fresh for me to be impressed. All around lay heaps of stones. Some were old and tumbled into piles, gathered from the ruins for reuse in new walls. Others were freshly hewn, being shaped with care as facings, corners, and pillars.

Even that makeshift king's house was not my destination. After being presented to King Omri, a man in plain military garb, I was taken back to the village. My palace was to be a mudbrick house, slightly larger than the others and set within a walled compound but otherwise completely ordinary. My lord Ahab's first wife, Ishah-ahav, and her children already lived there. I did not unpack all my fine things but decorated my chamber with only a bright hanging, a special rug, and a few dishes.

I was surprised by Ishah-ahav's seeming indifference to my special status. Had I not replaced her as principal wife and would my sons not replace hers as princes? She told me bluntly not to expect the throne to pass from Omri to his son and to his son's son. Until my lord Ahab became king, I should remember I was a commander's wife. Until I had a son, I should not dream about princes. She had not lost anything to me. I should live in the present.

After some weeks of aloof seclusion that masked my homesickness and disappointment, I was drawn into the women's circles. My neighbors' lives needed mending from the civil war, as much as the palace walls. Many had been widowed by earlier purges or were managing their households and fields for absent husbands and sons in the army, adding to their

Tirzah

subsistence by supplying bread and cloth for the camp. They responded to my withdrawal with visits, smiles, and small gifts, but they did not treat me like a king's daughter or the wife of a crown prince. To them, I was a commander's wife, brought home from a foreign land, but no queen. I wanted their company, but it was hard for me not to treat them like servants, because they did all the work for themselves. I knew how to direct the tasks of servants, but not how to cook. I could spin flax into linen from an ivory distaff and choose colored threads to weave a fine garment for the goddess's image, but I could not card weedy fleece or spin sheep-smelling wool on a rough stick. Ishah-ahav gave me directions in the shared tasks of our house, and I followed them, even as my own servant did.

But I learned to be grateful for the village. The king's house in the ruins was always clouded by dust blown up from the camp. Horses and chariots rattled, workers shouted, masons' metal tools struck the stones hour after hour. There were no families up there, only men. I was much freer to walk outside the village than I had been in Tyre, even into the hills with other women and their older children to gather herbs for seasoning and sage to boil in water for a drink that calms the stomach, which I was needing more often.

And, eventually, I grew to admire the women's skills and wisdom. They worked, they exchanged necessities with each other, they adapted to hardship with understated wit. They included me in their trade network and made me familiar with the paths between houses—who spun the softest wool, who grew the strongest mint, whose ewe had twin lambs to spare for meat, whose dye made the brightest threads for needlework, and who had all the news. I returned their goodwill with samples of weaving and embroidery, with patterns from the looms of Tyre. And I tried, with roughened hands, to spin wool on a stick weighted with a ring of hardened clay.

The village sat on a rocky slope above the valley fields. It looked out over a wide ravine where the creeks from the two springs joined and flowed east, down through a path of green toward the Jordan River. Israel's soil was rich, and, where it had water, it produced abundantly. Even some dry rounded hills were farmed. Stepped terraces curved around the slopes like tracks from a potter's fingers on a spinning lump of clay. They were planted with single rows of vines or olives, fed by winter rains and summer heat. Sheep and goats grazed the upper hillsides and cleared the harvest stubble in the valley. Villagers could live here with little knowledge of a world beyond their springs.

But King Omri saw much farther. Tirzah's creek bed made a highway to the east, toward the valley of the Jordan and to Gilead beyond. Throughout the hill country, the valleys were Israel's roads. Tyre's ships made their own highways across flat seas, between islands and along coasts to western ports where metals could be found. To share these metals, Israel could trade its fruits with Tyre—its wine and olive oil and wool and grain—but it could also rule traffic on the valley-roads. North and south, east and west, all routes would pass through the valleys controlled by Israel, the Israel of Omri's ambition.

Hillside village and valley-road, army camp and unfinished palace—my memory of Tirzah sees them now as the foundation stones of Omri's kingdom. But these were not the thoughts of a sixteen-year-old bride.

I did not see my lord Ahab as often as I had expected. He was usually away with the army or slept in the camp. With knowing smiles, however, my neighbors said he came to our village house more often than he used to, and not just to visit his boys. Others might see him as only a commander, but in my chamber he was welcomed as a prince. He came to me smelling of leather and horses and left with my fragrant oils in his beard. And when the women learned I no longer bled with the moon but drank the boiled sage water for my stomach every morning, they told me: I was pregnant.

Tirzah

Jizebul Writes to Ethbaal: The Birth of Atalyah

881 BCE

To Ethbaal king of Tyre. Your daughter Jizebul, your servant in the House of Omri, sends to greet my lord and your household. I hope you are well. Here with me everything is fine. I bless you to Baal Shamem, the Lady Astarte, and all the gods of Tyre.

Our household is increasing. The scribe Abdi-Ptah arrived with the woman you sent to help me with the child. I am glad to hear from them how Tyre prospers. Abdi-Ptah reported seeing many wagons at Akko and bundles from Damascus waiting to be loaded for the ship's return to Tyre. My lord Ahab says to tell you that he blesses you to YHWH for sending such a skillful scribe. He has put Abdi-Ptah at the head of the scribes in the king's house, to oversee their work and to organize archives for letters and accounts.

The child is a girl. My travail was not difficult because she is small. My lord Ahab gave her a majestic name, Atalyah, "YHWH is exalted." May she be the sister of many brothers.

I ask you to send me two women skilled in spinning, dying, and weaving wool, with their looms, to instruct the weavers of Tirzah. They weave well but now work only for themselves on rough frames. They could produce more garments, and finer ones, for Israel and the markets of Tyre.

Do not chide me, my lord and father, for being slow to respond to your letter. My words to you are not carried as quickly as they are written. The messengers of Israel travel east from Tirzah down the ravine to the Jordan, then turn north to Rehov and west to Akko. This will change when we move to the new city in the west. My lord Ahab says King Omri is building it on the hill of Shemer, where your architects are making a king's house for all of us.

Sealed by my own hand.

The Jezebel Letters

Names and Gods

881 BCE

Atalyah, "Yhwh is exalted," was my lord Ahab's name for her, but the women called her "Little Sister." My child's names carried the thoughts of others.

My lord Ahab was disappointed, and he rebuked me saying, "I planted the seed of a son in your womb!" A soldier blames his wife more easily than his god. What does Yhwh, the god of desert mountains and battles, know about bringing seeds into fruit? "Yhwh bless it!" was my lord Ahab's response to news of her birth, but he meant just the opposite, as everyone heard in his angry tone. I suspect his naming held the same double sense.

The women's name for her also carried two meanings. Atalyah was the little sister to my lord Ahab's sons by Ishahahav. That was her reality, and mine, as my daughter grew up in the same household with her half brothers and their mother, to whom I was like a little sister. Now that my womb had been opened, I could look to my sons of the future, the gods willing. But which gods?

Silver-plated bronze statue from Tirzah

The Lady had been honored at Tirzah for many generations. Women showed me clay plaques, broken chalices, and even a silver-plated statue found in Tirzah's rubble when the new foundations were dug. Abdi-Ptah said it was the Lady Hathor, with her hair curled upon her shoulders, but no one at Tirzah knew that name. It was hard for me to call upon Lady Astarte, whom I knew at the blue-green sea of Tyre, when there were only hills and fields around me. Families of the village invoked their own Lady, the Lady Asherah—Yhwh's Asherah, they called her. No one gave her name to their child, but without her sustenance, what son would live to carry the family's line?

Tirzah

The Israelites also knew Baal, or at least their baals. At grape vats and olive presses carved into the terraced bedrock, shrine niches held small stone pillars. Offerings were made on hilltop platforms to insure the rains. But these were little baals, not Baal Shamem, the Rider of Clouds whose storms swept in from the Great Sea—the Baal of Tyre. My family's very names invoke him. I am Ji Zebul, "Where is the Prince?"—the Lady Anath's cry as she searches for Baal in Mot's realm of death. My father was Eth Baal, "Baal exists"—the shout that marks Baal's return and the earth's relief after Mot's season of dryness and heat.

But where at Tirzah was the sanctuary to Baal Shamem to honor Israel's covenant with Tyre? There was no longer any major temple at Tirzah, only a small shrine room at the king's house and a rough altar of field stones at the camp, where priests offered sacrifice to Yhwh of Hosts each time the commanders left for battle.

Less than half a day's travel to the south was an old sanctuary at Shechem, in the valley between two mountains. That temple was dedicated to El Berith, God of the Covenant, whose great standing stone witnessed to treaties like those made on Baal's Headland. Shechem's priests had brokered agreements among Israel's clans long before kings arose, and they were suspicious of royal arrangements that bypassed kinship loyalties and their priestly seniority. People at Tirzah were reluctant to speak of Shechem. King Jeroboam, an early ruler of Israel, had trouble with those priests. When he rebuilt his towns after the invasion of Shishak of Egypt, he moved his capital away from there, across the Jordan to Penuel in Gilead. Another ruler moved back to these highlands, to Tirzah, still keeping distance from the vipers in Shechem's stony den.

Yhwh had many shrines. Israelite stories called him Fear of Isaac, and the older high places west of Tirzah invoked his presence with small metal images of a bull calf.○ To further weaken Shechem's power, King Jeroboam had established his royal shrine at Beth-el as the true "House of El," empowering the priests and prophets of his Ephraimite heritage and rewarding Israelite loyalties in that southern region so close to Jerusalem. At Beth-el, too, the bull was Yhwh's throne, or was it the pedestal of Bull El from the old stories?

This all seemed very strange to me—not the many gods, but the moving capital without a major temple. To be a king like my father, one needs a city with all the offices at the center, not in the territory of one or another group. The king should be there, the temples and priests of all the gods should be there under his eye, with the scribes and commanders and merchants. The priests of the chief gods should be kept beholden to the king. Or, like my father, whose priestly family had marriage ties to an earlier generation of Tyre's kings, they might take the throne if the nobles were displeased. Perhaps that was why Israel's kings tried to isolate Shechem, where the priests had a longer lineage and authority of governing than any king. If Jerusalem's kings had faced their own problem—for their priests⁰ have deeper roots than the House of David—Atalyah might still be alive.

The move from Tirzah to Samaria would stop the wandering of Israel's capital. Samaria would be King Omri's city, at the crossroads of Israel's valley-roads, founded on new beginnings in stone and in flesh. I hoped the gods of Tyre would receive there the homage they deserved.

Tirzah, Omri's foster mother, was to be left as a small village and an unfinished palace. I, too, was fostered there and learned much about Israel's people. The weavers sent by my father worked in a shed in our courtyard, teaching women to refine their threads and patterns, showing carpenters how to build the better looms. If Israelite women could weave this way, in their houses as they did in Tyre but with wool instead of linen, they could bring returns from a market outside their village. At Tirzah, however, there was too little wool, since local

Tirzah

sheep were slaughtered young to feed the army. I hoped that at Samaria, the crossroads might bring more wool to Israel's looms and to Tyre's cargoes.

At Tirzah, the Lady, by whatever name, had delivered my daughter, beautiful and small. I wrapped Atalyah in a fine cloth embroidered with the greens and blues of my Lady's sea. I called her by the name of the darting blue-green bird that shines among the olives, my "Little Green Bee-eater."

Bronze bull statue from Dothan area

4
Samaria

King Omri Acquires Samaria

881 BCE, EVENTS IN THE NORTHERN KINGDOM OF ISRAEL,
AS DESCRIBED MUCH LATER BY PRIESTLY SCRIBES FROM JERUSALEM

In the thirty-first year of Asa king of Judah, Omri began to reign over Israel; for twelve years [he reigned]. In Tirzah, he reigned six years. Then, he bought the hill of Shomron from Shemer for two talents of silver; he fortified the hill, and he called the name of the city that he built by the name of Shemer, the owner of the hill—Shomron.

Omri's Vision for Israel

879 BCE

THE HILL OF SHEMER—Shomron, Samaria—was the hub around which the wheel of King Omri's empire turned, as chariots and wagons moved in all directions from its gleaming palace. The new city would become the center of covenants, the throne room from which threats and rewards struck bargains for cooperation and profit. Building the city was the prelude to building alliances, posting diplomats, deploying an army of scribes and couriers, merchants and spies. Just as in the old stories when Baal celebrated his victories by building a house, so Omri truly became king of Israel in Samaria.

The army was extending Israel's boundaries across the fertile lowlands of Jezreel and incorporating the highlands of the Galil and northern valleys of Chinneroth, the inland sea.○ Partly by arms, mostly by agreement with Ben-hadad of Damascus, my lord Ahab's forces took control of the Aramaean posts north of Chinneroth, even to fortified Hazor and to Dan, where springs gush out at the foot of Mount Hermon to form the Jordan River. The Aramaeans ruling at the headwaters were displaced from their privileges at Ben-hadad's court, demoted to supplying units for his army. What had once been a territory contested among Tyre, Israel, and Aram became their common domain—patroled by Israel, open to Tyre's agricultural settlements, crossed by increasing shipments from Damascus. Much more than local food and cloth traveled the valley-roads. Metals arrived at Akko's port, destined for inland forges, to become tools and weapons and chariot frames and horses' harnesses. Horses themselves and charioteers moved from pastures to ports and camps and battlefields. Luxury spices and oils flowed from inland Arab traders to the coastal cities and ships. Raw woods and ivory and shell passed from harbors to the workshops of Damascus and returned as banquet couches, ceremonial chairs and tables, and inlays, already finished or emerging under the hands of mobile artisans in noble houses of cedar and hewn stone.

King Omri, supported by my father Ethbaal, achieved his advances by force and favor, uncontested by larger kingdoms. To the south, Egypt was withdrawing into its own problems. To the north, rulers in the Land Between the Rivers were consolidating their power and only beginning to covet the new western kingdoms. Damascus traded towns in its western region to Israel in return for open frontiers there, gaining profits and freedom to shift its army to the northern plains where Assyria might threaten. Omri had also thwarted the ambitions of the Philistines, who, from their coastal cities, had established footholds in the Jezreel and Jordan valleys. Philistines, too, had ports and traded in metals. Their leaders, too, could coordinate military and economic ventures. From his highland base, Omri had pushed the Philistines back to the citadel at Gibbethon, now firmly under Israel's control.

Header-stretcher wall at Samaria

To the east, across the Jordan, Moab's warlords still clung to their local power. Their infighting and scattered militias made them easy targets for Israel's standing army across Moab's open terrain. How the gods must have laughed to see them resist Israel's rule, when eventually they would succeed only by imitating the very ways they opposed—a monarchy whose goods flowed to a king and his favorites on the way to markets beyond.○

And what of the House of David in Jerusalem? In Tyre's stories, Solomon son of David was King Hiram's ally, ceding control of Akko's plain to Tyre and opening trade from the hill country. The people of Israel tell a different story. Unified under Saul against the Philistines, Israel's clans hoped for larger successes. David, from somewhere south of Israel's frontier in Benjamin, used mercenaries and a professional army to dash that hope and enslave the people of Ephraim.○

David surrounded Israel with a chain of hostile regions—Geshur across the Chinneroth and Ammon across the Jordan, with a few cities of Gilead between, plus the Philistines at Gath, and even Tyre. Pressured on all sides after Saul's death and his sons' demise at the hands of David's cronies, northern leaders submitted to David, only to have their people taxed and put to hard labor for Jerusalem's gain. David's favorite son, Absalom, courted the north with promises of relief but lost his bid for the throne to Solomon, who oppressed them mightily. Restive under Solomon's burdens, Israel shook off what Jerusalem now claims was brotherly dominion when he died. But Israel knows its fathers to be Jacob and Joseph. David's "Judah" is not in their stories; perhaps the priests who shape his chronicles invented that "brother."○

Before Omri's successes, Asa of Jerusalem had paid Benhadad of Damascus to harrass Israel's northern territories, while Asa's troops skirmished on its southern frontier. But Omri's strength and prospects outweighed Jerusalem's silver and gold, and Aram changed sides, eager for the link with Tyre. David's chain was reforged and closed around Jerusalem from all sides—Tyre, Israel, Aram, Gilead, Moab.

Those in Jerusalem who now counsel their king to repeat Asa's strategy, to bribe Damascus at the expense of their own nobles, should open their eyes. The true brotherhood established between our Houses after Asa's death was a fruitful bond of mutual aid and prosperity. Heed this story and be instructed. Covenant loyalty to your neighbor is better than paying the distant enemy of your enemy to be your friend.

Jizebul Writes to Ethbaal: The Move to Samaria

879 BCE

To Ethbaal, king of Tyre and king of the Sidonians. Your daughter Jizebul, your servant in the House of Omri in Samaria, sends to greet my lord and your household. The children and I are well. I bless you to Baal Shamem, the Lady Astarte, and all the gods of Tyre. May the gods keep you well as you raise your scepter over Sidon and the cities of the coast.

I send this letter from the king's house on the hill of Shomron. The architects and skilled workers you sent, together with the men of Israel, have built a city more noble than any in the hill country, but it is no rival to the Tyre I remember. The commanders are here. The merchants from Damascus and agents from across the Jordan are arriving and establishing their places. They will not be with us in the king's house, but the hill is large and will serve them better than Tirzah.

My lord and father, your wisdom toward the House of Omri is well rewarded. The king has appointed ministers to manage the affairs of the kingdom. The scribes and couriers are organized at Samaria. The strength of the army under my lord Ahab is supported by servants of the king in cities he is fortifying. And the messenger who brought your gift for my son reported how many warehouses are being built at Akko to hold goods in transit to Tyre.

But I must warn you about something disturbing. Not everyone in Israel blesses the name of King Omri. When the plan to leave Tirzah became known, several captains from Gilead came to speak against it. The pastures of Gilead are home to Israel's chariot soldiers and war horses, and iron comes from their mines. As Israel's frontiers extend, the men of Gilead fear that their loyalty to the old kings Saul and Jeroboam counts for nothing, that their voice in the king's ear is no longer heeded. Such unrest from within the army has brought down former kings of Israel, as Omri knows well. He placed my lord Ahab at the head of the commanders to build their loyalty. An older son of Omri, Nimshi "the weasel,"○ oversees the trading and training of horses for the chariots, with his eye on Gilead. My lord Ahab says opposition in Gilead will pass when Samaria's success brings wealth to the eastern lands as well as to the western hills.

And not everyone in Samaria blesses the name of my lord and father. Before the acknowledgment ceremony for my son Ahaziah, King Omri summoned me. He spoke harshly to me because Tyre accepted the invitation from Ashurnasirpal king of Assyria to attend his palace dedication at Calah.○ I assured my lord the king that the request showed Assyria's desire to honor Tyre, not Tyre's need to please Assyria. Perhaps, I said, Tyre's gifts to Ashurnasirpal were merely road taxes, not tribute. The king permitted the naming ceremony to proceed and Tyre's kinship to be acknowledged. Will you not send word of your steadfast friendship to Omri, lest those who think too highly of Israel's strength alone should poison the king's heart against you?

For my part, I am confident of your wisdom. May my son Ahaziah possess the kingdom of Omri in the third generation, from Samaria, a city that brings glory to Tyre. May my lord Ethbaal live long to see Tyre's partners flourish and his offspring multiply.

Sealed by my own hand.

The View from Samaria

879 BCE

AHAZIAH. My lord Ahab showed his thoughts in naming our son. A man of war, he always looked ahead to see the three ways, the four ways a battle might develop, and he had a strategy for each one. The outcome for the House of Omri was in my son's name: "YHWH possesses."

The move to Samaria established the command post. The old headquarters at Tirzah looked to the east, toward Gilead and Israel's stories of the past. The stones there were old and new, but the design was old, on the foundations of the old. Samaria was new in every part. It belonged to this House, and it looked in every direction, into the future.

From the rooftop, I looked out over the fields and groves in the surrounding valleys, as over green water, and I imagined myself on an island in a great lake.

Samaria viewed from north

The northern shore was the closest, where the road to Dothan began. Deep valleys ran east and west, toward Shechem and the coastal plain, meeting in the broad southern fields. At Tirzah, I was always looking east, down the valley toward Gilead, to escape the enclosing hills. My eyes were free at Samaria. I could see the dust of travelers in the far distance, approaching like sails on the horizon at Tyre. I could watch, too, as Baal's life-bringing clouds came, timely and full, from the west. But I never grew accustomed to the mountain chill of the rainy season, which lodged in stone and bone.

My eyes were free, but my feet were restrained. We lived in the king's house, not in a village. Ahaziah was to be raised as a prince. I unpacked all my fine things and received more that the craftsmen brought from Tyre: inlaid furniture made in Damascus and woven hangings for the stone walls, Tyrian clay dishes and bronze and silver drinking bowls. I arranged them in the residence and supervised adornment of the great hall where King Omri received messengers, many more than had ever come to Tirzah. I kept a rounded chip from the new walls of Samaria, along with a water-washed stone from Tirzah's spring and the pebble from Tyre, in a miniature chest from Damascus, of cedar inlaid with ivory—a gift from a Tyrian trader of my mother's kinsmen.

In Samaria, at least, I was more aware of royal matters because I was in the king's house. My lord Ahab was there too, when he was not in the field. He did not come to me now only for the times of pleasure but talked to me more about events and strategies, even some military matters. As Ethbaal's daughter, I had been taught to weigh affairs of state, and I fed upon news of cities and battlefields I would never see. My lord Ahab realized too, that if Ahaziah were to receive the throne before he came of age, I would be at his right hand as *gevirah* and regent, guiding him in these very matters. My lord was proud of me, proud of the king's house in which he was learning to live as a prince, strengthened by a sense of future beyond the battlefield.

My lord Ahab told me about other clouds—not the rain-bearing ones from the west but dark reports of danger coming from the east, which cast moving shadows across Samaria's bright stones and chilled my heart.

The Aramaeans of Damascus had seen it first—the ambition of Ashurnasirpal of Assyria pushing his armies westward toward the Great Sea, toward us. To stand against Ashurnasirpal, Damascus depended on Israel's friendship, receiving more in brotherhood with Samaria and Tyre than it had gained from Asa of Jerusalem's small purses.

South of Damascus, Israel's armies possessed the plains of Moab. Tribal rulers there had tried to unite under one warlord, but their loyalty was easily divided by Israel's overwhelming power and pledges of rewards for those who cooperated. And Moab had pastures for sheep, large herds that followed the seasons' forage and gave their wool for Israel's weavers, working now on better looms in many villages.

I did not doubt that Israel's army and merchant-ambassadors could enforce the oaths of Moab and Aram. I was less certain what force or promise could bind the unruly people within Israel's own realm.

From Tirzah, I had seen the plateau of Gilead rising out of the Jordan Valley. Many people at Tirzah had distant kin in the east, in the creek beds that cut the plateau toward the Jordan or on the eastern pastures. Men of Gilead controlled their western frontier at the Jordan fords, but the deep ravines of the Yarmuk in the north and the Jabbok in the south offered them little protection from the raids of Aram and Ammon. King Saul's militia had shielded them from Ammon, and, in return, they had tried to shield his sons from David's troops. Omri's small fortress at Ramoth-gilead kept watch over a shifting and permeable eastern frontier toward Damascus, strengthened more now by having a common cause with Aram than by superior arms.

The heritage of Gilead's traditions and the difference in their speech marked their territory with sharper boundaries than any on the ground.○ The stories defined a fierce and independent people. Tirzah's folk complained that their kin in Gilead called them deserters and exiles for having migrated to the richer western lands. According to Gilead's story, Yhwh the god of Israel favored the eastern tribes with the first gift of land. They sought to acknowledge that blessing with fervent and single-minded devotion to his ways, as they knew them. A capital at Penuel or Tirzah had sustained their self-importance, and they honored King Omri and my lord Ahab as warriors skilled in the deployment of their horses. But the capital at Samaria threatened to create a rift greater than the Jordan Valley. Omri began moving some families from their small plots in the western hills onto larger fields centered around towns in Gilead to gain loyalty for the throne and increase production, especially in the green valleys that opened into the Jordan.

To the south, Jerusalem's "kingdom" was puny—stony hills of dried weeds and scrub pines not to be compared to the groves of Israel and the cedars of Lebanon. Despite his neighbors' plans to ally against Assyria, Asa in Jerusalem remained antagonistic, unwilling to adapt to the threat or to yield the throne to his grown son Jehoshaphat. In Samaria's halls, scribes repeated the commanders' mocking words, that Jerusalem was now ruled by a sickness in the old king's loins. My lord Ahab boasted to me, however, that he and Jehoshaphat had exchanged private messages while their armies faced off in the fields of Benjamin, hinting at matters beyond their troops' stalemate. Would our son Ahaziah possess the allegiance of the House of David? My lord Ahab's designs were already in motion.

As if he knew he was special, Ahaziah was a demanding infant. He called for nursing with a loud rattling cry, waving his arms, red in the face. I often wrapped him in a blue cloth with purple trim and called him "Kingfisher."

Jizebul Writes to Ethbaal: Ashurnasirpal's Threat

876 BCE

To Ethbaal king of Tyre, king of the Sidonians. Your daughter Jizebul in the House of Omri in Samaria sends to greet my lord and your household. Are you well? All the children and I are well. I bless you to Baal Shamem, the Lady Astarte, and all the gods of Tyre. May they guard you and keep you well.

I received your generous gift for my son Joram. He is lean and strong, and he grows quickly. The one who carried your letter also brought word that the gods have favored you with a new prince in your house, Baal-azzor. I rejoice with you. *Be pleased to receive a soft weaving from my own hand for his comfort and special wine from our royal vineyard for your table.*

While our sons play, their fathers think of war. No doubt you have heard of the great danger from the north. Ashurnasirpal of Assyria is massing troops and supplies in Bit-Adini. My lord Ahab says they cannot reach this far south, but if they strike through Hattina to the Great Sea, you will see it.

What will you do? I have told my lord Ahab that Tyre's defense is its wealth, not an army. The Israelites do not understand that your ships follow many currents and that you must pay transit fees to carry goods from all the lands. King Omri still remembers that your envoys attended Ashurnasirpal's dedication ceremonies at Calah. I know that even if you must send gifts to the Assyrians, you will not bow down to them or assist them against Israel. Your message of brotherhood to Omri for Joram's naming ceremony was timely and well received.

Sealed by my own hand.

Ashurnasirpal II's Inscription

875 BCE, ASSYRIAN DESCRIPTION OF THE CAMPAIGN TO THE WEST

I departed from the country Bit-Adini and crossed the Euphrates at the peak of its flood by means of rafts made buoyant with inflated goatskin bottles. I advanced towards Carchemish. There I received from himself the tribute of Sangara, the king of the Hittites amounting to: 20 talents of silver, an object of gold, a ring of gold, golden daggers, 100 talents of copper, 250 talents of iron, furthermore bull-images of copper, copper basin-and-ewer sets for washing, a copper brazier—all his own furniture, the weights of which were not taken separately—furthermore beds of boxwood, chairs of boxwood, tables of boxwood, all inlaid with ivory, also 200 young females clad in linen garments with multicolored trimmings made of dark and reddish purple-dyed wool, also alabaster, elephants' tusks and even a shining chariot and a golden chair with panels—his own royal insignia. I took over the chariot-corps, the cavalry and the infantry of Carchemish. The kings of all surrounding countries came to me, embraced my feet and I took hostages from them and they marched with me towards the Lebanon forming my vanguard.

I departed from Carchemish, taking the road between the mountains Munzigani and the Hamurga, leaving the country Ahanu on my left. I advanced toward the town Hazazu which belongs to Lubarna from Hattina. There I received gold and linen garments.

I proceeded and crossed the river Apre where I passed the night. From the banks of the Apre I departed and advanced towards the town Kunulua, the royal residence of Lubarna from Hattina. Afraid of the terrible weapons of my ferocious army, he embraced my feet to save his life. Twenty talents of silver the equivalent of one talent of gold, 100 talents of tin, 100 talents of iron, 1,000 heads of big cattle, 10,000 sheep, 1,000 linen garments with multicolored trimmings, easy chairs of boxwood with insets and mountings, beds of boxwood, beds provided with insets, tables with ivory inlay on boxwood—all his own furniture, the weights of which were not taken separately, also female singers . . . , large instruments and other great objects I received from him as his tribute, and himself I pardoned. I took over the chariot-corps, the cavalry and the infantry of Hattina and seized hostages from him.

At that time I received also the tribute of Gusi from Iahani consisting of: gold, silver, tin, iron, large and small cattle, linen garments with multicolored trimmings. From Kunulua, the royal residence of Lubarna from Hattina, I departed; I crossed the river Orontes and passed the night on the banks of the Orontes. From the banks of the Orontes I departed, taking the road between the mountains Iaraqi and Iaturi, and crossed over the . . . mountains to pass the night on the banks of the Sangura River. From the banks of the Sangura River I departed, taking the road between the mountains Saratini and Duppani, and passed the night on the banks of the . . . lake. I entered Aribua, the fortress of Lubarna from Hattina, and seized it as my own town. I harvested the grain as well as the straw of the Luhuti country and stored them therein. In his own palace I performed a festival and then settled natives of Assyria in it the town. **While I stayed in Aribua, I conquered the other towns of Luhuti, defeating their inhabitants in many bloody battles. I destroyed them, tore down the walls and**

burned the towns with fire; I caught the survivors and impaled them on stakes in front of their towns.⁰ At that time I seized the entire extent of the Lebanon mountain and reached the Great Sea of the Amurru country. I cleaned my weapons in the deep sea and performed sheep-offerings to all the gods. The tribute of the seacoast—from the inhabitants of Tyre, Sidon, Byblos, Mahallata, Maiza, Kaiza, Amurru, and of Arvad which is an island in the sea, consisting of: gold, silver, tin, copper, copper containers, linen garments with multicolored trimmings, large and small monkeys, ebony, boxwood, ivory from walrus tusk—thus ivory a product of the sea—this their tribute I received and they embraced my feet.

I ascended the mountains of the Amanus and cut down there logs of cedars, stone-pines, cypresses and pines, and performed sheep-offerings to my gods. I had made a sculptured stela commemorating my heroic achievements and erected it there. The cedar beams from the Amanus mountain I sent to the temple Esarra for the construction of a sanctuary as a building for festivals serving the temples of Sin and Shamash, the lightgiving gods.

Impaled captives from Assyrian relief sculpture

Sons of the Prophets

875 BCE

THE WHIRLWIND FROM ASSYRIA PASSED TO THE NORTH. Like a blast of heat and dust from the desert, Ashurnasirpal stripped towns in his path of their animals and harvest, toppled their walls, dismembered their people, and cleared their palaces of fine things. The whirlwind blew to the Great Sea and turned north, sucking tribute from the coast of the Lebanon into its wake. In ruined cities, Assyria left garrisons to mark the path for future strikes. We shall be ready, my lord

Samaria

Ahab vowed. But the next storm would not come for at least fifteen years.

The elder generation of rulers looked to their sons and prepared. My long-lived father publicly designated my new brother Baal-azzor as crown prince with an appointed regent. Asa, that sick old king in Jerusalem, finally passed active rule to Jehoshaphat with the army's approval. Omri leaned more and more upon the arm of my lord Ahab for the daily decisions of our growing kingdom. And my lord Ahab looked to his own future. I had two princes now. My lord Ahab praised his god for his son Joram, "Yhwh is exalted," and this time he meant it. His two sons by Jizebul daughter of Ethbaal of Tyre assured Omri's royal lineage to the third generation, the gods willing.

The Assyrian storm struck north of us, but its rumbling was heard in Gilead. If the Assyrians established permanent supply bases in Hattina, they would next look to march south through Damascus, to Hauran, to Gilead, then west through Jezreel's valley to the sea. The Israelites in Gilead lived among Aramaeans, whose sense of security came from Damascus, not Samaria. Who would offer better protection, Ben-hadad or Ahab? For the moment, they were allies. The Gileadites had once been confident of their priority with Israel's kings at Tirzah, but Omri's move to Samaria had left them feeling abandoned and vulnerable in spite of the fort at Ramoth-gilead.

It was difficult to sympathize with their fear when all they showed was hostility. At first, bands of men calling themselves "Sons of the Prophets" came to Samaria from time to time. While several chanted and beat a rhythm on hand-held drums, one would fall into a trance: "Yhwh says this, Yhwh says that." For a warrior god, their Yhwh showed surprisingly little regard for the military advantage gained by my lord Ahab on many fronts—in battle, through alliances, and by trade.

Everything was upside down to these "prophets" from Gilead. In the stones of Samaria's mighty walls—huge blocks squared and fitted close without mortar—they saw a sign of weakness, because they were not the rough-hewn stones of Israel's past. To them the rich furnishings of the king's house, few as they were, bespoke a growing softness, not the lean strength of poor steppe herders. And the increasing yield of Israel's expanded estates, clearly a sign of the gods' favor, was said to be an offense to Y<small>HWH</small> of Hosts!

"They are harmless," my lord Ahab said. "Let them fall down of their own accord," he mocked at their trances. I was more anxious, chiding him for the welfare of his sons. How could these wild men speak against the king without consequences? They might look like fools in their skin garments, living in caves or with gullible people. But fools are allowed to speak what is in the minds of others more cunning than they. I felt uneasy for my children whenever I heard the drums.

My new prince Joram was healthy but not large and boisterous like his brother. He turned his head to watch everything with quiet intensity. When I first held him, my heart sank at the birthmarks near his left eye: one like a path of tears running straight down his cheek and another from the corner of his eye to his ear. "They will be covered by his hair and beard," the midwife whined at me when I turned on her. Abdi-Ptah came to write my letter to my father as I sat holding the child. He gasped, then knelt before us. "Horus," he whispered, "the eye of Horus!"○

Joram was my hovering falcon, my "Kestrel."

Eye of Horus amulet from Megiddo

5
Baal's Headland

Ahab Becomes King of Israel

874 BCE, EVENTS IN THE NORTHERN KINGDOM OF ISRAEL,
AS DESCRIBED MUCH LATER BY PRIESTLY SCRIBES FROM JERUSALEM

Now the rest of the acts of Omri that he did, and the mighty deeds that he did, are they not written in the Book of the Daily Affairs of the Kings of Israel? Omri slept with his fathers, and was buried at Samaria; Ahab his son ruled after him.

In the thirty-eighth year of Asa king of Judah, Ahab the son of Omri began to reign over Israel; he reigned in Samaria twenty-two years.

And as if it had been a trifling thing for him to walk in the sins of Jeroboam son of Nebat, he took a wife—Jezebel daughter of Ethbaal, king of the Sidonians—and went and served Baal, and bowed himself to him. He erected an altar for Baal in the house of Baal, which he built in Samaria. Ahab also made an Asherah.

King Ahab's Beginnings

874 BCE

KING OMRI had come to the throne by civil war. He was always looking over his shoulder, watching for remnants of

Tibni's rival faction. My lord Ahab came to the throne with the army's support. He had been one of them for sixteen years and had earned their loyalty. Even with Omri's death, the older commanders were already assured that my lord Ahab would increase their power. They would be little princes in fortified cities, while younger men led in battle.

A ring of forts had served as Israel's frontier markers. My lord Ahab had long wanted to increase the national draft, not only for the standing army but also for laborers for building. Like the reinforced corners of Samaria's wall, the renovated forts protected the corners of the realm. Gezer, near the former Philistine city of Gibbethon, controlled the valley-roads into the hill country of Jerusalem. Megiddo guarded the coastal highway's crossing into the Jezreel Valley. Hazor and Dan faced Aram in the north, along the route by which trade or troops came from Damascus. Other cities strengthened regions of the highlands.

The lands east of the Jordan River were different. Without the natural defense of Israel's hills and valleys, the eastern plateaus and their mixed peoples were more difficult to rule. In the plains of Moab, Israelite tribal elements clustered around Ataroth. Omri's fort there was reinforced, and a line of outposts was extended east along the Arnon Gorge to Jahaz. Resistance to my lord Ahab's succession came from Chemosh-yatti, the Moabite warlord in Dibon who now called himself "king" and claimed Ataroth in his territory. North of Moab, the Israelite clans in Gilead had helped to give Omri influence as well as control over the Aramaean villages. Now, dissent increased as the clans' old ways and mobility were curbed by the reins of my lord Ahab. Ramoth-gilead was the fortified gate in an otherwise unfenced pasture on Israel's open frontier to the Hauran.

Forts showed the closed fist of power; prosperity offered the open hand of reward. My lord Ahab increased his father's practice of moving some Israelites from the highlands into towns in Gilead. Farmers with large families, who tried to subsist on small plots of uncertain yield, often could not meet the full exactions of crops required by the king and also feed themselves. The prospect of watered land and royal subsidies overcame their reluctance to leave the stony terraces of their fathers. They were given special status—Tishbites, "settlers"—and encouraged to weave their family stories into the tales of Gilead's first Israelites, specially favored by Yhwh.[9]

Ravine in Gilead

Unfortunately, they were attracted, too, by the fervor of the Sons of the Prophets, who proclaimed Gilead's traditional interests. Relocated and thriving by royal initiative, the Tishbites of Omri's time refrained from open criticism of the king's new ways. Their sons were not so restrained with my lord Ahab, especially when they saw the small plots their fathers had yielded to the king consolidated and given as larger estates to new owners under royal patronage.

At Samaria, my lord Ahab and I redirected the builders to our plan for a larger capital. He needed more space for his other army—the scribes and agents who oversaw the kingdom's trade. Districts had to supply produce for the capital and the royal cities, and surpluses for trade. Outfitting the army required long-term agreements for breeding and acquiring horses, for chariots and weapons, as well as for drafting and training soldiers and feeding them. The program of joining small plots into larger estates for the growing nobility—estates tended by young debt slaves and sons without inheritance—had managers at Samaria and the royal cities.

Regular visitors from Tyre had often complained to me that there was no temple to our Baal Shamem on the hill of

Shomron. How could the guarantor of Tyre's prosperity be approached in Israel without a temple? Yhwh had royal shrines now at Beth-el and the frontier city of Dan, an enclave as El Berith at Shechem, and altars in the royal precinct at Samaria. The local baals were honored with Yhwh at high places across the hills, wherever their productive and protective favor was needed. The Lady Asherah's tree was in many shrines and her figure was in many houses. But the sole covenant shrine for Baal Shamem of Tyre—the stones and altars on Baal's Headland—was not enough. With my lord Ahab's accession to the throne, we remedied that.

Construction began immediately. The outer wall of the royal precinct became an inner wall as the city's perimeter was extended to the north and strengthened with a casemate fortification.○ North of the royal quarters, just over the crest of the hill, priests from Tyre located an auspicious site for the sanctuary on a broad natural terrace, where the western breeze would carry the smoke of sacrifice away from the king's house. The platform was laid out, built up, the temple itself founded and enclosed by its own wall around the large courtyard. Baal Shamem and Astarte of Tyre at last found their home in Samaria, even if the Israelites called them Baal and Asherah. This brought me new duties: overseeing the maintenance of the priests and the furnishings of the temple, especially the weavings.○

I also had another, more private, building project in mind. My lord Ahab's plans included enlarging Megiddo's outpost at Jezreel because it was closer to the pass below Mount Gilboa that linked the Jordan Valley to the coast. Jezreel was warmer—much warmer than Samaria—during the winter rains. I encouraged him to remodel the fort at Jezreel to become his spring quarters, a better post for couriers to the northern and eastern armies during the annual campaigns. He could leave Samaria's palace under the management of Obadiah the steward. The children and I would spend the rainy season and spring with our attendants on a newly designated royal estate, close enough to the fort to find protection if necessary, but away from Samaria's chill and the commotion of building. He agreed.

We were unpacking at the Jezreel estate, anticipating the rainy season, when bad news came. A band of the Sons of the Prophets had attacked the covenant shrine of Baal Shamem on Baal's Headland. They had pulled down the pillars, torn apart the altars, and killed the resident priests, burning their house over them. Their leader, a Tishbite, sent a priest's terror-stricken servant to Jezreel with a message. "Say to the king, say Eliyahu, 'Yhwh is my God,' has done this in reprisal for Samaria's waywardness. Tyre's gods and Tyre's goods shall not pollute the inheritance of Yhwh."

It could not have come at a worse time. A delegation from my father Ethbaal was at Jezreel to acknowledge my lord Ahab's rule and renew the covenant. Eliyahu's desecration had effectively nullified the treaty and cast grave doubts on my lord Ahab's ability to govern his own people, to say nothing of the neighboring territories. The ambassadors returned to Tyre for consultations. And Baal Shamem's wrath was swift and unmistakable. The winter rains did not arrive.

My lord Ahab sent search parties, but Eliyahu and his pack of chanting "Sons" had ducked like rock badgers into their crevices. As we heard later, one of his holes was in Jerusalem's territory, near Beer-sheba. Suspecting that a remnant of Tibni's opposition might still be at work with support from sick Asa of Jerusalem, Ahab changed his leniency toward the Sons of the Prophets into an immediate death warrant and hunted them down. It was not enough for Baal Shamem. The rains did not come.

Fortification tower at Jezreel

The Jezebel Letters

Jizebul Writes to Ethbaal: A Plea for Covenant Renewal

873 BCE

To Ethbaal king of Tyre, king of the Sidonians. Your daughter Jizebul, your servant in the House of Omri in Samaria, sends to greet my lord and my brother Baal-azzor at your right hand. Are you well? We are well. I bless you to Baal Shamem, the Lady Astarte, and all the gods of Tyre. May they guard you and keep you well.

By now you will have received the delegation from my lord Ahab, offering covenant loyalty to Tyre according to the agreement you made with his father Omri. I write to petition, with full knowledge of my lord Ahab, that you will renew the covenant with a ceremony at Baal's Headland.

My lord and father, soon it will be ten years since I stood for you in the covenant rites on Baal's Headland. All that you desired has come to pass. King Omri's victories opened highways from Moab to Damascus and from Damascus to the Great Sea. Israel's fields and herds have been fruitful, and I have been fruitful. The House of Omri is established in Samaria and in my sons. The peoples subdued by Omri have sworn allegiance to my lord Ahab. But there is unease at the new conditions of his rule. The drought also creates great discontent.

Let our two kingdoms meet again at Baal's Headland. Together let us repair the altars and standing stones that the Sons of the Prophets threw down. Let us conduct the ritual of Baal's return from the realm of Mot, which is celebrated in your very honored name. Let us invoke the Baal Shamem of our mutual covenant with pleasing sacrifice and pray that he will no longer chastise our lands for the Tishbite's blasphemy. May he return to us with the rains of life.

I entreat you to send noble sons of your house to the ceremony, that they may visit with my lord Ahab and bring us news of your renewed accord.

Sealed by my own hand.

Baal's Headland

Eliyahu on Baal's Headland

<small>871 BCE, EVENTS IN THE NORTHERN KINGDOM OF ISRAEL,
AS DESCRIBED MUCH LATER BY PRIESTLY SCRIBES FROM JERUSALEM</small>

After many days the word of Yhwh came to Eliyahu, in the third year of the drought, saying, "Go, show yourself to Ahab and I will give rain on the ground." So Eliyahu went to show himself to Ahab.

The famine was severe in Samaria. Ahab called Obadiah, who was over the king's house. (Now Obadiah revered Yhwh greatly; when Jezebel was cutting off the prophets of Yhwh, Obadiah took a hundred prophets and hid them, fifty men to a cave, and provided them with bread and water.)

Then Ahab said to Obadiah, "Go through the land to all the springs of water and to all the creek beds; perhaps we may find grass to keep alive the horses and mules, and not lose some of the animals." So they divided the land between them to pass through it; Ahab went on one path by himself, and Obadiah went on another path by himself.

As Obadiah was on the path, Eliyahu met him; Obadiah recognized him, fell on his face, and said, "Is it you, my lord Eliyahu?"

And he said to him, "It is I. Go, say to your lord that Eliyahu is here."

And he said, "How have I sinned, that you would give your servant into the hand of Ahab, to kill me? As Yhwh your god lives, there is no nation or kingdom to which my lord has not sent to seek you; and when they would say, 'He is not here,' he would require of the kingdom or nation to swear, that they had not found you. But now you say, 'Go, say to your lord that Eliyahu is here.' As soon as I have gone from you, the spirit of Yhwh will carry you I know not where, so when I come to tell Ahab and he does not find you, he will kill me, although your servant has revered Yhwh from my youth. Has it not been told to my lord what I did when Jezebel killed the prophets of Yhwh, how I hid a hundred of the prophets of Yhwh, fifty men to a cave, and provided them with bread and water? Yet now you say, 'Go, say to your lord that Eliyahu is here'; he will surely kill me."

Eliyahu said, "As Yhwh of Hosts lives, before whom I stand, surely today I will show myself to him." So Obadiah went to meet Ahab, and told him, and Ahab went to meet Eliyahu.

When Ahab saw Eliyahu, Ahab said to him, "Is it you, you troubler of Israel?"

He answered, "I have not troubled Israel; but you have, and the House of your father, because you have forsaken the commandments of Yhwh and followed the baals. Now therefore send, gather to me all Israel at Baal's Headland, with the four hundred fifty prophets of Baal and the four hundred prophets of Asherah, who eat at the table of Jezebel."

So Ahab sent to all the Israelites, and gathered the prophets at Baal's Headland. Eliyahu then came near to all the people, and said, "How long will you go limping with two different opinions? If Yhwh is God, follow him; but if Baal, then follow him."

The people did not answer him a word.

Then Eliyahu said to the people, "I, I alone, am left a prophet of Yhwh; but the prophets of Baal—four hundred fifty men. Let them give two bulls to us; let them choose one bull for themselves, cut it in pieces, and lay it on the wood, but put no fire to it; I will prepare the other bull and lay it on the wood, but put no fire to it. Then you call on the name of your god and I will call on the name of Yhwh; the god who answers by fire, that one is God."

All the people answered, "Well spoken!"

Then Eliyahu said to the prophets of Baal, "Choose for yourselves one bull and prepare it first, for you are many, and call on the name of your god, but put no fire to it."

So they took the bull that was given them, prepared it, and called on the name of Baal from morning until noon, crying, "O Baal, answer us!" But there was no voice, and no answer. They limped around the altar that they had made.

At noon, Eliyahu mocked them, saying, "Cry with a loud voice! Surely he is a god; either he is 'doing his business,' or he has wandered away, or he is on a journey, or perhaps he is asleep and must be awakened."

Then they cried with a loud voice, and they cut themselves according to their custom with swords and spears until the blood gushed on them. As midday passed, they raved on until the time of the offering of the oblation, but there was no voice, no answer, and no attention.

Then Eliyahu said to all the people, "Come closer to me"; and all the people came closer to him.

First he repaired the altar of Yhwh that had been torn down; Eliyahu took twelve stones, according to the number of the tribes of the sons of

Baal's Headland

Jacob, to whom the word of Yhwh came, saying, "Israel shall be your name"; with the stones he built an altar in the name of Yhwh. Then he made a trench, large enough to contain two measures of seed, around the altar. Next he put the wood in order, cut the bull in pieces, and laid it on the wood.

He said, "Fill four jars with water and pour it on the burnt offering and on the wood."

Then he said, "Do it a second time"; and they did it a second time.

Again he said, "Do it a third time"; and they did it a third time, so that the water ran all around the altar and filled also the trench with water.

At the time of the offering of the oblation, Eliyahu the prophet came near and said, "O Yhwh, God of Abraham, Isaac, and Israel, today let it be known that you are God in Israel, that I am your servant, and that by your word I have done all these things. Answer me, O Yhwh, answer me, so that this people may know that you, O Yhwh, are God, and that you have turned their hearts back."

Then the fire of Yhwh fell and consumed the burnt offering, the wood, the stones, and the dust, and even licked up the water that was in the trench.

When all the people saw it, they fell on their faces and said, "Yhwh, that one is God; Yhwh, that one is God."

Eliyahu said to them, "Seize the prophets of Baal; do not let one of them escape."

Then they seized them; and Eliyahu brought them down to the creek bed of Kishon, and killed them there.

Eliyahu said to Ahab, "Go up, eat and drink; for there is a sound of a turbulent downpour."

So Ahab went up to eat and to drink.

Eliyahu went up to the top of Baal's Headland; there he bowed himself down upon the earth and put his face between his knees.

He said to his servant, "Go up now, look toward the sea."

He went up and looked, and said, "There is nothing."

He said, "Go again," seven times.

At the seventh time, he said, "Look, a little cloud like a man's hand is rising out of the sea."

The Jezebel Letters

Then he said, "Go say to Ahab, 'Harness your chariot and go down before the rain stops you.'"

In a little while, the heavens grew black with clouds and wind; there was a great downpour. Ahab rode off and went to Jezreel.

But the hand of Y<small>HWH</small> was on Eliyahu; he girded up his loins and ran in front of Ahab to the entrance of Jezreel.

Ahab told Jezebel all that Eliyahu had done, and how he had killed all the prophets with the sword.

Then Jezebel sent a messenger to Eliyahu, saying, "So may the gods do to me, and more also, if by this time tomorrow I do not make your life like the life of one of them."

Then he was afraid; he got up and fled for his life, and came to Beer-sheba, which belongs to Judah. . . .

View toward Jezreel Plain from Baal's Headland (Mount Carmel)

Covenant Renewal and Rain

871 BCE

I KNOW WHAT THEY ARE SAYING IN JERUSALEM ABOUT ELIYAHU'S "victory" on Baal's Headland. *Sheqer!* A lie! He is one of many who claim credit for breaking the drought, but he is the one who caused it! How the priests in Jerusalem twist the story! Let it be known that they make this false report to increase the honor of the family who sheltered Eliyahu from my lord Ahab's search, the family of King Jehoash's supposed mother, Zibiah of Beer-sheba.

Eliyahu did not govern Israel and call all the people together. He certainly did not talk face-to-face with my lord Ahab and walk away. His only confrontation was a furtive raid, and his only fire a torch that ignited the priests' house. His band made a cowardly attack upon the monuments, then ran away to their caves. Eventually, he found his way to those in Jerusalem who plant unrest in Israel, both then and by their stories now, and they found him a hiding hole in Beer-sheba. His desecration caused the drought and brought great harm to those whose name he bore, those Tishbite farmers and herders of Gilead upon whom Baal Shamem's vengeance fell without mercy. And the life-giving rains did not return at the hand of Eliyahu's Yhwh of Hosts.

Those who read the annals of Tyre will be instructed that the prayers of my father Ethbaal were answered with a downpour that ended the drought.○ Indirectly, perhaps, that may be true, because he had the wisdom finally to send a delegation, including brothers I had known, to the ceremony on Baal's Headland. He had waited so long, he wrote, to be sure my lord Ahab's rule was secure. My father may well have been praying in Baal Shamem's sanctuary at Tyre, as I and many others were also praying for rain in Samaria's temple, at the hour appointed by the priests. But those on the heights of Baal's Headland acted for all of us.

My lord Ahab met Tyre's ambassadors at Megiddo, and together their parties climbed to the high place, armed against possible intruders. An advance group of priests and consecrated workers had repaired the covenant site—clearing away the priests' house, rebuilding the altar, resetting the pillars. Looking back over the valley toward Megiddo, my lord Ahab told me later, he saw the flatland, dry and dusty as a beaten path. On the mountain, gazelles had chewed the bark of every shrub and tree to their necks' reach, and goats had climbed to strip the highest limbs. Great clumps of their black hair hung from broken branches, limp flags against a clear sky.

The ritual of Baal's return from Mot's deathly realm was completed in good order. No raving prophets, no jars of water, no fire from heaven. The treaty was read out, sworn, and witnessed by the stones of the sanctuary. My lord Ahab and my brothers from Tyre ate and drank, invoking the brotherhood of their fathers.

And in the bare trees, tufts of black hair began to wave as a breeze rose from the sea before the Rider of Clouds.

Hymn of Praise to Baal[○]

O Baal my God, you are very great.
    You are clothed with honor and majesty.
Who is wrapped in light as with a garment,
    who stretched out the heavens like a tent,
who set the beams of his chambers on the waters,
    who makes the clouds his chariot,
who rides on the wings of the wind,
    who makes the Winds his messengers,
    Fire and Flame his ministers.
Who set the earth on its foundations,
    so that it shall never be shaken.

You cover it with the Deep as with a garment;
    the Waters stood above the mountains.
At your rebuke they flee;
    at the sound of your thunder they take to flight.
They rose up to the cosmic mountains,
    ran down to the depths,

Baal's Headland

to the place that you appointed for them.
You set a boundary that they may not pass,
    so that they might not again cover the earth.

Who makes Springs gush forth in the valleys;
    they flow between the hills,
giving drink to every wild animal;
    the wild asses quench their thirst.
By the streams the birds of the air have their habitation;
    they sing among the branches.
Who waters the mountains from his lofty abode;
    with the fruit of his work
    the earth is satisfied.
Who causes the grass to grow for the cattle,
    and plants for people to use,
He brings forth food from the earth,
    and wine to gladden the human heart,
oil to make the face shine,
    and bread to strengthen the human heart.

Ivory plaque with goats and tree of life in Phoenician style

The trees of Baal are watered abundantly,
    the cedars of Lebanon that he planted.
In them the birds build their nests;
    the stork has its home in the fir trees.
The high mountains are for the wild goats;
    the sheltering rocks for the rock badgers.

You have made the Moon to mark the seasons;
    the Sun knows its time for setting.
You make darkness, and it is night,
    when all the animals of the forest come creeping out.
The young lions roar for their prey,
    seeking their food from God.
When the Sun rises, they withdraw
    and lie down in their dens.
People go out to their work
    and to their labor until the evening.

O Baal, how manifold are your works!
With the Lady you have made them all;
    the earth is full of your creatures.○
The One of the Sea, great and wide,
    who put creeping things innumerable,
    living things both small and great.
Who made the ships,
    and Leviathan that you formed to sport in it.
These all look to you
    to give them their food in due season;
when you give to them, they gather it up;
    when you open your hand, they are filled with good things.
When you hide your face, they are dismayed;
    when you take away your Breath, they die and return to their dust.
When you send forth your Breath,
    they are created;
    and you renew the face of the ground.

May the glory of Baal endure forever;
    may Baal rejoice in his works—

Baal's Headland

who looks on the earth and it trembles,
> who touches the mountains and they smoke.

I will sing to Baal as long as I live;
> I will sing praise to my God while I have being.

May my meditation be pleasing to him,
> for I rejoice in Baal.

6
Jezreel

Jehoshaphat Becomes King in Jerusalem

<small>869 BCE, EVENTS IN JERUSALEM,
AS DESCRIBED MUCH LATER BY PRIESTLY SCRIBES THERE[○]</small>

Now the rest of all the acts of Asa, and all his power, and all that he did, and the cities that he built, are they not written in the Book of the Daily Affairs of the Kings of Judah? But at the time of his old age, he was diseased in his "feet."[○] Then Asa slept with his fathers and was buried with his fathers in the City of David his father; Jehoshaphat his son reigned in his place.

Jehoshaphat son of Asa began to reign over Judah in the fourth year of Ahab king of Israel. Jehoshaphat was thirty-five years old when he began to reign, and twenty-five years he reigned in Jerusalem. His mother's name was Azubah daughter of Shilhi.

He walked in all the way of Asa his father; he did not turn from it, doing right in the eyes of Y<small>HWH</small>; but the high places were not taken away—the people still sacrificed and burned incense on the high places.

Jehoshaphat also made peace with the king of Israel.

Jezreel

Shalom with Jehoshaphat

869 BCE

VAYYASHLEM. And he made peace.

Jehoshaphat of the House of David did not only stop the frontier skirmishes and remove the military threat. As my lord Ahab expected, Jehoshaphat established right relations with the House of Omri. He wanted our families to unite. He asked for Atalyah for his son Jehoram. Their betrothal would not be consummated until she was fifteen, a year younger than I was when I married my lord Ahab.

Unlike his father Asa, Jehoshaphat wanted his kingdom to be expansive, not isolated. His secret talks with my lord Ahab had convinced him that Israel's power could also be to Jerusalem's advantage. Let Israel control the routes north to Damascus and east to Moab. With an alliance, Jehoshaphat received control of some contested cities in Ephraim, so my lord Ahab could attend to the north. Jehoshaphat directed his efforts to securing the south, at Beer-sheba and the Negev, where the routes brought copper from Edom and spices from the Arabs, and at Ezion-geber whose port offered access to the sea. Even from its hill country, Jerusalem could develop a sea trade with the help of Israel and Tyre. Jehoshaphat could hold the outposts on the Sinai routes to Egypt. The flow of goods to Israel and Tyre would enrich many in Jerusalem and her towns along the way. If Assyria resumed its western marches, Jehoshaphat would not be fighting on his own land but defending it from behind a shield of many armies in his allies' territory far to the north.

Shalom, right relations. The gods rewarded our partnership. Gezer, on Israel's border with Jerusalem and Philistia, could be built as more than a garrison. The regional centers flourished in Israel and the southern hill country. The fields recovered from the drought, and, in the hills, plots of oak and pine were harvested for timber, replaced by new terraces for olive groves and vineyards on a scale not known by the families who had left them.

Terraced hillsides

My attention turned to preparing Atalyah. Small and restless, she shared my sense of confinement even in the Samaria quarters. The olive grove at our Jezreel estate was her favorite place, where chameleons disguised themselves as lichen-covered rocks on the low stone walls and little green bee-eaters flashed among the silver leaves. I had a large booth constructed among the trees so her tutors and I could find shelter from sun or rain.

She played at being queen. A remnant of fine blue cloth, just big enough for a sash, was her royal vestment. She sat enthroned on the gnarled base of an ancient tree, dictating letters and directing the servants of her household in the grove. The sun, filtered through olive leaves, decorated her robe with ever-shifting circles of light, like disks embroidered in silver thread on the Lady's shimmering vestments in Samaria's temple.

I, too, had visitors under the booth in the grove—guests from the Tyrian towns of the Galil° and merchants seeking to have their wares exhibited as furnishings in the king's house. I know how my enemies spread malicious gossip about those guests, especially about the young man who brought dyed cloth for my inspection and who sat with me for long hours in the shade. My special friend—not to give his name to harm, I shall write as I called him—*Achli*, my brother.

> Perfume and incense make the heart glad,
> and the sweetness of a friend is better than one's own counsel.°

His speech was strangely familiar, more intimate in accent than in the words themselves. He was, I discovered, a son of

Jezreel

the Tyrian trader who had brought me the little ivory chest from Damascus, a distant kinsman from my mother's house, merchants from Achziv, north of Akko.

> O that you were like a brother to me,
> > who nursed at my mother's breast!
> If I met you outside, I would kiss you,
> > and no one would despise me.○

Achli and I were never alone, never out of the sight of servants and guests; we touched each other only with words and eyes. *Sheqer!* A lie! to say we did anything more. He wove pictures for me with his stories—how Tyre had changed since I left, how the royal women of Damascus furnished their chambers, how cormorants (he called me by my family name) and egrets fished in the papyrus swamps of the Huleh. I called him "Stork"—for his broad shoulders, long legs, well-oiled beard, and his coming to Jezreel in spring when migrating storks followed mowers in the king's fields. Once he learned how I used the ivory box for my memory-stones, he brought me three rounded river-rocks, one from each of the streams that merge into the Jordan on his route to Damascus. Dull in my hand, they glowed, rich with color, in a dish of water, just as I glowed in his company.

And he brought me news, old but still troubling, rumors from other traders that Eliyahu had lived during the drought with a widow at Zarephath between Sidon and Tyre. A clever refuge—who would think to look for the enemy of Tyre at

Phoenician traders from Assyrian relief sculpture

Tyre's back gate? What trouble was Eliyahu stirring among the Sidonians? Were food and lodging all the widow provided for him? Had my father Ethbaal or my lord Ahab killed her husband or taken his land, that she needed a wild man's comfort?

The land around Jezreel was changing hands. As my lord Ahab used the fortress at Jezreel more often for his royal seat, provisions were needed to feed the officials and visitors there. Formerly a small winter house for the family, our estate was expanding to supply the garrison with produce. Local family heads, like those around Samaria, were also granted larger portions in return for their contributions. Small plots not directly contracted to the court were taxed in kind. To relieve these farmers of extra mouths, my lord Ahab drafted their sons for the army, the estates, and the court. Younger sons had an alternative to their father's poor subsistence. Families that could not meet their tax quotas reduced their own needs and met their debt by substituting their children's labor, or even, in last resort, yielding the land itself. Thus, many family farms were absorbed into royal estates and grants, especially around regional centers, where the commanders and officials followed Samaria's model. To succeed in the new contracts for trade, all Israel's efforts were directed to production—for the king, the army, the officials, and for export. Surely, this benefited all!

And the new ways worked. Israel prospered as a sign of the gods' approval. Truly, this was *shalom*, with the gods, the king, and the land in right relations. And the House of David shared our peace.

Naboth's Vineyard

869 BCE, EVENTS IN THE NORTHERN KINGDOM OF ISRAEL,
AS DESCRIBED MUCH LATER BY PRIESTLY SCRIBES FROM JERUSALEM

Later, the following events took place: Naboth the Jezreelite had a vineyard in Jezreel, beside the palace of Ahab king of Samaria.

Jezreel

And Ahab said to Naboth, "Give me your vineyard, that it may be a garden of greens for me, because it is near my house; I will give you in its place a better vineyard than it; or, if it is good in your eyes, I will give you silver, the price of this one."

But Naboth said to Ahab, "Far be it from me—by Y<small>HWH</small>!—that I should give the inheritance of my fathers to you."

Ahab went to his house resentful and vexed because of what Naboth the Jezreelite had said to him; for he had said, "I will not give you the inheritance of my fathers." He lay on his bed, turned away his face, and would not eat food.

Jezebel his wife came to him and said to him, "Why is your spirit sullen, that you will not eat food?"

He said to her, "Because I spoke to Naboth the Jezreelite and said to him, 'Give me your vineyard for silver; or, if you prefer, I will give you another vineyard in its place'; but he said, 'I will not give you my vineyard.'"

Jezebel his wife said to him, "Do you now reign over Israel? Get up, eat some food, and let your heart be glad; I will give you the vineyard of Naboth the Jezreelite."

So she wrote letters in the name of Ahab and sealed them with his seal; she sent the letters to the elders and the nobles who lived with Naboth in his city.

She wrote in the letters, "Call a fast, and seat Naboth at the head of the assembly; seat two men—sons of worthlessness^O—opposite him, and have them testify against him, saying, 'You have "blessed" God and the king.'^O Then take him out, and stone him to death."

The men of his city, the elders and the nobles who lived in his city, did as Jezebel had sent word to them. Just as it was written in the letters that she had sent to them, they called a fast and seated Naboth at the head of the assembly. The two men, sons of worthlessness, came in and sat opposite him; and the worthless ones testified against Naboth before the assembly, saying, "Naboth 'blessed' God and the king." So they took him outside the city, and stoned him with stones, and he died. Then they sent to Jezebel saying, "Naboth has been stoned; he is dead."

As soon as Jezebel heard that Naboth had been stoned and was dead, Jezebel said to Ahab, "Get up, take possession of the vineyard of Naboth the Jezreelite, which he refused to give you for silver; for Naboth is not alive, but dead."

As soon as Ahab heard that Naboth was dead, Ahab got up to go down to the vineyard of Naboth the Jezreelite, to take possession of it.

Then the word of YHWH came to Eliyahu the Tishbite, saying: Get up, go down to meet Ahab the king of Israel, who rules in Samaria; he is now in the vineyard of Naboth, where he has gone to take possession. You shall say to him, "Thus says YHWH: Have you killed, and also taken possession?" You shall say to him, "Thus says YHWH: In the place where dogs licked up the blood of Naboth, dogs will lick up your blood, even yours."

Ahab said to Eliyahu, "Have you found me, O my enemy?"

He answered, "I have found you. Because you have sold yourself to do evil in the eyes of YHWH, behold, I will bring evil upon you; I will consume those after you, and will cut off from Ahab everyone who pees against a wall, bond or free, in Israel; and I will 'give' your house—like the house of Jeroboam son of Nebat, and like the house of Baasha son of Ahijah—to the anger with which you have angered me, for you have caused Israel to sin. Also concerning Jezebel YHWH said, 'The dogs shall eat Jezebel within the district of Jezreel.' Anyone belonging to Ahab who dies in the city the dogs shall eat; and anyone of his who dies in the field the birds of the air shall eat."

When Ahab heard those words, he tore his clothes and put sackcloth over his bare flesh; he fasted, lay in the sackcloth, and went about dejectedly.

Then the word of YHWH came to Eliyahu the Tishbite: "Have you seen how Ahab has humbled himself before me? Because he has humbled himself before me, I will not bring the evil in his days; but in the days of his son, I will bring the evil on his house."

Stopping the Blight at Jezreel

869 BCE

How easily words are twisted, even when the message is written!

Jezreel

View from Jezreel over valley
(photo by Robert Haak)

    A wilting blight struck the vineyards near Jezreel. The wildfire of devastation blackened the fields as leaves spotted, darkened, and fell; in some places, it jumped over one plot only to burn another.

    Jezreel's local elders and the nobles of outlying estates called for a solemn assembly. Like elders purging a village of bloodguilt for a murder by an unknown assailant,○ they would seek absolution. The day before the assembly, the men fasted, including my lord Ahab, even though he would not attend the ceremony. Wearing sackcloth over empty stomachs, they tried to avert further harm without knowing its cause.

    But I knew the culprit. My lord Ahab had tried to acquire the nearby plot of Naboth, planted with vines, for a vegetable garden. Vines would grow just as well on more distant hillsides, which my lord Ahab offered. Naboth's watered field in the lowland was better suited for vegetables for our table and for the king's house at Jezreel. But he refused to negotiate with the stewards.

    It was more than a simple stalemate. Naboth held his family zealously to the old ways, clinging to a particular field as God's gift to his fathers, which he would not release, no matter what compensation was offered. Why could he not acknowledge that the king was also God's gift, the agent divinely commissioned to distribute land for greatest blessing to all? Was it because of Eliyahu, who, it was rumored, had once been seen leaving Naboth's house at first light? The stewards had reported to me Naboth's defiant curse at their offers: Naboth had cursed the king by the divine Name so revered among Israelites, so honored they would only say "bless" instead of curse.

Since the fast required landowners to abstain from all normal work, even by my lord Ahab, I wrote on his behalf, addressing the assembly with this letter:

*To the elders and nobles of Jezreel. Jizebul, wife of Ahab king in Samaria, sends to greet you. May you be blessed by Y*HWH *and his Asherah.*

*Receive with every courtesy the men who deliver this letter, for they are stewards over the king's estate at Jezreel. They are witnesses to the blasphemy of Naboth the Jezreelite, whose "blessing" of Y*HWH *and the king has sparked God's anger. Because he would not give his vineyard for exchange or silver but gave only a curse, God has given your vineyards to the blight. When you seek to appease God's anger, seat Naboth at the head of your assembly, and let these witnesses testify against him. Then take him out and stone him to death with those who share his guilt, according to your laws.*

Sealed by my own hand with the seal of the king.

So it happened. Jezreel's assembly recognized the truth and their danger. They found Naboth guilty of a trespass against their God, one that would pollute all their fields. They stoned Naboth and his sons who, by proximity and as heirs to the field, shared his guilt.º The stewards had Naboth's vines dug out and burned, even though they looked clean, and the blight spread no further.

Jozacar and Jehozabad have told me how the story is repeated now by priestly scribes in Jerusalem—that Naboth refused my lord Ahab's request by saying it would be *halilah*, a profane thing against Y<small>HWH</small>, for him to release his fathers' field to the king. With wordplay they have changed his unmentionable curse, his *qelalah,* into a righteous word! The royal stewards, sons of a landless father greatly respected in their service to my lord Ahab, have become "sons of worthlessness," as if being landless made them also liars. The Eliyahu of their story, speaking Jerusalem's words instead of YHWH's, curses my lord Ahab and me, actually repeating Naboth's offense! Jerusalem's scribes cried out "remember Naboth's vineyard" as they divided my murdered Atalyah's royal estates to buy friends for Jehoiada the priest. The same scribes were lax in their accounts of revenues, filling the priests' treasury at the expense of the nobles.○ They used Naboth's loss for their own profit. May their vineyards burn with fire and blight, like those of Jezreel!

When he came to the throne in Jerusalem, King Jehoash was too young to understand Jehoiada the priest's moves to set the kingdom under priestly rule and against Israel. Perhaps the king will see his danger now, when he needs the loyalty of noble families to face Hazael.

7
Beth-hakkherem

Jehoshaphat's Beginnings

869 BCE, EVENTS OF JEHOSHAPHAT'S REIGN
AS DESCRIBED IN THE POSTEXILIC WORK OF THE CHRONICLER[○]

The fear of Y<small>HWH</small> was upon on all the kingdoms of the lands around Judah, and they did not make war against Jehoshaphat. From the Philistines, they brought Jehoshaphat gifts and silver for tribute; also the Arabs also brought him seven thousand seven hundred rams and seven thousand seven hundred male goats. Jehoshaphat went from great to greater. He built in Judah fortresses and storage cities. He carried out great works in the cities of Judah. He had soldiers, mighty warriors, in Jerusalem. These were their numbers by fathers' houses: Of Judah, the commanders of the thousands: Adnah the commander, and with him three hundred thousand mighty warriors; and next to him Jehohanan the commander, and with him two hundred eighty thousand; and next to him Amasiah son of Zichri, the one making a freewill offering to Y<small>HWH</small>, and with him two hundred thousand mighty warriors. **Of Benjamin: Eliada, a mighty warrior, and with him two hundred thousand armed with bow and shield; and next to him Jehozabad, and with him 180,000 armed for war. These were the ones serving the king,**[○] besides those whom the king had given in the fortified cities throughout all Judah.

Beth-hakkherem

Now Jehoshaphat had great riches and honor; and he made a marriage alliance with Ahab.

A Covenant Hymn○

How very good and pleasant it is
>   when kindred live together in unity!
It is like the precious oil on the head,
>   running down upon the beard,
>   on the beard of Aaron,
>   running down over the collar of his robes.
It is like the dew of Hermon,
>   which falls on the mountains of Zion.
For there Y<small>HWH</small> ordained his blessing,
>   life forevermore.

A spring at Dan

The Jezebel Letters

Atalyah's Marriage

866 BCE

 Mattan, the priest who accompanied Atalyah to her wedding and her new home, took with him the covenant hymn. It is still used in Jerusalem—changed, of course, to eliminate reference to Ijon of the north and to make Zion's narrow ridge into the mountain of God.○ Our brother Jehoshaphat and his son Jehoram heard our hymn with glad hearts during the ceremony at Beth-el.

> Behold, how good and how pleasant
> > the dwelling of brothers as one!
> Like sweet oil upon the head
> > going down upon the beard,
> Like the dew of Hermon
> > which runs down upon the mountains of Ijon.
> For there, God confers the blessing:
> > life, forevermore.○

There—between Baal's Headland in the west, where his sweet rains first anoint the land, and Hermon, the snow-capped mount from whose roots gush the fountains that fill Chinneroth—there, where Tyre and Israel and Aram met in brotherhood, the blessing was granted. And when Jerusalem, whose little Gihon spring trickles through the rock below her ridge like seepage from a cracked pot, when Jerusalem dwells in covenant with Israel, the blessing overflows upon her also.

Jerusalem's priests may say that *shalom* is the blessing of their Yhwh alone. In Samaria, as in Tyre, the songs speak of another—of Lady Anath, sister-consort to Baal—who brings *shalom*. In the old stories, it was she, not a priest, over whose body the precious fluids ran down. After her warring contests or before her feasting with Baal,

Beth-hakkherem

    she draws some water and bathes;
        sky-dew, fatness of earth,
           spray of the Rider of Clouds;
    dew that the heavens do shed,
        spray that is shed by the stars.
    She rubs herself with ambergis
        from a sperm-whale whose home's in the sea.

Baal invited the warring Lady to his feast after her ablutions, saying:

    Take war away from the earth,
        banish all strife from the soil;
    pour peace into earth's very bowels,
        much amity into earth's bosom.○

    I taught Atalyah our stories of *shalom*. We sat in the booth in Jezreel's grove with our Tyrian guests listening to a singer who chanted the story of that other garden, the garden of God on a mountain like Hermon, with trees like the forests of the Lebanon. The tree of life grew on that mount of Eden, rooted in the cosmic waters,

    with fair branches and forest shade,
        and of great height,
           its top among the clouds.
    The Waters nourished it,
        the Deep made it grow tall,
    making its rivers flow
        around the place it was planted,
    sending forth its streams
        to all the trees of the field.
    So it towered high
        above all the trees of the field;
    its boughs grew numerous

and its branches long,
> from abundant water in its shoots.
> In its boughs all the birds of the air made their nests;

(Yes, Atalyah, even the little green bee-eater was there.)

Ivory plaque with tree of life design

> under its branches all the animals of the field
> > gave birth to their young;
> and in its shade
> > all the great peoples lived.
> It was beautiful in its greatness,
> > in the length of its branches;
> for its roots went down
> > to abundant water.
> The cedars in the garden of God
> > could not rival it,
> > > nor the juniper trees equal its boughs;
> the plane trees were as nothing
> > compared to its branches;
> no tree in the garden of God
> > was like it in beauty.

(Yes, Atalyah, more beautiful than the ivory trees in the king's house.)

> With its mass of branches,
> > it was the envy of all the trees of Eden
> > that were in the garden of God.○

Such a peace was desired by our gods. Israelites, too, honor the Lady with trees at her shrines and on their altars. Even Jerusalem's priests tell of that garden from which waters flowed downhill in four directions, where the great tree stood and all creatures lived in harmony.○ In their wilderness stories, was not the lampstand of the tabernacle of Yhwh fashioned as a tree of life, with its branches of flowers and fruits?○

Beth-hakkherem

When men are in right relations as brothers, their peace is shared by fields and herds. Earth grieves at the disputes of men and rejoices at their covenants.○ To that end, we sent our daughter to Jerusalem, that we all might prosper. I gave her my wedding bracelet, the one with the tree of life drawn in grains of gold. Israel and Jerusalem had ended their warfare; in peace, we were ready to receive the sky-dew, the sweet oil of earth. And Atalyah could give birth to Jehoram's sons, who would carry this blessing for the House of David into future generations.

This, men of Jerusalem, is the inheritance you shunned by listening to Jehoiada the priest and his son Zechariah when they killed the *gevirah* Atalyah and rejected brotherhood with Israel. The ruler in Samaria may not yet admit his folly either. Be ever watchful for your opportunity to remove obstacles to peace.

Jehoshaphat's Administration

865 BCE, ASPECTS OF JEHOSHAPHAT'S REIGN
AS DESCRIBED IN THE POSTEXILIC WORK OF THE CHRONICLER○

Jehoshaphat his son reigned in Asa's place, and he strengthened himself because of Israel.○ He placed forces in all the fortified cities of Judah and set garrisons in the land of Judah, and in the cities of Ephraim that his father Asa had taken.

Jehoshaphat resided at Jerusalem; then he went out again among the people, from Beer-sheba to the hill country of Ephraim, and brought them back to Yhwh, the God of their fathers. He appointed judges in the land in all the fortified cities of Judah, city by city. He said to the judges, "Watch what you are doing, for you judge not on behalf of human beings but on Yhwh's behalf; he is with you in the matter of judgment. Now let the fear of Yhwh be upon you; take care what you do, for there is no perversion of justice with Yhwh our God; there is no partiality, or taking of bribes."

And also in Jerusalem, Jehoshaphat appointed some Levites and priests and heads of families of Israel, to give judgment for Yhwh and to decide disputed cases. They returned to Jerusalem. He charged them, saying: "This is how you shall act: in the fear of Yhwh, in faithfulness, and with your whole heart°; whenever a case comes to you from your brothers who live in their cities, concerning bloodshed, ritual law or commandment, statutes or ordinances, then you shall instruct them, so that they may not incur guilt before Yhwh and wrath may not come on you and your brothers. Do so, and you will not incur guilt. See, Amariah the chief priest is over you in all matters of Yhwh; and Zebadiah son of Ishmael, the governor for the house of Judah, in all the king's matters; and the Levites will serve you as officers. Act with strength, and may Yhwh be with the good!"

Jizebul Writes to Atalyah: Concerns in Jerusalem

865 BCE

To Atalyah, wife of Jehoram of the House of David in Jerusalem. Your mother Jizebul sends to greet you. Are you and the child well? We are well. I bless you to Baal Shamem and the Lady Astarte. May they guard you and keep you well.

I received news of the birth with great joy. Your lord Jehoram shows his love for our House by naming his son after your brother Ahaziah. You also are blessed to have received a son as your firstborn. May these thoughts lift your spirits.

The birth announcement arrived before I could reply to your last letter and the sadness in your heart. News of the child has cleared my thoughts.

I know how it grieves you that Jerusalem is not a noble city like Samaria. I, too, was disappointed when I was a bride in Tirzah. Season your troubled mind with patience. Our brother Jehoshaphat rules in a manner new to his hill country, as your grandfather Omri did in Israel. He strives to build fortified cities, to gather an army and laborers by conscription, to secure the loyalty of great men by granting estates, and to require exaction for the royal stores. He

Beth-hakkherem

has just begun to take thought to make a fine city. By the time your son is grown, it will be different. What are you to do now?

I am sending with this messenger another letter, to our brother Jehoshaphat. I ask that he will receive builders from us, not only for the royal precinct in Jerusalem but also to make a house for you and your lord Jehoram outside the city. Surely there is an estate nearby that supplies the king's table, like our estate at Jezreel. It will be better for you and the child to live there, away from the king's house that you call a cage of stone in the noise and dirty streets of Jerusalem. I shall send craftsmen to make a beautiful house for you, and you shall have arbors for shade, where you can sit in the afternoon breezes. May the thought of these pleasures help your sadness to pass.

About the matter of judges, keep me informed. Your father Ahab made judges from his friends the commanders and nobles assigned to the fortified cities, alongside the elders in towns such as Jezreel. You report that our brother Jehoshaphat gives many of these offices to priests. Your father chose to keep the priests apart, to appoint his own priests at Beth-el and Samaria, and to have those from old families at Shechem and elsewhere each seek his favor one by one. But you say that the priests who make judgments in the highland towns are brothers to those in Jerusalem, and that they must give gifts to the king's shrine there and to its priest, who governs the council for appeals. Does this not establish another line of nobles, standing before the king but not dependent on him? And he keeps in Jerusalem the head men of fathers' houses from the cities that your father Ahab ceded to him—as judges or hostages?

You are right to be concerned about the priests' power. You are now the mother of a prince in the House of David. Tell your lord Jehoram what you see, so he may be watchful and preserve your son's birthright. And tell me more about how it goes with Mattan, the priest who serves at our covenant altar there.

Sealed by my own hand.

The Jezebel Letters

The Fruits of *Shalom*

858 BCE

ATALYAH GOT HER OWN HOUSE. Halfway to Beth-lehem, on a hill looking north toward Jerusalem, the builders raised walls of large squared stones quarried from the hill itself—Beth-hakkherem, House of the Vineyard. Built as both stronghold and winery, the wall was doubled by the rooms built into it: storerooms for abundance or fortification for defense. The terraces and farm houses of the estate spread around it—Samaria in miniature.○

Atalyah had married into a House of David with many branches. Unlike King Omri, our brother Jehoshaphat had received the throne from his father, and with it came an extended clan throughout the southern hill country and an hereditary priesthood in Jerusalem's shrine. Jehoshaphat leaned heavily upon his kindred and their priests. Six of Jehoshaphat's sons were his deputies in the fortified cities, while crown prince Jehoram assisted in Jerusalem.○

King Omri had built Israel's governance upon his comrades in the army, some of whom were related, like my lord Ahab and Omri's son Nimshi, who oversaw the chariot horses. Since becoming king, my lord Ahab had new wives and offspring, so many that some said he was blessed by the Lady as in the old stories, with seventy sons! These would be the officials of the next generation. I had expected this, a sign of his power, but he was still drawn to my chamber, to rest in what he called his fragrant garden, his bed of spices. My two boys were of age now, princes among my lord Ahab's sons, tutored in the noble households at Samaria. Ahaziah involved himself in the affairs of the king's house. My "Kingfisher" used the power of his voice and large presence to mark his path as he swooped from room to room. Joram, my "Kestrel," hovered in silence but with long-sighted eyes. He took his place in the army, winning the loyalty of his fellow officers and observing the ways of the commanders.

Beth-hakkherem

The fruits of peace were plentiful throughout our lands. Moab sent its fleece to our weavers in the villages. Our brother Jehoshaphat controlled the southern routes for Edomite copper and Arab spice caravans. Metals and woods and ivory and shell came from Tyre's sea trade through our valley-roads to supply Damascus with materials for its rich furnishings. Olives and vines flourished on newly built terraces, lowland fields had multiple harvests, and Gilead's iron and pastures supplied the weapons and horses of war. Samaria was adorned with all their bounty.

Left alone, the covenant of brothers produced its blessings, but our good fortunes were shaken by a new threat from the Land Between the Rivers. Ashurnasirpal's son Shalmaneser took the throne already enriched by his father's victories and cast his eyes toward our kingdoms in the west. After more than fifteen years without Assyrian attack, we faced an unrelenting foe.

The regions far to the north were his first objective, as Shalmaneser pushed into the mountains of Nairi and reopened the path of destruction cut by his father across Hattini to the Great Sea. And, as he had placated Ashurnasirpal with gifts, so my father Ethbaal shielded the coastlands with generous presentations to the one who called himself "the king of the world." My dear friend Achli told me what he had seen at the Rock, how the horseheaded sea-wagons of Tyre left the northern harbor as my aged father watched, to deliver bales of goods to the mainland. How Shalmaneser gloated over that offering, as if it came by force of his arms, rather than by my father's wit.

But we were not caught off guard. The prosperity of our peace had been forged into swords as well as plowshares, as we prepared to face "the king without rival."

Ethbaal sending tribute to Shalmaneser, from Assyrian bronze gate

The Jezebel Letters

Shalmaneser III's First Year

858 BCE, ASSYRIAN DESCRIPTIONS OF THE CAMPAIGN TO THE WEST

I am Shalmaneser, the legitimate king, the king of the world, the king without rival, the "Great Dragon," the only power within the four rims of the earth, overlord of all the princes, who has smashed all his enemies as if they be earthenware, the strong man, unsparing, who shows no mercy in battle—the son of Ashurnasirpal, king of the world, king of Assyria, grandson of Tukulti-Ninurta, likewise king of the world, king of Assyria, a conqueror from the Upper Sea to the Lower Sea, to wit the countries Hatti, Luhuti, Adri, Lebanon, Que, Tabali, Militene; who has visited the sources of both the Tigris and the Euphrates.○

At that time Ashur, the great lord . . . gave me scepter, staff . . . necessary to rule the people, and I was acting only upon the trust-inspiring oracles given by Ashur, the great lord, my lord, who loves me to be his high priest and . . . all the countries and mountain regions to their full extent. I am Shalmaneser . . . conqueror from the sea of the Nairi country and the sea of the Zamua country which is nearer to Assyria as far as the Great Sea of Amurru. I swept over Hatti, in its full extent making it look like ruin-hills left by the flood . . . thus I spread the terror-inspiring glare of my rule over Hatti.

On my continued march to the sea, I made a stela representing myself as the supreme ruler and set it up beside that of the god Hirbe. . . . I marched to the Great Sea, washed my weapons in the Great Sea; I offered sacrifices there to my gods. I received the tribute from all the kings of the seacoast. I made a stela representing myself as king and warrior and inscribed upon it the deeds which I had performed in the region of the seacoast; I set it up by the sea.○

I received the tribute brought on ships from the inhabitants of Tyre and Sidon.○

Beth-hakkherem

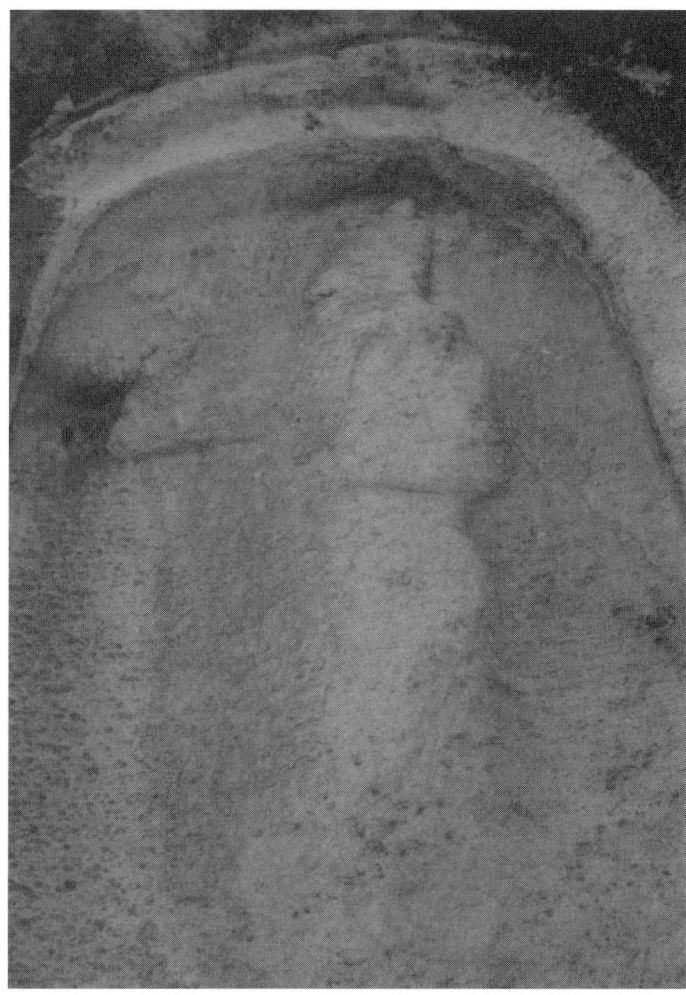

An Assyrian monument (Shalmaneser's?) on cliffs above the Dog River, Lebanon.

8
Karkar

Jizebul Writes to Baal-azzor: Tyre's Covenant with Israel

855 BCE

 To Baal-azzor king of Tyre and king of the Sidonians. Your sister, Jizebul daughter of Ethbaal—may his name be preserved in honor—wife of Ahab son of Omri, king of Israel in Samaria, sends to greet you. I bless you to Baal Shamem, the Lady Astarte, and all the gods of Tyre. May they guard you and keep you well.

 My lord, you have come to the throne of our father Ethbaal with your eyes turned to the north, to Hattini and the path of the Assyrians to the west. The gods have been merciful to the coastlands, granting us peace for almost twenty years, while you grew to manhood. Our father purchased that peace with gifts each time the Assyrians reached the Great Sea, the year after your birth and three years ago. You will surely follow in his ways to secure Assyria's favor for Tyre.

 What do you see when you look to the south? Do not forget our father's plan. He saw the wealth of the south coming to Tyre through the House of Omri. My lord Ahab has fulfilled that vision, uniting lands on both sides of the Jordan, from Damascus to the port of Ezion-geber. But the peoples allied to Israel for commerce and prosperity are now preparing to defend themselves against Assyria. Will the new king of Tyre stand with us?

By now you will have received the delegation sent from my lord Ahab to renew the covenant between the House of Ethbaal and the House of Omri. If you reject the covenant of our father in order not to offend Shalmaneser, will that not cut off the trade whose profits give Tyre its influence with Assyria? If Shalmaneser is permitted to march to Damascus and to Samaria, that too will diminish Tyre— Assyria will take for itself what was destined for Tyre and still require your tribute. Our kingdoms need the cargoes from Tyre's sea trade to defend the land routes of Tyre's prosperity. The House of Omri has shown itself worthy of Tyre's confidence for two generations, as it will also to the third, in your kinsmen, my sons. Will you not add the horseheaded sea-wagons of Tyre to our army of chariots?

My brother, it is well known that our father passed over other sons to give the throne to you, the son of his old age. Friendship with the House of Omri and all our allies will strengthen your hand against any who oppose your rule. May you have the wisdom to follow the path of friendship for both our Houses.

Sealed by my own hand.

Jizebul Writes to Atalyah: Preparations for War

853 BCE

To Atalyah, wife of Jehoram son of Jehoshaphat king in Jerusalem. Your mother Jizebul sends to greet you and your son Ahaziyah. I bless you to Baal Shamem and the Lady Astarte. May they guard you and keep you well.

Here, we are preparing for the spring battles that are sure to come. As you know, our brother Jehoshaphat has come to Samaria for the gathering of commanders. Your father Ahab says that Shalmaneser will aim for Damascus this time, coming south from Aleppo to the banks of the Orontes at Karkar. All the kingdoms have pledged to send troops against him, headed by Ben-hadad of Damascus. At the great banquet, our brother Jehoshaphat promised, "As your people, so are my people."○ *For once, it seems, those who skirmished at each other's frontiers—Aram and Israel and Jerusalem—are united against a common enemy from afar; even Moab and Ammon send forces under Israel's command. Our "Kestrel" Joram will also go to Karkar, leaving me and Ahaziah as regents at Samaria.*

Our brother Jehoshaphat's absence from Jerusalem gives you and your lord Jehoram great power and great danger. We have received reports that not everyone in Jerusalem favors this war. The family of Heman the king's seer is known to oppose Jerusalem's alliance with any other kingdom. Hanani son of Heman rebuked King Asa for relying on Aram, and his son Jehu has opposed Israel since the days of Baasha.○ *How can such opposition be tolerated? Are all who claim to speak in the name of God protected, regardless of their treasonous words? Even sick King Asa only put Hanani in stocks rather than killing him!*

Beware, then, of those who seek the ear of your lord Jehoram, to argue against Jerusalem's covenants. They will say that Jerusalem's holy Mount Zion and her god are greater than any army.○ *They will mean that Jerusalem alone is too small and unimportant to interest Assyria, and she should not become Assyria's enemy by joining the wars of others.*○ *In the days of King Asa, that may have been true. But now the covenant with Israel has strengthened our brother Jehoshaphat so that he controls Edom and the Arab routes in the Negev, even to the port at Ezion-geber, and the Philistines acknowledge him with gifts. The well-being of Jerusalem depends upon our brotherhood, for our joint prosperity in peace has made us both targets for war.*

Be watchful, therefore, lest the strength of the House of David be diminished by those who speak against their brothers in Israel. They undermine the standing of your husband and your son to inherit the throne of our brother Jehoshaphat. Your father Ahab counsels that you and your lord Jehoram should rely on the loyalty of Jehozabad, the king's commander from Benjamin, who serves in Jerusalem. The men of Benjamin under him know the power of Israel from the frontier wars with Asa, and many of them have more kinsmen in our Ephraim than in David's Hebron.

And do not neglect offerings to Baal Shamem at the covenant altar served by Mattan our priest, especially now. Zion has been beautified by the architects of

Tyre, and all who worship there can see the blessings of brotherhood in its very stones.

Sealed by my own hand.

Shalmaneser III's Monolith Inscription

853 BCE, Assyrian description of the battle at Karkar

In the year of Daian-Ashur, in the month Aiaru, the fourteenth day, I departed from Nineveh. I crossed the Tigris and approached the towns of Giammu on the river Balih. **They became afraid of the terror emanating from my position as overlord, as well as of the splendor of my fierce weapons, and killed their master Giammu with their own weapons.** I entered the towns Sahlala and Til-sha-Turahi and brought images of my gods into his palaces. I performed in his own palaces. I opened his treasury, inspected what he had hidden; I carried away as booty his possessions, bringing them to my town Ashur. From Sahlala I departed and approached Kar-Shalmaneser. I crossed the Euphrates another time at its flood on rafts made buoyant by means of inflated goatskins. In Ina-Ashur-utir-asbat, which the people of Hattina call Pitru, on the other side of the Euphrates, on the river Sagur, I received tribute from the kings of the other side of the Euphrates—that is, of Sanagara from Carchemish; Kundashpi from Commagene; of Arame, man of Gusi; of Lath from Melitene; of Haiani, son of Gabari; of Kalparuda from Hattina; and of Kalparuda of Gurgum—consisting of silver, gold, tin, copper, copper containers. I departed from the banks of the Euphrates and approached Aleppo. The inhabitants of Aleppo were afraid to fight and seized my feet in submission. I received silver and gold as their tribute and offered sacrifices before the Adad of Aleppo. I departed from Aleppo and approached the two towns of Irhuleni from Hamath. I captured the towns Adennu, Barga, and Argana his royal residence. I removed from them his booty as well as his personal possessions. I set his palaces afire. **I departed from Argana and approached Karkara. I destroyed, tore down, and burned down Karkara, his royal residence. He brought along** to help him 1,200 chariots, 1,200 cavalrymen, 20,000 foot soldiers of Adad-'idri○ of Damascus; 700 chariots, 700 cavalrymen, 10,000 foot soldiers of Irhuleni from Hamath; 2,000 chariots, 10,000 foot soldiers of Ahab, the Israelite;○ 500 soldiers from Que; 1,000 soldiers from Musri; 10 chariots, 10,000 soldiers from Irqanata; 200 soldiers of Matinu-ba'lu from Arvad; 200 soldiers from Usanata; 30 chariots, 1,000 soldiers of Adunu-ba'lu from Shian; 1,000 camel-riders of Gindibu', from Arabia; [. . .],000 soldiers of Ba'sa, son of Ruhuhi, from Ammon—all together **these were twelve kings**. They rose against me for a decisive battle. I fought with them with the support of the mighty forces of Ashur, which Ashur, my lord, has given to me, and the strong weapons which Nergal, my leader, has presented to me, and I did inflict a defeat upon them between the towns Karkara and Gilzau. I slew 14,000 of their soldiers with the sword, descending upon them like Adad when he makes a rainstorm pour down. I spread their corpses everywhere, filling the entire plain with their widely scattered fleeing soldiers. During the battle I made their blood flow down the channels [. . .] of the district. The plain was too small to let all their souls descend into the nether world, the vast field gave out when it came to bury them. With their corpses I spanned the Orontes before there was a bridge. Even during the battle I took from them their chariots, their horses broken to the yoke.

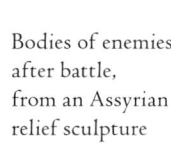

Bodies of enemies after battle, from an Assyrian relief sculpture

The Lessons of Karkar

853 BCE

Men of Jerusalem and nobles of the hill country, why do your priestly scribes not remind you that my lord Ahab defended you, that your wise king Jehoshaphat joined in defeating the Assyrians?○ Have thirty years blotted out the stories of your fathers, blown to the wind like words scratched in sand?

The armies of the western alliance held their ground at Karkar. All Shalmaneser's boasts cannot disguise the truth: his forces did not march beyond the Orontes. "The ruler of all lands" turned back without receiving tribute from the twelve kings!

Men of Jerusalem, ask the sons of your commanders: who had the largest force at Karkar? The scribes should boast that your king Jehoshaphat's friendship with my lord Ahab helped Israel send more chariots than Aram, as many soldiers as Hamath. Even Moab and Edom fought with us. Israel's covenant with Ben-hadad of Damascus made Aram the friend of Jerusalem, not the foe who now takes your silver with Hazael's threats of invasion. As long as the kings of Samaria and Jerusalem fought together, Jerusalem never saw an invading army near her, whether from Assyria or Aram.

Such resistance was bought at a great price. For war, the nobles of Israel and the southern hill country pressed their lands and people for more goods and soldiers. Horse breeders met quotas; farmers gave their harvests and first mowings.○ Many sons were lost on the battlefield, and their plots went unredeemed into their neighbor's estate, where their widows and orphans became servants.

Those who spoke against the wars could not see the outcome of their words. My lord Ahab warned them. If Assyria could not be stopped before Damascus, then Israel and all the hill country would see the terrors Shalmaneser had inflicted on others: captives tortured and dismembered, pillars of skulls raised in front of burning cities, tens of thousands of people deported for resettlement and service in Assyrian provinces, chariot troops commandeered for Assyria's army. Better for the House of David to join the House of Omri and fight at Karkar than to have our own lands devastated.

Nobles of the hill country, people of the land upon whose estates great demands were made, you would have been the victims of Assyria's atrocities if our brother Jehoshaphat had not agreed to the covenant. Was it any more than the price you have been paying for isolation under King Jehoash, to enrich the priests' treasury in Jerusalem and the looting of Hazael? Now that you see the wisdom of your *gevirah* Atalyah, are you really so helpless, like young birds whose mother is caught in a snare, leaving you naked and shrieking in the nest?

The Death of Ahab

853 BCE, EVENTS IN THE NORTHERN KINGDOM OF ISRAEL, AS DESCRIBED MUCH LATER BY PRIESTLY SCRIBES FROM JERUSALEM

Now the rest of the acts of Ahab, and all that he did, and the house of ivory that he built, and all the cities that he built, are they not written in the Book of the Daily Affairs of the Kings of Israel?

So Ahab slept with his fathers; and Ahaziah his son ruled in his place.

Ahab's *Marzeaḥ*

853 BCE

When my lord Ahab went to Karkar to meet Shalmaneser, we had a plan in case, the gods forbid, he should not return. He directed our troops from the side of the battlefield, while Joram rode with the commanders. Ahaziah and I managed affairs in Samaria with the royal guards close at hand, prepared to install him as king immediately if necessary.

My lord Ahab returned in safety but shaken. The kings of the western lands had fought as fiercely on the open plain, he said, as if defending their own besieged city. And, as in siege warfare, the well-supplied Assyrians could wait at the river-wall of the Orontes, to move again year after year as the city-lands weakened in materials and will. The first attack was thwarted. How long, O gods, would the siege continue? How long would the coalition fight as one with such great losses? He never regained the confidence I had seen in him for almost thirty years.

Six months later when he began falling and losing speech, we took our places again. My lord Ahab passed quickly. There was little time for dissenting factions to gather and plot. I anointed his body with the scented oils of our bed and buried him in the royal tomb cut under the western end of the king's house.° Joram secured the army. Ahaziah ordered all the sons of Omri and the nobles to come at once to Samaria to pledge loyalty to him and renew their estate grants.

Behind the scenes, I directed preparations for the feast. The nobles were accustomed to celebrating the *marzeaḥ*° in their cities. A royal *marzeaḥ*, however, would put them together under our eyes and impress them with the unbroken power of the House of Omri to the third generation, in the line of Ahab.

The banquet couches and tables were brought from storage and arranged in the central court, the ivory beds at the front. Bronze and silver drinking bowls were set out. Fatted calves, lambs, goats, and wild game were slaughtered. Male and female musicians and servants were assembled and instructed. Many large storage jars° were set around the courtyard and filled with wine.

The images from my childhood in Tyre's temple brought their blessings to the meal, carved into the ivory inlay of the couches and tables and inlaid into the cedar-paneled walls. The Lady at the window looked out from the legs of the ivory couches. That Lady, who greets the deceased king from her window in the sky, was also there as the long-horned cow to bless the new king—the Lady Hathor suckling the king as the wild cow nurses her newborn, the Lady Anath yearning for

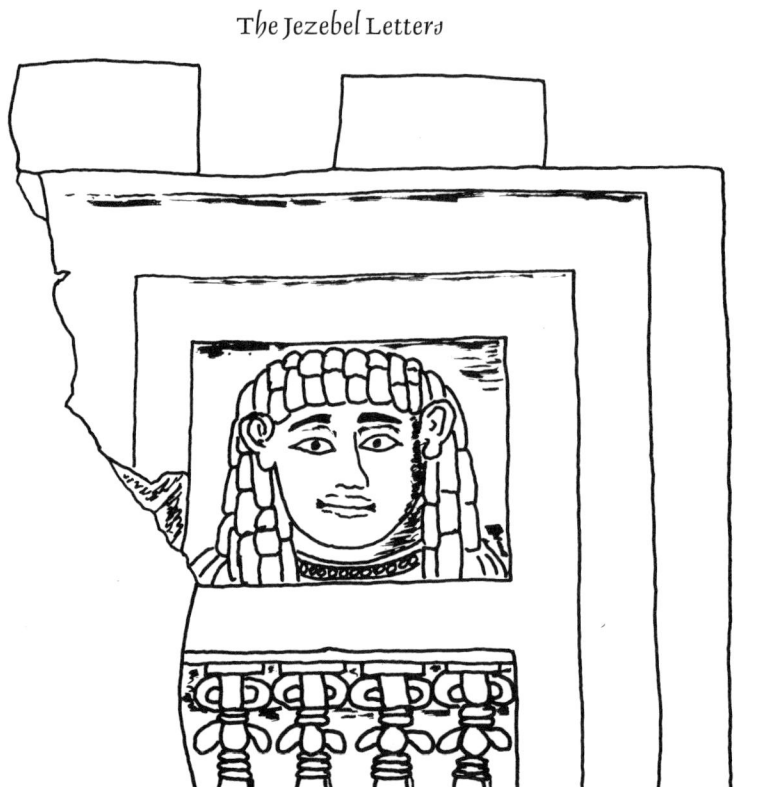

Ivory plaque with woman at the window

Baal as a cow for her calf. Death and birth were for one moment inseparable, like the kid, the lamb, or the calf stewed in its mother's milk.° But the god and the king were reborn in the new king, like the infant Horus on the lotus. The king's throne was protected by winged cherubim, guardians of the tree of life, which was sculpted on the couches and in curving volutes on stone pillars around the courtyard. And his vitality would be that of the stag, the hart leaping upon the mountain of spices— the venison upon which he feasted—carved upon the couches as ivory deer drinking in the garden of the gods.

When all was in readiness, the men's procession began. From outside the city wall, it moved up the hill toward the king's house, first circling the temple where the Lady's figure looked out from her elaborate window.○ I watched their slow march from behind the lattice of my upper chambers: Joram and another son led a pair of royal horses, in full silver and ivory bridles, that pulled my lord Ahab's chariot, empty except for his armor; Ahaziah rode in a chariot flanked by the royal guard; then the sons of the king walked with the nobles and kinsmen from Jerusalem, and the commanders followed.

Behind the screen, I wept. *Gevirah*, queen mother at last, but without the partner who had created a kingdom greater than any seen before in the highlands. Could our son face the Assyrians and maintain his father's throne?

The feast invoked more guests than those reclining on the banquet couches. My lord Ahab's victories had been purchased with the blood of many men. This *marzeaḥ* served not only to honor my lord Ahab and his fathers but also to recall those fallen with him, whose family names might cease to be remembered. The House of Omri was built upon the loyalty of the noble houses, now gathered to name their departed. The wine flowed for each song, each cup of remembrance, and splashed on the walls and the store jars. Under the tables, dogs gorged themselves on choice morsels, fallen from the revelers' hands. I dressed in my royal robes and joined the feast briefly—

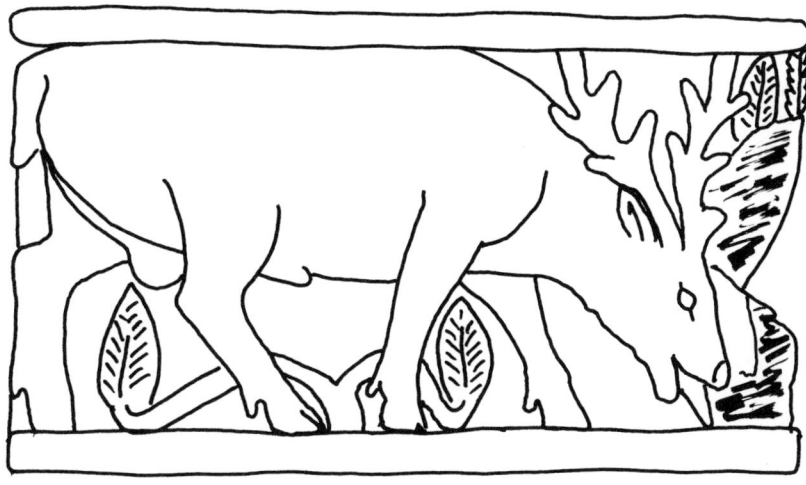

Ivory plaque with drinking stag

The Jezebel Letters

as *gevirah*, when Ahaziah raised his cup to the name of my lord Ahab—then returned to my chambers.

I took the precaution of posting guards throughout the king's house. Had not Zimri—that usurper for seven days—killed king Elah and slaughtered all the house of Baasha while they were drunk at such a meal, gathered in one room?° The House of Omri had come to power out of that turmoil. We would not be so overcome ourselves. But as songs echoed in the palace halls, I heard from a distance—or was it in my mind—drumming.

Ivory plaque with infant Horus on lotus

9
Ekron

Ahaziah Becomes King in Israel

853 BCE, EVENTS IN NORTHERN KINGDOM OF ISRAEL,
AS DESCRIBED MUCH LATER BY PRIESTLY SCRIBES FROM JERUSALEM.○

Ahaziah son of Ahab began to reign over Israel in Samaria in the seventeenth year of King Jehoshaphat of Judah; he reigned two years over Israel.○ There was no king in Edom; a deputy was king. Jehoshaphat made ships of the Tarshish type to go to Ophir for gold; but they did not go, for the ships were wrecked at Ezion-geber. Then Ahaziah son of Ahab said to Jehoshaphat, "Let my servants go with your servants in the ships," but Jehoshaphat was not willing.

Moab rebelled against Israel after the death of Ahab.

Jizebul Writes to Atalyah:
Ahaziah's Beginnings

852 BCE

To Atalyah, wife of Jehoram son of Jehoshaphat king in Jerusalem. Your mother Jizebul sends to greet you and your son Ahaziyah. I bless you to Baal Shamem and the Lady Astarte. May they guard you and keep you well.

The Jezebel Letters

Your father Ahab has been buried less than a year, and already Ahaziah is violating the covenant with our brother Jehoshaphat. You write that Jehoshaphat is failing, that your lord Jehoram sits daily at his right hand. You are now in a position to help our kingdoms. Ahaziah alienates many in Samaria as well as in Jerusalem by seeking advantage in the south. We must hold our Houses in unity.

It was agreed that our brother Jehoshaphat should appoint the deputy over Edom and that the Negev routes and the port at Ezion-geber should be under his control. Jehoshaphat was right to refuse to let Ahaziah share in that venture. It must strain the goodwill of those in Jerusalem who admired your father Ahab to see how his son tries to lord it over them.

I am distressed that Ahaziah also seeks greater ties to the Philistines, especially at Ekron. The House of David has always favored the Philistines at Gath and, with our backing, attained power among the other cities. But Ahaziah courts the ruler of Ekron, promising to help him regain the glory lost in the days of Hiram and Solomon and setting him against Jerusalem. Despite my strongest protests, he is bringing to Samaria the daughter of Ekron. As I write, they are preparing the wedding feast.

Imposing mound of Tell es-Safi (Gath)

Ahaziah and his young men do not acknowledge the wisdom of their fathers, who knew that reward binds a friend more loyal than one who is beaten into obedience.○ Let your lord Jehoram know that Jehoshaphat still has covenant brothers in Samaria, who want him to prosper and harvest the fruits of his own lands. May the gods help us turn Ahaziah's feet back to that path before the House of David abhors him.

Sealed by my own hand.

Ekron

A Royal Wedding Song from Samaria○

[SINGER'S INTRODUCTION]
My heart overflows with a goodly theme;
> I address my verses to the king;
> my tongue is like the pen of a ready scribe.

[TO THE KING]
You are the most handsome of men;
> grace is poured upon your lips;
> therefore God has blessed you forever.

Gird your sword on your thigh,
> O mighty one,
> in your glory and majesty.

In your majesty ride on victoriously for the cause of truth
> and to defend the right;

let your right hand teach you dread deeds.
Your arrows are sharp
> in the heart of the king's enemies;
> the peoples fall under you.

The eternal, everlasting God has enthroned you.
Your royal scepter
> must be a scepter of equity;

you must love righteousness and hate wickedness,
> because God, your God, has anointed you.

Your garments are the oil of gladness;
> your robes are all fragrant with myrrh and aloes and
>> cassia.

From ivory palaces
> stringed instruments make you glad;

daughters of kings are among your ladies of honor;
> at your right hand stands the queen in gold of Ophir.

[TO THE BRIDE]
Hear, O daughter, consider and incline your ear;
> "forget your people and your father's house,

and the king will desire your beauty.
>   Since he is your lord, bow to him.
A Tyrian robe is among your gifts,
>   the guests court your favor."
All her garments are royal robes,
>   inside woven with gold;
The maiden is led to the king;
>   behind her, her companions follow.
With joy and gladness they are led along
>   as they enter the palace of the king.

[To the king]
In the place of your fathers shall be your sons;
>   you will make them princes in all the earth.
I will cause your name to be celebrated in all generations;
>   therefore the peoples will praise you forever and ever.

The Death of Ahaziah

852 BCE, EVENTS OF THE NORTHERN KINGDOM OF ISRAEL
AS DESCRIBED MUCH LATER BY PRIESTLY SCRIBES FROM JERUSALEM○

Ahaziah had fallen through the lattice in his upper chamber in Samaria, and lay injured; so he sent messengers, telling them, "Go, inquire of Baal Zebul, the god of Ekron, whether I shall recover from this injury."○

But the messenger○ of Yhwh said to Eliyahu the Tishbite, "Get up, go to meet the messengers of the king of Samaria, and say to them, 'Is it because there is no God in Israel that you are going to Baal "Zebub," the god of Ekron?' Now therefore thus says Yhwh, 'You shall not leave the bed to which you have gone, but you shall surely die.'" So Eliyahu went.

The messengers returned to the king, who said to them, "Why have you returned?"

They answered him, "There came a man to meet us, who said to us, 'Go back to the king who sent you, and say to him: Thus says Yhwh: Is it because there is no God in Israel that you are sending to inquire of

Ekron

Baal "Zebub," the god of Ekron? Therefore you shall not leave the bed to which you have gone, but shall surely die.'"

He said to them, "What sort of man was he who came to meet you and told you these things?"

They answered him, "A hairy man, with a leather belt around his waist."

He said, "It is Eliyahu the Tishbite."

Then the king sent to him a captain of fifty with his fifty men. He went up to Eliyahu, who was sitting on the top of a hill, and said to him, "O man of God, the king says, 'Come down.'"

But Eliyahu answered the captain of fifty, "If I am a man of God, let fire come down from heaven and consume you and your fifty." Then fire came down from heaven, and consumed him and his fifty.

And again the king sent to him another captain of fifty with his fifty. He went up and said to him, "O man of God, thus says the king: 'Come down quickly!'"

But Eliyahu answered them, "If I am a man of God, let fire come down from heaven and consume you and your fifty." Then the fire of God came down from heaven and consumed him and his fifty.

Again the king sent the captain of a third fifty with his fifty. So the third captain of fifty went up, and came and fell on his knees before Eliyahu, and entreated him saying, "O man of God, please let my life, and the life of your servants, these fifty, be precious in your eyes. Look, fire came down from heaven and consumed the first two captains of fifty men with their fifties; but now let my life be precious in your eyes."

Then the messenger of Yhwh said to Eliyahu, "Go down with him; do not be afraid of him."

So he set out, and went down with him to the king, and said to him, "Thus says Yhwh: Because you have sent messengers to inquire of Baal 'Zebub,' the god of Ekron—is it because there is no God in Israel to inquire of his word?—therefore you shall not leave the bed to which you have gone, but you shall surely die."

So he died according to the word of Yhwh that Eliyahu had spoken. And his brother Joram ruled in his place, because Ahaziah had no son.[○] Now the rest of the acts of Ahaziah that he did, are they not written in the Book of the Daily Affairs of the Kings of Israel?

The Jezebel Letters

How Ahaziah Died

852 BCE

> In the place of your fathers shall be your sons;
>   you will make them princes in all the earth.
> I will cause your name to be celebrated in all generations;
>   therefore the peoples will praise you forever and ever.

 THE GROOM'S BLESSING HAS TAKEN A STRANGE TURN, I thought when I listened to Ahaziah's wedding and remembered my own. My son was king and my name as *gevirah* should also be great, but instead, I grieved at my offspring's folly. Soon, I grieved at his death.

I started the rumor that Ahaziah fell through the lattice, but, in truth, he was pushed. My "Kingfisher" could not fly.

He had antagonized many in a short time. The Moabite rebels occupied the army's attention under his brother Joram, but Ahaziah would not send enough men and supplies to subdue them fully, shaming the commanders. Eager to please the nobles with more wealth, he diverted the army toward greater southern trade. He pushed Israel's frontier farther south along the Philistine coast, past Gezer to Ekron, where he imagined a center to press the hill country's olives.º He established outposts on the overland route in Sinai between the gulf port of Ezion-geber and the south Philistine coast.º

Olive oil production area at Ekron

Ekron

He wanted a share of the fleet at the port itself. His expansions put him into direct competition with our brother Jehoshaphat, whom my lord Ahab had left to manage those routes to Jerusalem's benefit in return for contributions to our coalition.

While looking to the south, Ahaziah seemed blind to the north and east. Shalmaneser was regrouping for another push toward the Great Sea. With Israel's troops floundering in Moab and posted along southern routes, Ben-hadad of Damascus took the lead to rebuild the western coalition. Israel's commanders admired Damascus. Especially in Gilead, where the military drew its best captains and horsemen, Ahaziah's neglect was keenly felt. And the Sons of the Prophets, who had been dispersed for condemning my lord Ahab's reliance on Tyre, reappeared with new oracles against Ahaziah's increasing ties to the Philistines. They chanted threats against what they called Baal "Zebub" of Ekron, whose shrine was soon to be built at Samaria for the bride and covenant. Some servants of the king in Samaria, loyal to my lord Ahab's strategy for the region, privately agreed with their outrage.

While our brother Jehoshaphat declined in Jerusalem, his son Jehoram, Atalyah's husband, ruled as coregent over the House of David. He answered Ahaziah's aggression by executing some of Israel's officials in the Negev, whom he suspected of intercepting westbound caravans.○ The two young kings, my son and my son-in-law, had brought us to the brink of open warfare.

Ahaziah was in the royal women's quarters at Samaria to visit his new Philistine wife. The daughter of Ekron was expected to bear Israel's next crown prince, much to the dismay of old courtiers. Two eunuchs entered the newlyweds' room at a vulnerable moment and, in their struggle, pushed Ahaziah through the latticed window of the upper chamber. Had they only stabbed him and the girl as intended, they might have had time to escape, for no one else would have disturbed the king at such a moment, but his fall roused the guard.

The attackers were captured, of course. Before their execution, they implicated Obadiah, Ahab's aged overseer of the king's house, who had promised them safety after the deed, but he could not be found. There were reports of his having left Samaria escorted by two captains, heading east. I secured the palace with the royal guard and sent for Joram to return immediately from Moab. He was in Samaria when Ahaziah's broken body failed. The commanders were pleased with Joram, so pleased that one might suspect they were complicit in Ahaziah's death. Others even accused me of conspiracy to kill the girl, of a plot gone awry when Ahaziah defended her!

My "Kestrel" Joram became a royal falcon, as Abdi-Ptah's prescient bow before the infant with the eye of Horus had foreshadowed. That loyal servant had been retired by Ahaziah but remained in my household. His neck permanently bent forward as if over a scroll and with crippled hands, he was always a wise counselor. He too died, soon after Joram's accession.

Joram called back the southern forces and repaired the alliance with Jehoram in Jerusalem. Defending against Shamaneser's attacks would take the lifeblood of both Houses—every horse and man, every jar of oil and wine and grain, the cloth of every loom, the metal of every forge. In five years, the men of Samaria and Jerusalem and the western kingdoms would meet Shalmaneser three more times at the Orontes, and three times they would stop him there.

Ivory plaque with eye of Horus, from Samaria

10
Dibon

Joram's Troubles with Moab

850 BCE, EVENTS RELATING TO THE NORTHERN KINGDOM OF ISRAEL, AS DESCRIBED MUCH LATER BY PRIESTLY SCRIBES FROM JERUSALEM.○

Joram son of Ahab became king over Israel in Samaria in the eighteenth year of Jehoshaphat king of Judah; he reigned twelve years.○ He did what was evil in the eyes of Yhwh, though not like his father and mother, for he removed the pillar of Baal that his father had made. Nevertheless he clung to the sin of Jeroboam son of Nebat, which he caused Israel to commit; he did not depart from it.

Now Mesha king of Moab was a sheep breeder, and he used to pay to the king of Israel one hundred thousand lambs, and the wool of one hundred thousand rams. But when Ahab died, the king of Moab rebelled against the king of Israel. So King Joram marched out of Samaria at that time and mustered all Israel.

As he went, he sent word to the king of Judah, saying, "The king of Moab has rebelled against me; will you go with me to Moab for battle?"

He answered, "I will go; I am yours, my people are as your people, my horses are as your horses." Then he asked, "By which way shall we march?"

Joram answered, "By the way of the wilderness of Edom."

So the king of Israel, the king of Judah, and the ruler of Edom° set out; and when they had made a roundabout march of seven days, there was no water for the army or for the animals that were with them.

Then the king of Israel said, "Alas! Yhwh has called us, three kings, only to be given into the hand of Moab!"

But the king of Judah said, "Is there no prophet of Yhwh here, through whom we may inquire of Yhwh?"

Then one of the servants of the king of Israel answered, "Elisha son of Shaphat, who used to pour water on the hands of Eliyahu, is here."

The king of Judah said, "The word of Yhwh is with him."

So the king of Israel and the king of Judah and the ruler of Edom went down to him.

Elisha said to the king of Israel, "What have I to do with you? Go to the prophets of your father and the prophets of your mother."

But the king of Israel said to him, "No; it is Yhwh who has called us three kings, only to be given into the hand of Moab."

Elisha said, "As Yhwh of Hosts lives, whom I serve, were it not that I have regard for the king of Judah, I would neither look toward you nor see you. But get me a musician."

And then, while the musician was playing, the power of Yhwh came on him. And he said, "Thus says Yhwh, 'I will make this dry creek bed full of pools.' For thus says Yhwh, 'You shall see neither wind nor rain, but the dry creek bed shall be filled with water, so that you shall drink, you, your cattle, and your animals.' This is only a trifle in the eyes of Yhwh, for he will also give Moab into your hand. You shall strike every fortified city and every choice city; every good tree you shall fell, all springs of water you shall stop up, and every good piece of land you shall ruin with stones."

The next day, about the time of the morning offering, suddenly water began to flow from the direction of Edom, until the country was filled with water.

When all the Moabites heard that the kings had come up to fight against them, all who were able to put on armor, from the youngest to the oldest, were called out and were drawn up at the frontier. When they rose early in the morning, and the sun shone upon the water, the Moabites saw the water opposite them as red as blood. They said, "This is blood; the

Dibon

kings must have fought together, and killed one another. Now then, to the spoil, Moab!"

But when they came to the camp of Israel, the Israelites rose up and attacked the Moabites, who fled before them; as they entered Moab they continued the attack. The cities they pulled down, and on every good piece of land each man threw a stone, until it was covered; every spring of water they stopped up, and every good tree they felled.º Only at Kir-haresheth did the stone walls remain, until the slingers surrounded and attacked it.

When the king of Moab saw that the battle was going against him, he took with him seven hundred swordsmen to break through, opposite the ruler of Edom; but they could not. Then he took his son, the firstborn who was to succeed him, and offered him as a burnt offering on the wall.

And great wrath came upon Israel, so they withdrew from him and returned to their own land.

Soldiers cutting trees in battle, from Phoenician drinking bowl

The Mesha Inscription

850 BCE, RELATIONS BETWEEN MESHA KING OF MOAB AND THE RULERS OF ISRAEL AND JERUSALEM, AS INSCRIBED ON A STONE MONUMENT IN DIBON (MOAB'S CAPITAL) FROM LATE IN MESHA'S REIGN, PERHAPS AROUND 830 BCEº

I am Mesha, son of Chemoshit king of Moab, the Dibonite—my father had reigned over Moab thirty years, and I reigned after my father, who made this high place for Chemosh in Qarhoh . . . because he saved me from all the kings and caused me to triumph over all my adversaries. As for Omri king of Israel, he humbled Moab many days, for Chemosh was angry at his land. And his son followed him and he also said, "I will humble Moab." In my time he spoke thus, but I have triumphed over him and over his house, while Israel has perished forever! Now Omri had occupied the land of Medeba, and Israel had dwelt there in his time and half the time of his son Ahab, forty years; but Chemosh dwelt there in my time.

And I built Baal-meon, making a reservoir in it, and I built Qaryaten. Now the men of Gad had always dwelled in the land of Ataroth, and the king of Israel had built Ataroth for them; but I fought against the town and took it and slew all the people; the town belonged to Chemosh and Moab. And I brought back from there the altar-hearth of his Beloved, dragging it before Chemosh in Kerioth, and I settled there men of Sharon and men of Maharith. And Chemosh said to me, "Go, take Nebo from Israel!" So I went by night and fought against it from the break of dawn until noon, taking it and slaying all, seven thousand men, boys, women, girls, and maid-servants, for I had devoted them to destruction for the god Ashtar-Chemosh. And I took from there the altar-hearths of Yhwh, dragging them before Chemosh. And the king of Israel had built Jahaz, and he dwelt there while he was fighting against me, but Chemosh drove him out before me. . . .

It was I who built Qarhoh, the wall of the forests and the wall of the citadel. . . . And I cut beams for Qarhoh with Israelite captives. . . .

And as for Hauronen, there dwelled in it the House of David . . . and Chemosh said to me, "Go down, fight against Hauronen." And I went down and I fought against the town and I took it, and Chemosh dwelled there in my time.

Insurrections

845 BCE

LIKE THE ARMORED PLANKS of a city gate cracking under a battering ram, so the kingdoms of the western coalition weakened and splintered under Shalmaneser's repeated blows. And, like deserters fleeing a besieged city by a less guarded back gate, so the Moabites broke away from our rule, soon to be followed by Edom.

The results were devastating. Unable to receive enough Moabite wool, our looms were often empty. Men and horses from the rebellious areas did not join us against Shalmaneser's third push toward the south. Moab and Edom's example was followed by Libnah of the Philistines in the western foothills of Jerusalem's own hill country! Unable to rely on Edom's copper or control the Arab trade through Philistia, we lost the inland profits.

The defeat in Moab set off more unrest in Gilead. It was rumored that "King" Mesha son of Chemosh-yatti sacrificed his crown prince to Chemosh on the walls of Dibon. The Gileadites had their own story about such a human offering in war, a story rehearsed each year in a four-day women's ritual for girls of marriageable age.○ Usually men of strategy and courage, the men of Gilead explained Moab's victory by blaming it on Mesha's sacrifice, despite the obvious factor of scarce water and supplies on the roundabout approach. But they seemed to tell Moab's story with too much sympathy. Were they recounting Moab's resistance to Israel and YHWH, whose shrines in Moab were destroyed, as a mask for their own rejection of the covenant with Tyre and the shrine of Baal Shamem that honored it? It was no longer Eliyahu who ranted against this alliance but Elisha his servant, whose whereabouts seemed all too familiar to some of Joram's officials.

In Tyre, my brother Baal-azzor postponed renewing the covenant with Joram, waiting to gauge his strength. In Samaria, men muttered in corners of the king's house about sending tribute to Shalmaneser rather than fighting him.

The Jezebel Letters

Jizebul Writes to Atalyah: Advice about Jehoram

845 BCE

To Atalyah, wife of King Jehoram of the House of David in Jerusalem. Your mother Jizebul sends to greet you. I bless you and your son Ahaziyah to Baal Shamem and the Lady Astarte. May they guard you and keep you well.

You will receive this letter from the hand of my kinsman—the man we called "Stork"—whom you will remember from our happy days at Jezreel. His friendship has been a great solace to me since the death of your father, and he brings you some gifts from me. Be sure he is presented to your lord Jehoram and to Ahaziyah. He has influence among Tyrians in the port of Dor, which may be useful to Jerusalem if the Philistine ports are cut off—I hear of troubles there.

After the loss in Moab, messengers from Jerusalem weary my heart with more bad news. Our brother Jehoshaphat established the throne of David on secure legs, with the help of your father Ahab. But your lord Jehoram trembles on a footstool of fear. Does he believe that your brother Ahaziah was killed at the order of your brother Joram? Is that why Jehoram massacred his own brothers at their fortified cities?○ Now, instead of sending the cities' wealth to the king and the army, his nobles fight among themselves for power. I would not trust them, even to defend the king's sons who were sent to replace his dead brothers as tokens of Jerusalem's presence. In the east, your lord Jehoram removed the officials of Israel from their posts in Edom, fearing their power at his back, and now Edom is lost to both kingdoms. By rededicating the high places and taking their offerings for war, he challenges Jerusalem's priests, always a greedy band under our brother Jehoshaphat. Giving his daughter Jehosheba in marriage to Jehoiada the priest will not heal that open wound in the capital.

The pain in your lord Jehoram's bowels reminds me of his grandfather Asa, whose fears festered in his loins. But he was wise enough to prepare his son. You must do the same. Insist that your son Ahaziyah stand by the king's throne and act as regent when he is not well. Let your father Ahab and our brother Jehoshaphat be the models for Ahaziyah. You say the priests have arranged for Ahaziyah to marry a woman of Beer-sheba, to strengthen loyalty on the Negev *frontier. Let us send him a bride from Samaria, so that he and his offspring may renew their trust in the House of Omri.*

Who is left in Jerusalem to help you? I commend to you again the family of Jehozabad, a man of Benjamin upon whom our brother Jehoshaphat relied. He was a commander of thousands in Jerusalem, a soldier known and respected by your father Ahab. Jehozabad's son Shomer would be a suitable companion for Ahaziyah, as the father would be a reliable tutor to any grandsons of Jehoshaphat, to instill confidence in our kingdoms' mutual interests and teach them strategies for joint ventures. You must preserve that generation that it may serve Ahaziyah and keep the House of David alive.

You must insure that Ahaziyah does not withdraw, infected by your lord Jehoram's sickly fear. Ahaziyah is the grandson of Ahab and Jehoshaphat. So much that his fathers built is falling away before the Assyrians. I pray that by the time he reaches the throne, the power of our brotherhood will again have brought shalom *to both Houses.*

Sealed by my own hand.

Jehoram's Administration

845 BCE, EVENTS IN JERUSALEM
AS DESCRIBED IN THE POSTEXILIC ACCOUNTS OF THE CHRONICLER[○]

Jehoshaphat slept with his fathers and was buried with his fathers in the city of David; Jehoram his son ruled in his place.

He had brothers, the sons of Jehoshaphat: Azariah, Jehiel, Zechariah, Azariah, Michael, and Shephatiah; all these were the sons of Jehoshaphat king of Judah.[○] Their father gave them many gifts, of silver, gold, and valuable possessions, together with fortified cities in Judah; but he gave the kingdom to Jehoram, because he was the firstborn. When Jehoram took over the kingdom of his father and was established, he killed all his brothers with the sword, and also some of the officials of Israel.

Jehoram was thirty-two years old when he began to reign; he reigned eight years in Jerusalem. He walked in the way of the kings of Israel, as the house of Ahab had done; for a daughter of Ahab was his wife.

In his days, Edom revolted against the rule of Judah and set up a king of its own. Then Jehoram crossed over with his commanders and all his chariots. He set out by night and attacked the Edomites, who had surrounded him and his chariot commanders. So Edom has been in revolt against the rule of Judah to this day. At that time, Libnah also revolted against his rule.

Moreover he made high places in the hill country of Judah.

Yhwh aroused against Jehoram the anger of the Philistines and of the Arabs who are near the Cushites. They came up against Judah, invaded it, and carried away all the possessions they found that belonged to the king's house, along with his sons and his wives, so that no son was left to him except his youngest son.○

After all this Yhwh struck him in his bowels with an incurable disease.

11

Damascus

Elisha and Hazael of Aram

843 BCE, EVENTS RELATING TO DAMASCUS,
AS DESCRIBED MUCH LATER BY PRIESTLY SCRIBES FROM JERUSALEM○

Elisha went to Damascus while Ben-hadad king of Aram was sick. When it was told him, "The man of God has come here," the king said to Hazael, "Take in your hand a present and go to meet the man of God. Inquire of Yhwh through him, saying, 'Shall I recover from this sickness?'"

So Hazael went to meet him, taking a present in his hand, all kinds of good things of Damascus, forty camel loads. When he entered and stood before him, he said, "Your son Ben-hadad king of Aram has sent me to you, saying, 'Shall I recover from this sickness?'"

Elisha said to him, "Go, say to him, 'You shall certainly recover'; but Yhwh has shown me that he shall certainly die."

He fixed his gaze and stared at him, until he was ashamed. Then the man of God wept. Hazael asked, "Why does my lord weep?"

He answered, "Because I know the evil that you will do to the sons of Israel; you will set their fortresses on fire, you will kill their young men with the sword, dash in pieces their children, and rip up their pregnant women."

Hazael said, "What is your servant, who is a mere dog, that he should do this great thing?"

Elisha answered, "YHWH has shown me that you will be king over Aram."

Then he left Elisha, and went to his lord Ben-hadad, who said to him, "What did Elisha say to you?"

And he answered, "He told me that you would certainly recover."

But the next day he took the netted bedcloth and dipped it in water and spread it over the king's face until he died. And Hazael ruled in his place.

Jizebul Writes to Baal-azzor: Concerns about Hazael

843 BCE

To Baal-azzor king of Tyre and king of the Sidonians. Your sister, Jizebul daughter of Ethbaal and giverah of the House of Omri in Samaria, sends to greet my lord and brother. I bless you to Baal Shamem, the Lady Astarte, and all the gods of Tyre.

I entreat you, my brother, to accept the offer of Joram king of Israel, my son, to renew the covenant of your fathers in this, the tenth year after my lord Ahab's death. Why do you hesitate to pledge brotherhood with your kinsmen, the kings in Samaria and Jerusalem? Have they not proven worthy of your confidence by blocking the Assyrians, time after time? I know that Tyre must seek goodwill and rights of commerce by sending gifts to Assyria. So also did our father Ethbaal keep open routes to the north, while still pledging friendship to the southern kings. Does Shalmaneser threaten you for befriending us? You are indispensable to him; surely, he will not harm you.

The king's servants whisper to me that Tyre has also sent messengers to Damascus, to the usurper Hazael. What have you to do with him? Do you seek alliance with that son-of-a-nobody who, though defending Damascus, would hide in his house and let Shalmaneser march to the sea? Are you renouncing the covenant of our father, to make Hazael your brother and guardian of the inland routes rather than the House of Omri?

Damascus

Our father Ethbaal trusted King Omri and my lord Ahab to open the way for Tyre to Philistia and the southern hill country, to Moab and Edom, even to Aram. But the wars have been costly. For ten years, we have fought the Assyrians with all our sons and our horses and our goods. Surely you shall see our trade flowing to Tyre again, when the danger from the north has been thwarted. If you seek to open these paths with gifts of silver to Aram, the roads will be made slippery with the blood of your kinsmen.

If you reject the alliance, how shall I honor you and pray for our father's house before the pillar of Baal Shamem in Samaria? It will be torn down! Will you leave me and my children and my children's children without an altar to the god of our father? Do not abandon us! May the gods of Tyre keep us ever before your face.

Sealed by my own hand.

Jizebul Writes to Atalyah: Growing Dangers

843 BCE

To Atalyah, wife of Jehoram king of the House of David in Jerusalem. Your mother Jizebul sends to greet you. I bless you and your son Ahaziyah to Baal Shamem and the Lady Astarte. May they guard you and keep you well.

I regret that the party bringing Ahaziyah's bride Bat-ahav from Samaria must also carry this heavy letter. Receive her kindly, as a daughter. The House of Omri and the House of David need each other greatly in these days.

Is there no end to the bad tidings? The foundations that your father Ahab established for our kingdoms are shaken. Baal-azzor, the son of my father whom I called brother, turns his back on Tyre's covenant with Israel, to barter with Damascus like a woman selling herself at the threshing floor. Hazael rules in Aram, a usurper who bribes the nobles of Damascus with promises of silver from Tyre, to hide behind his walls before the Assyrians while sending threats to

Samaria. Edom has loosed itself from the reins of Jerusalem, and Moab slays the Israelite men of Gad in Medeba. The Philistines and Arabs have turned against your lord Jehoram, and, you say, there is unrest among the inhabitants of Jerusalem who blame Israel for their misfortunes.

In Samaria, Joram has removed the pillar of Baal Shamem of Tyre from its public place in the temple, as Baal-azzor removed himself from the covenant. It is stored in the innermost citadel, with the vestments and sacred vessels. Privately, Baal-azzor assures us that he will trade with Israel, but there is little to exchange. Men here talk more openly of bowing to Shalmaneser if Assyria will shield us from Hazael's attack. How can the Assyrian enemy of your father Ahab be a friend to us against the vengeful Hazael, whose father's city of Dan was given to us by our brother Ben-hadad? Everything is turned upside down.

Your good news about the agreement with Dor gives me hope. Baal Shamem's covenant priest from Samaria has moved to Dor, where he may remain in our service among the Tyrians. Your priest Mattan also knows those men and can keep open that path to the coast. If all else fails, neither Shalmaneser nor Hazael is likely to march there, so Samaria and Jerusalem will have an outlet on the sea.

The Lady is still honored in Samaria. Keep her altar well supplied in Jerusalem. May she grant long life to the fruit of Ahaziyah and his bride, for the blessing of both our Houses.

Sealed by my own hand.

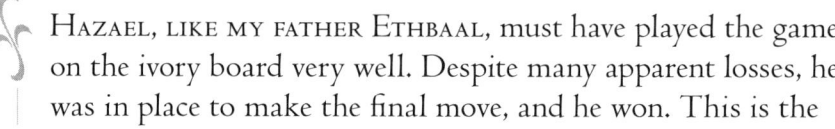

Hazael's Opportunity

Events of 843–841 BCE

Hazael, like my father Ethbaal, must have played the game on the ivory board very well. Despite many apparent losses, he was in place to make the final move, and he won. This is the man, nobles of the hill country, to whom the priests would entrust your safety.

When my lord Ahab and Ben-hadad of Damascus agreed that Israel and Aram would join forces—was it thirty-five years before the coup?—Dan with its territory was ceded to King Omri. Hazael's father, warlord of Dan, revolted when my lord Ahab took the throne, and the rebel lost both his office and his life. The boy Hazael was taken to Damascus to become Ben-hadad's servant. Not quite a hostage, trained as a soldier, and useful as a messenger, he was often sent on errands for the king, away from the center of power. But the servant outwitted his master. He used his journeys to listen and learn, to plot a different course for Aram. He was liked by other noble sons, who saw many of their generation displaced from their inheritance by Ben-hadad or die in battle against Shalmaneser.

My dear one, Achli, came regularly to Samaria to visit me. We had time alone now, but our conversations were somber. He reported murmurs of unrest in Damascus, when the young men spoke freely, tongues loosened by wine, with the Tyrian traders. The army captains and local merchants' sons said Aram was strong enough to defend its own cities but was weakened by the standoffs in the north with others. The ambitious Aramaeans were yoked with armies no longer pulling their share of the load. Why not take what they needed from their neighbors rather than granting concessions for help that was no help? Shalmaneser was campaigning in many distant lands. He would not always look toward the Great Sea. And when his back was turned, men of Damascus could be the rulers of the west, enriching themselves and their Tyrian friends. If only Ben-hadad would abandon the way of covenants that could obviously no longer succeed.

But as we now know, Ben-hadad did not change, and, after a fourth clash in the north with Shalmaneser, he became very ill. He relied on his chief aide Hazael, who smothered him to

The Jezebel Letters

death on his sickbed. Hazael's noble friends supported him. Then he turned against us, marching to reclaim his father's city, trying to evict Israel from the Aramaean frontiers of the Galil and Gilead. Shalmaneser seemed to be busy elsewhere.

Hazael chose to attack when our troops were reduced, for Jehoram in Jerusalem had just died of his sickness, and Ahaziyah was taking the throne. The battle against Hazael went badly. Joram was wounded and returned to Jezreel. But, as if he had been waiting for our infighting, Shalmaneser turned again to the west, where there was no longer a great army to meet him at the Orontes. Hazael withdrew to defend Damascus against the Assyrians.

Our commanders had time to regroup with reinforcements from Ahaziyah, all now under Jehu, grandson of my lord Ahab's brother Nimshi.º They waited at Ramoth-gilead for the next attack. Would it be Shalmaneser or Hazael? And if it was Shalmaneser, should we fight or pay?

Battle scene with enemy under chariot, from Assyrian relief sculpture

Damascus

Shalmaneser III's Description of Hazael

845–841 BCE, SHALMANESER III'S INSCRIPTION ON A BASALT STATUE○

I defeated Hadadezer○ of Damascus together with twelve princes, his allies. I stretched upon the ground 20,900 of his strong warriors, the remnants of his troops I pushed into the Orontes River and they dispersed to save their lives; Hadadezer himself perished.

Hazael, a son of nobody, seized the throne, called up a numerous army and rose against me. I fought with him and defeated him, taking the chariots of his camp.

He disappeared to save his life. I marched as far as Damascus, his royal residence, and cut down his gardens.

Ahaziyah Becomes King in Jerusalem

841 BCE, EVENTS DESCRIBED MUCH LATER IN THE POSTEXILIC WORK
OF THE CHRONICLER AND BY PRIESTLY SCRIBES FROM JERUSALEM○

In the course of time, at the end of two years, Jehoram's bowels came out because of the disease, and he died in great agony. His people made no fire in his honor, like the fires made for his fathers. He was thirty-two years old when he began to reign; he reigned eight years in Jerusalem. He departed with no one's regret. They buried him in the city of David, but not in the tombs of the kings.

The inhabitants of Jerusalem made his youngest son Ahaziyah king in his place; for the troops who came with the Arabs to the camp had killed all the older sons. So Ahaziyah son of Jehoram reigned as king of Judah.

In the twelfth year of Joram son of Ahab king of Israel, Ahaziyah son of Jehoram king of Judah began to reign. Ahaziyah was twenty-two years old when he began to reign: he reigned one year in Jerusalem. His mother's name was Atalyah daughter of Omri king of Israel.○ He walked in the way of the house of Ahab, for he was son-in-law to the house of Ahab.

The Jezebel Letters

He went with Joram son of Ahab to wage war against Hazael king of Aram at Ramoth-gilead, where the Aramaeans wounded Joram. Jehoram the king returned to be healed in Jezreel of the wounds that the Aramaeans had inflicted on him at Ramah, when he fought against Hazael king of Aram.

Ahaziyah son of Jehoram king of Judah went down to see Joram son of Ahab in Jezreel, because he was wounded.

View toward east from Jezreel

12

Ramoth-gilead

Hazael's Victories: The Tel Dan Inscription

841 BCE, VICTORIES DESCRIBED ON AN ARAMAIC INSCRIPTION ON STONE FROM TEL DAN, FOUND BROKEN INTO SEVERAL PIECES IN A WALL AND DEBRIS JUST OUTSIDE THE CITY GATE, ATTRIBUTED TO HAZAEL°

[. . .] MR '[. . .] and made (a treaty)? [. . .]
[. . .]-el my father, went up [against him when] he was fighting in A[bel? . . .]
and my father passed away; he went to [his ancestors.] Now the king of I[s]rael entered
formerly into the land of my father; [but] Hadad made me myself king
and Hadad went before me; [and] I departed from [the] seven [. . .]
of my kingdom; and I slew mig[hty ki]ngs, who harnessed thou[sands of cha-]
riots and thousands of horsemen, [so that then was killed° Jo]ram, son of [Ahab,]
king of Israel, and [was] killed [Ahazi]yahu, son of [Joram, kin-]
g of the house of David; and I set [their cities to ruins?? and I turned]

The Jezebel Letters

their land into de[solation? And I slew all of it and I settled in it]
    other [men].
and to the tem[ple I devoted it. And Jehu son of Omry ru-]
led over Is[rael . . . and I laid down a]
siege upon [. . .]

Area outside Dan gate where inscription was found

Jehu's Revolt

841 BCE, EVENTS IN THE NORTHERN KINGDOM OF ISRAEL,
AS DESCRIBED MUCH LATER BY PRIESTLY SCRIBES FROM JERUSALEM

Then the prophet Elisha called to one of the Sons of the Prophets and said to him, "Gird up your loins; take this flask of oil in your hand, and go to Ramoth-gilead. When you arrive, look there for Jehu son of Jehoshaphat son of Nimshi; go in and get him to leave his companions, and take him into an inner chamber. Then take the flask of oil, pour it on his head, and say, 'Thus says Yhwh: I anoint you king over Israel.' Then open the door and flee; do not linger."

So the young man, the prophet's servant, went to Ramoth-gilead. He arrived while the commanders of the army were in council, and he announced, "I have a message for you, commander."

Jehu said, "For which one of us?"

Ramoth-gilead

And he said, "For you, commander."

So Jehu got up and went inside the house; the prophet poured the oil on his head, saying to him, "Thus says Yhwh the God of Israel: I anoint you king over the people of Yhwh over Israel. You shall strike down the house of your lord Ahab, so that I may avenge the blood of my servants the prophets, and the blood of all the servants of Yhwh from the hand of Jezebel. For the whole house of Ahab shall perish; I will cut off from Ahab everyone who pees against a wall, bond or free, in Israel. I will make the house of Ahab like the house of Jeroboam son of Nebat, and like the house of Baasha son of Ahijah. The dogs shall eat Jezebel in the territory of Jezreel, and no one shall bury her." Then he opened the door and fled.

When Jehu came back to his lord's officers, one said to him, "Is it *shalom*? Why did that madman come to you?"

He answered them, "You know the sort and how they babble."

They said, "*Sheqer*! A lie! Now, tell us!"

So he said, "This is just what he said to me: 'Thus says Yhwh, I anoint you king over Israel.'"

Then hurriedly each took his cloak and spread it for him on the bare steps; and they blew the ram's horn, and proclaimed, "Jehu is king."

Thus Jehu son of Jehoshaphat son of Nimshi conspired against Joram. Joram with all Israel had been on guard at Ramoth-gilead against Hazael king of Aram; but King Joram had returned to be healed in Jezreel of the wounds that the Aramaeans had inflicted on him, when he fought against Hazael king of Aram.

So Jehu said, "If this is your wish, then let no one slip out of the city to go and tell the news in Jezreel."

Then Jehu mounted his chariot and went to Jezreel, where Joram was lying ill. Ahaziyah king of Judah had come down to visit Joram.

In Jezreel, the sentinel standing on the tower saw the company of Jehu arriving, and said, "I see a company."

Joram said, "Take a horseman; send him to meet them, and let him say, 'Is it *shalom*?'"

So the horseman went to meet him; he said, "Thus says the king, 'Is it *shalom*?'"

Jehu responded, "What have you to do with *shalom*? Fall in behind me."

The sentinel reported, saying, "The messenger reached them, but he is not coming back."

Then he sent out a second horseman, who came to them and said, "Thus says the king, 'Is it *shalom*?'"

Jehu answered, "What have you to do with *shalom*? Fall in behind me."

And again the sentinel reported, "He reached them, but he is not coming back. It looks like the driving of Jehu son of Nimshi; for he drives like a madman."

Joram said, "Get ready." And they got his chariot ready.

Then Joram king of Israel and Ahaziyah king of Judah set out, each in his chariot, and went to meet Jehu; they met him at the property of Naboth the Jezreelite.

When Joram saw Jehu, he said, "Is it *shalom*, Jehu?"

He answered, "What *shalom* can there be, so long as the harlotries of your mother Jezebel and her sorceries are so many?"

Then Joram reined about and fled, saying to Ahaziyah, "Treachery, Ahaziyah!"

Jehu drew his bow with all his strength, and shot Joram between the shoulders, so that the arrow pierced his heart; and he sank in his chariot.

Jehu said to his third officer Bidkar, "Lift him out, and throw him on the plot of ground belonging to Naboth the Jezreelite; for remember, when you and I rode side by side behind his father Ahab how Yhwh uttered this oracle against him: 'For the blood of Naboth and for the blood of his sons that I saw yesterday, says Yhwh, I swear I will repay you on this very plot of ground.' Now therefore lift him out and throw him on the plot of ground, in accordance with the word of Yhwh."

When Ahaziyah king of Judah saw this, he fled in the direction of Beth-haggan. Jehu pursued him, saying, "Shoot him also!"

And they shot him in the chariot at the ascent to Gur, which is by Ileam. Then he fled to Megiddo and died there. His officers carried him in a chariot to Jerusalem, and buried him in his tomb with his fathers in the city of David.

When Jehu came to Jezreel, Jezebel heard of it; she painted her eyes, and adorned her head, and looked down out of the window.

Ramoth-gilead

As Jehu entered the gate, she said, "Is it *shalom*, Zimri, murderer of his lord?"

He looked up to the window and said, "Who is with me? Who?"

Two or three eunuchs looked out at him.

He said, "Throw her down."

So they threw her down; some of her blood spattered on the wall and on the horses, and he trampled on her.

Then he went in and ate and drank; he said, "See to that cursed woman and bury her; for she is a king's daughter."

But when they went to bury her, they found nothing of her except the skull and the feet and the palms of her hands.

When they came back and told him, he said, "This is the word of YHWH, which he spoke by his servant Eliyahu the Tishbite, saying, 'In the territory of Jezreel the dogs shall eat the flesh of Jezebel; the corpse of Jezebel shall be like dung on the field in the territory of Jezreel, so that they shall not say, This is Jezebel.'"

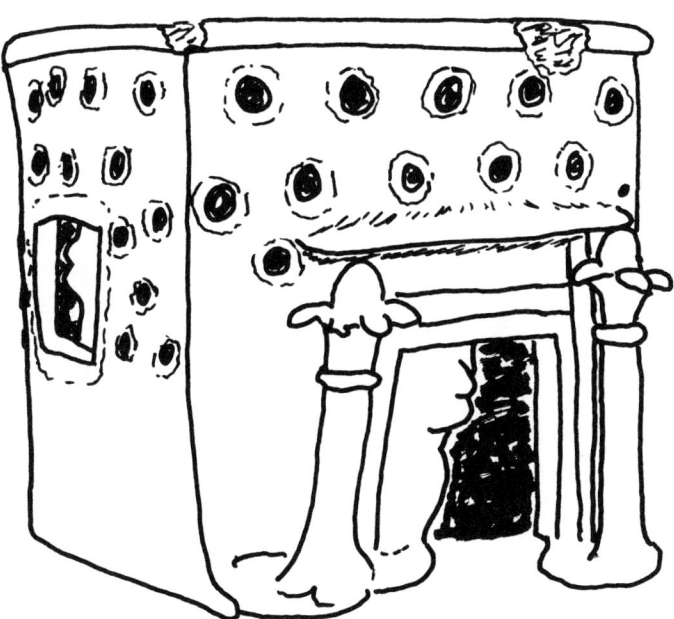

Model shrine with image at door and window

The Jezebel Letters

What Did Not Happen at Jezreel

841 BCE

Sheqer! A lie!

There was no trampled body to bury because I was not at Jezreel when Jehu arrived. Joram had recovered enough from his wound that I was packing at our estate, preparing to join Ahaziyah in Samaria where he was acting as regent in Joram's absence. Several messengers arrived all at once with news—of Jehu's murder of Joram at Jezreel, of the uprising against Ahaziyah in Samaria, of Shalmaneser's approach to Gilead from Hauran. I took refuge at Megiddo.

Jehu did not honor my son Joram with a *marzeaḥ*. Instead, those who tell Jehu's story defame the house of Ahab with their mockery of the feast and praise themselves like Assyrians.○

There was no procession past a woman at the window in Jezreel. Joram's chariot, like Ahab's, should have paraded below the Lady's image in the window of her Samaria temple. Cups of remembrance, not my blood, should spatter on the walls. Dogs fight under the table for banquet scraps, not over my flesh in the street. And like dogs, Jehu's braggarts steal boasts from their Assyrian master's table, with their claims of arrows in the back and enemies run over by chariots.

But Jehu's tale puts right words in my mouth, that *shalom* could not come from this one who betrayed his lord the king. And I hope the bones he claims were left—skull, hand, foot—will be all that is left of me, or less, after my cremation.

Why do men incite each other in battle by insulting their mothers? To inflame them and cloud their judgment at the moment of combat? Surely no one believes such taunts about the mother. And as for his hope that there will be no one to raise a cup and say, "This is Jizebul, may her name be preserved in honor," time will tell whose name survives.

But although I escaped, the house of my lord Ahab did not. Those who wanted to bow to Shalmaneser found their

Ramoth-gilead

king in another son of Omri, in Jehu grandson of Nimshi son of Omri. Called "Weasel" for his guile in horsetrading, Nimshi bequeathed his cunning to Jehu.○

"Is it *shalom*? Is it *shalom*? Is it *shalom*?" Joram and Ahaziyah had instructed Jehu to negotiate with the Assyrians as they approached Ramoth-gilead.○ What terms did Shalmaneser's envoy dictate for Israel's tribute? The death of all my lord Ahab's offspring—revenge for my lord's prowess in blocking Shalmaneser at Karkar—was the price Jehu was willing to pay!○ Or, rather, those who feared Shalmaneser and hoped he would strike down Hazael were willing for Jehu to offer such a "gift." Shalmaneser, not an unnamed prophet of Yhwh, incited Jehu to kill the king. How dare he claim the protection of anointing for himself when he has killed an anointed one!○

Joram, my royal falcon, and Ahaziyah, grandson who came to Samaria as king of the House of David in Jerusalem—gone! All my princes have been swallowed by Death! Is there no end to my lament?

> Mot has come up into our windows.
> He has entered our palaces,
> to cut off the children from the streets
> and the young men from the squares.○

Jehu's Purges

<small>841 BCE, EVENTS IN THE NORTHERN KINGDOM OF ISRAEL, AS DESCRIBED MUCH LATER BY PRIESTLY SCRIBES FROM JERUSALEM AND IN THE POSTEXILIC WORK OF THE CHRONICLER○</small>

Now Ahab had seventy sons in Samaria. So Jehu wrote letters and sent them to Samaria, to the officials of Jezreel, to the elders, and to the supporters of Ahab, saying, "When this letter reaches you—since the sons of your lord are with you and you have chariots and horses, a fortified city, and weapons—select the best and most suitable of the sons of your lord, set him on the throne of his father, and fight for the house of your lord."

But they were utterly terrified and said, "Look, the two kings could not stand up to him; how then can we stand?"

So the steward of the king's house, and the governor of the city, along with the elders and the supporters, sent word to Jehu, saying: "We are your servants; we will do anything you say to us. We will not make anyone king; do whatever seems good to you."

Then he wrote them a second letter, saying, "If you are on my side, and if you are ready to obey me, take the heads of your lord's sons and come to me at Jezreel tomorrow at this time."

Now the king's sons, seventy persons, were with the leaders of the city, who were rearing them. When the letter reached them, they took the king's sons and killed them, seventy persons; they put their heads in baskets and sent them to him at Jezreel.

When the messenger came and told him, "They have brought the heads of the king's sons," he said, "Make two heaps of them at the entrance of the gate until morning."

Decapitation of captives and piling of heads, from Assyrian relief sculpture

Then in the morning when he went out, he stood and said to all the people, "Are you innocent? Behold, it was I who conspired against my lord and killed him; but who struck down all these? Know then that there shall fall to the earth nothing of the word of Yhwh, which Yhwh spoke concerning the house of Ahab; for YHWH has done what he said through his servant Eliyahu."

So Jehu killed all who were left of the house of Ahab in Jezreel, all his nobles, close friends, and priests, until he left him no survivor.

Then he set out and went to Samaria. On the way, when he was at Beth-eked of the Shepherds, Jehu met kinsmen of Ahaziyah king of Judah and said, "Who are you?"

They answered, "We are kinsmen of Ahaziyah; we have come down to visit the sons of the king and the sons of the queen mother."

He said, "Take them alive." They took them alive, and slaughtered them at the pit of Beth-eked, forty-two men; he did not spare a single man of them.

When he came to Samaria, he killed all who were left to Ahab in Samaria, until he had wiped them out.

In those days YHWH began to cut off part of Israel. Hazael defeated them throughout the frontier of Israel: from the Jordan to the rising of the sun, all the land of Gilead, of the Gadites, the Reubenites, and the Manassites, from Aroer, which is by the Wadi Arnon, that is, Gilead and Bashan.

When Jehu was executing judgment on the house of Ahab, he met the officials of Judah and the sons of Ahaziyah's kinsmen, who attended Ahaziyah, and he killed them.

He searched for Ahaziyah, who was captured while hiding in Samaria and was brought to Jehu, and put to death.

They buried him, for they said, "He is the son of Jehoshaphat, who sought YHWH with all his heart."

And the house of Ahaziyah had no one to keep the power of the kingdom.

Jizebul Writes to Atalyah: Jehu's Coup

841 BCE

To Atalyah gevirah *in the House of David in Jerusalem. Your mother Jizebul sends to greet you in haste. Ask the messenger who delivers this letter for the token I sent with him. You will recognize it. If he does not have anything, beware.*

He is not the same man to whom I gave the letter.

There is treachery all around! Our sons are murdered; the kings of Samaria and Jerusalem are dead! Your brother Joram, wounded by Hazael, has died at the hand of Jehu in Jezreel. Your son Ahaziyah tried to keep the power of both kingdoms in Samaria. The kinsmen you sent from Jerusalem to assist him were intercepted and massacred. The nobles in Samaria executed the king's sons in conspiracy with Jehu. Ahaziyah fled but did not reach the safety of Megiddo. All are bowing to Jehu, who is in league with Shalmaneser.

Act immediately! Guard the son of Ahaziyah by Bat-ahav of Samaria. Hold the throne as regent for him until he is of age. The officers who remain loyal to you and to the House of David are returning to Jerusalem with Ahaziyah's body. Jehu is not strong enough to extend his forces beyond the hills of Samaria while Shalmaneser passes. You will be secure for a time unless there is also a conspiracy in Jerusalem.

Do not believe the reports of my death. I send this letter from Megiddo, but I cannot stay here. While Jehu gathers strength in Samaria, he lets his lord Shalmaneser march uncontested from the Hauran through Gilead, to Megiddo and the sea. I will send word to you from another place.

May the gods guard you and keep you well.

Written and sealed by my own hand.

Shalmaneser III's Victory

841 BCE, SHALMANESER III'S REPORT FROM AN ANNALISTIC TEXT

In the eighteenth year of my rule I crossed the Euphrates for the sixteenth time. Hazael of Damascus put his trust upon his numerous army and called up his troops in great number, making the mountain Senir, a mountain facing the Lebanon, into his fortress. I fought with him and inflicted a defeat upon him, killing with the sword 16,000 of his experi-

Ramoth-gilead

enced soldiers. I took away from him 1,121 chariots, 470 riding horses as well as his camp.

He disappeared to save his life but I followed him and besieged him in Damascus, his royal residence. There I cut down his gardens outside of the city, and departed. I marched as far as the mountains of Hauran, destroying, tearing down, and burning innumerable towns, carrying booty away from them that was beyond counting.

I also marched as far as the mountains of Baal's Headland which is at the side of the sea and erected there a stela with my image as king. **At that time I received the tribute of the inhabitants of Tyre, Sidon, and of Jehu, son of Omri.**○

Shalmaneser's report from the Black Obelisk○

The tribute of Jehu, son of Omri; I received from him silver, gold, a golden bowl, a golden vase with pointed bottom, golden tumblers, golden buckets, tin, a staff for a king, and wooden valuables.

Jehu (?) bowing to Shalmaneser on the Black Obelisk

Jehu's Losses

840 BCE

From my window on the sea, I watched Israel fall. I took refuge at Dor, a port ruled by my kinsman, grandson of one of my older brothers from Tyre. My dear Achli, whose grown sons traded cloth dyed in Dor, arranged my transit from Megiddo.

When Shalmaneser marched through the valley to Baal's Headland, the twin piles of rotting heads at Jezreel's gate proclaimed Jehu's alliance to him, as if the Assyrians themselves had conquered the fortress. But the gods make their own agreements. In return for Jehu's tribute of gold and skulls, Shalmaneser offered little, taking Israel's gifts but failing to defend it against Hazael. Jehu's supporters in Gilead—settlers and Sons of the Prophets who opposed the house of Ahab— were the very ones to be cut off from Israel, surrendered to Hazael's repeated incursions. Dan and Hazor were taken, garrisons from which Hazael kept Jehu confined to the hills.

I know how the scribes of Samaria now describe Jehu's coup: heroic, single-handed, and divinely ordained. Usurpers must create the story that makes them legitimate, to cover the truth. It is laughable, how Jehu claims credit for removing Baal from Samaria. The pillar and vestments of Baal Shamem had been put away years earlier by my son Joram, when Baal-azzor refused to renew the covenant. Jehu called a sham assembly of nobles friendly to Tyre, as if to reopen the covenant, then murdered all. But Tyre would have little to do with insignificant Jehu once Hazael's strength became clear. If Yhwh of Hosts was so pleased with Jehu, why did he allow his servants in Gilead to be overrun by Hazael and his god Hadad?

My father Ethbaal had great hopes for the house of Omri through my lord Ahab. Now the house of Omri was ruled by the son of a weasel. The legacy of my lord Ahab retreated to Jerusalem with the body of Ahaziyah, to be vested in the infant son who alone was rightful heir to the two kingdoms.

13
Jeruʃalem

Atalyah Becomes Queen in Jerusalem

841 BCE, EVENTS IN JERUSALEM
AS DESCRIBED IN THE POSTEXILIC WORK OF THE CHRONICLER○

Now when Atalyah, Ahaziyah's mother, saw that her son was dead, she set about to destroy all the royal offspring of the house of Judah. But Jehosheba, the king's daughter, took Jehoash son of Ahaziyah, and stole him away from among the king's sons who were being killed; she put him and his nurse in a storeroom for the banquet couches. Thus Jehosheba, daughter of King Jehoram and wife of Jehoiada the priest—because she was a sister of Ahaziyah—hid him from Atalyah, so that she did not kill him; he remained with them six years, hidden in the house of God, while Atalyah reigned over the land.

How Atalyah Became Queen

841 BCE

 THE DESTINY OF KINGS is shaped as much by strategies in the women's quarters as by tactics on the battlefield.

Three sons were born in Jerusalem's royal precinct within weeks of each other that year, not including those of concubines: to Ahaziyah's wife Bat-ahav of Samaria, to his wife Zibiah of Beer-sheba, and to his half-sister Jehosheba, wife of Jehoiada the priest. Each child carried the hopes of a faction—those who favored Jerusalem's alliance with Israel, those who wanted more power for nobles in the fortified cities, and those who wanted priests to regain the privileges granted by Jehoshaphat.

Nobles of the hill country, you know how the House of David was cut down—not by Atalyah. Jehoram killed his brothers in their fortified cities, sending many of his sons and their mothers to take their places. Atalyah persuaded him to keep his sons' sons near Jerusalem, as hostages she said, to insure their fathers did not attempt to seize the throne and to keep them out of reach of disgruntled nobles. But she intended to train them as Ahaziyah's officials, and she oversaw their education. When Jehoram's sons in the cities were killed—by Philistines or by nobles who gave them up to weaken Jehoram? you would know—Atalyah's royal students were the few remaining shoots on David's tree. They were on their way to assist Ahaziyah in Samaria when Jehu cut them down.

Jehoram had alienated all who were once servants of Jehoshaphat—Jerusalem and countryside, nobles, commanders, priests. United in your opposition to him, you disagreed about his successor. The royal establishment prevailed, to proceed with Ahaziyah and the alliance with Israel.

Remember that Ahaziyah made his wishes known before leaving for the north: he favored a pact with Shalmaneser through Israel. Did Jehu's coup nullify that, or was the House of David still linked to Israel and the agreement with Assyria? Naming a successor would signal Atalyah's choice. Not that there seemed to be much choice. How could she maintain relations with Israel and be ally to Jehu, assassin of her brother and her son? But, how could she let the throne of Jerusalem leave our family by passing it to the offspring of Ahaziyah and the woman from Beer-sheba? And how could she stand alone against Assyria?

Like a clever Tyrian, she chose to bargain with all. She appeared to acquiesce to Jehu, calling herself "daughter of Omri"○ as Jehu styled himself "son of Omri," and she affirmed the covenant with Shalmaneser through Israel. How could she not, with the Assyrians at Jezreel? She made it known that the king-designate would be Ahaziyah's son by Bat-ahav of Samaria, with herself as regent, privately intending to nurture in Jerusalem a rival heir for Samaria, should Jehu falter. And she made independent arrangements by trading through Tyrian Dor, elevating Mattan the priest and the shrine of Baal Shamem in Jerusalem to special status. Many commanders and nobles found her ways practical, to give the hill country safety and a respite from war. Some priests and others wanting to sever ties to Israel disagreed.

Her enemies were quiet until the delayed *marzeaḥ* for Ahaziyah, when many from outside Jerusalem were in the royal precinct. In the few minutes of Atalyah's appearance for the toasts to Ahaziyah, deadly skirmishes erupted throughout the house from those who opposed her. Palace soldiers welcomed the temple guards coming to their aid, or so they thought. They let the temple guards escort the priest's wife Jehosheba, bloodied and disheveled, out of the royal women's quarters where she was visiting during the banquet. Only later was it discovered that the king's two wives and two young boys were dead—by stabbing, not by sword. Jehosheba raised a son all thought to be hers. Only much later did the question arise—was it her own?

For six years, Atalyah ruled alone, without knowing of any child. She sent the minimal exactions required by the weak Jehu or delayed them. Shalmaneser returned to the west for what would be the last time in her third year, but he did not damage the hill country. She retained the commanders' loyalty by giving them what they needed to resist Jehu's feeble pecking at the frontier. She did not allow Jerusalem's priests to control the countryside but gave you—the nobles and family heads—more power in your own lands, with local shrines. And she kept open Jerusalem's small path to the sea through Tyrians and Dor,○ again to benefit the landed ones. With Hazael pressing on Israel to the north and on lands east of the Jordan, she let the storm of Aram swirl around the frontiers, while she rebuilt the wealth of the hill country. And Hazael began to notice.

Atalyah could not count on Shalmaneser, who was no longer fighting in the west, and Jehu would be no help. If Hazael approached, she would stand for battle. And you people of the hill country knew you would be called once more to supply the army and send your sons to war, this time on your own land. Jehoiada the priest waited for his chance.

Jizebul Writes to Atalyah: Sad News

837 BCE

To Atalyah, gevirah of the House of David in Jerusalem. Your mother Jizebul sends to greet you from Dor. I bless you to Baal Shamem and the Lady Astarte. May they guard you and keep you well.

I received your letter and your gift of the gold bracelet. They reassure me that you have strengthened yourself on the throne well enough to think of your mother. The bracelet reminds me of the one I gave to Ahaziyah's bride, Bat-ahav, when she left Samaria. Do you remember? It was the four-winged beetle—the image you told me was to be embroidered in gold on Ahaziyah's blue wedding robe.○ How strange that the lowly Beetle rolls the Sun's good fortune into the heavens. How strange that our joy in the bride and her son failed like the weak sunlight of a short winter's day.

You have others more knowledgeable to advise you on the factions you described—priests in Jerusalem, army commanders, and officials of the fortified

Jerusalem

cities with landed nobles, heads of families, and their local high places. If you keep each of them dependent on you and any two of them set against the third, you will do well. You know my suspicions of the priests who were in Jerusalem before David. That they have men in arms who are not under the royal commanders is worrisome. My Little Green Bee-eater, may you devour those who would sting you.

There is nothing good to report from Samaria. I have not learned of any surviving sons of your father Ahab. The ruler of Dor, my Tyrian "host," keeps watch on me as if I were a prisoner. Does he act with Jehu's knowledge, to confine me here and restrict my letters? Perhaps those who fled to you from Jehu's slaughter know better, but I fear there is no man, young or old, left of my lord Ahab to challenge Jehu or to receive the crown from you. A pity that they thought to bring to Jerusalem archives of our family's rule but could not protect a living heir for Samaria's future. Shall we hope for a prince raised in secret, returning to claim his throne?○

The Tyrians traveling from Damascus say that Hazael is equipping his army for new campaigns. The Aramaeans boast that they will rule the highlands. They speak no longer of raids but of conquests. Samaria and Jerusalem together might have succeeded against him, but we have lost the best of your father's nobles, killed by Jehu, that son of a weasel. He may be vicious enough to kill the sons of the king like so many chicks, more for blood-sport than for food, but he cannot stand before Hazael. May the gods shorten his days by seven times the number of his murders.

Phoenician gold bracelet with four-winged beetle

And yet more sad news. Hazael welcomes most Tyrian merchants to Damascus under his agreement with Baal-azzor. But my dear friend Achli was detained and accused of spying for Jehu. Sheqer! A lie! Surely he, of all people, would not have gone near Samaria since Jehu's killings! Other traders have sought to find and ransom him, but they receive no answers. I fear I shall never see him and hear his sweet words again. And, I fear that I may see him and know he made my refuge at Dor a cage. I am consumed, grief upon grief.

Sealed by my own hand.

The Death of Atalyah

<small>835 BCE, EVENTS AS DESCRIBED MUCH LATER
BY PRIESTLY SCRIBES FROM JERUSALEM[○]</small>

But in the seventh year Jehoiada summoned the captains of the hundreds of the Carites and of the guards and had them come to him in the house of Yhwh.[○] He cut a covenant with them and put them under oath in the house of Yhwh; then he showed them the king's son.

He commanded them, saying, "This is what you are to do: one-third of you will go in on the sabbath and guard the king's house; another third will be at the gate Sur and a third at the gate behind the guards—you shall guard the house. And your two divisions that go out on the sabbath will guard the house of Yhwh on account of the king, each with his weapons in his hand; and whoever approaches the ranks is to be killed. Be with the king when he goes out and when he comes in."

The captains of the hundreds did according to all that Jehoiada the priest commanded; each brought his men who were to go off duty on the sabbath, with those who were to come on duty on the sabbath, and came to Jehoiada the priest. The priest delivered to the captains of the hundreds the spears and shields that had been King David's, which were in the house of Yhwh; the guards stood, every man with his weapons in his hand, from the south side of the house to the north side of the house, around the altar and the house, to guard the king on every side.

Then he brought out the king's son, put the crown on him, and gave him the insignia[○]; they proclaimed him king, and anointed him; they clapped their hands and shouted, "Long live the king!"

When Atalyah heard the noise of the guard and of the people, she came to the people, to the house of Yhwh; when she looked, behold, the king was standing by the pillar, according to custom, with the captains and the trumpeters beside the king, and all the people of the land rejoicing and blowing trumpets.

Atalyah tore her clothes and cried, "*Qesher! Qesher!* Conspiracy! Conspiracy!"

Then Jehoiada the priest commanded the captains of the hundreds who were set over the army, "Bring her out between the ranks, and kill with the sword anyone who follows her." For the priest had said, "Let her not be killed in the house of Yhwh."

So they laid hands on her; she went through the horses' entrance to the king's house, and there she was put to death.

Jehoiada cut a covenant between Yhwh and the king and people, that they should be Yhwh's people; also between the king and the people.

Then all the people of the land went to the house of Baal and tore it down; its altars and its images they broke in pieces, and they killed Mattan, the priest of Baal, before the altars.

The priest posted guards over the house of Yhwh. He took the captains of the hundreds, the Carites, the guards, and all the people of the land; then they brought the king down from the house of Yhwh, coming through the gate of the guards to the king's house.

He took his seat on the throne of the kings.

So all the people of the land rejoiced; and the city was quiet after Atalyah had been killed with the sword at the king's house.

Jehoash was seven years old when he began to reign.

Who Is King Jehoash?

835 BCE

The messenger from Jerusalem stepped back from my shrieks as grief and hope collided in my wailing.

"Atalyah is dead!? A royal heir is alive!?"

"Yes, they call him Jehoash, son of Ahaziyah by Zibiah of Beer-sheba. And to prove his royal birth, they showed a gold armband or bracelet of the four-winged beetle."

"The four-winged beetle? Do not lie to me!"

"Yes, the beetle with the sun."

Like storm waves breaking against the walls of Tyre, my heartbeat pounded in my ears. Must the gods be so cruel? I am the daughter of a priest who killed to take the throne. My daughter was killed by a priest who took her throne. But for whom? Who is this boy-king?

If he is Jehosheba's own son, he is not the seed of David. Jehoiada the priest can plant his seed in David's field, but it is only the priest's offspring.º By saying he is Ahaziyah's son by Zibiah of Beer-sheba, the priest used the boy to enlist the loyalty of the people of the land against Atalyah. If he is Ahaziyah's son by Bat-ahav of Samaria, he is the true heir, but not one wanted by a priest who rebelled against the covenant with Israel. All knew the beetle sign Ahaziyah favored, but no one besides Bat-ahav, Atalyah, and I knew the origin of that bracelet. Did someone take the bracelet from one mother and the child from another? Was Jehosheba's own son killed in the struggles? Was the living child she took playing with his own mother Bat-ahav's bracelet?

Until now, only a few in Jerusalem have known my hope for the one they call King Jehoash. His existence has not been a secret since the day Atalyah was killed, but his identity remains one.

As long as Atalyah had your loyalty—you nobles of the hill country—Jehoiada could not move against her. But Hazael's success and the lack of an heir in Jerusalem shifted the balance. You listened to the priest's words. If your wealth was to be protected, it must not go to an heirless *gevirah* preparing for war. And why should you support an empty agreement with Assyria through Israel and a Tyrian god's temple in Jerusalem? A smaller tax channeled through the house of Yhwh would be an easier burden, and part of it could be paid as tribute to keep Hazael away.

Not all followed Jehoiada with a whole heart. Among the commanders, the men of Benjamin held to their past, to tribal stories linking them in kinship to the north. King Saul, a warlord of Benjamin and father-in-law to David, led the highlands against the Philistines. On the frontier of Benjamin, Ahab and Jehoshaphat faced each other, befriended each other, and pledged brotherhood for their mutual interests. Our brother Jehoshaphat gave command of thousands to Eliada and Jehozabad of Benjamin, whose marriage ties to Israelite clans in Moab and Ammon made them especially useful.○ But Jehoiada the priest did not include their sons among his chief conspirators, as he did the sons of Jehoshaphat's other commanders Jehohanan and Zichri.○

Shomer son of Jehozabad of Benjamin○ escorted Ahaziyah's body from Megiddo to Jerusalem for burial. Atalyah gave him command of the troops in Benjamin to resist Jehu's weak sorties from the north, where he was when Jehoiada struck her down. Known to the priests for his family's devotion to Jehoshaphat, Shomer was not included in the purge of Atalyah's courtiers despite his service to the queen. He passed his father's loyalties, his military skills, and his name to his son, another Jehozabad. It was the son who brought me word of Atalyah's death.

The young Jehozabad learned from my grieving cries that the boy-king installed by the priests to serve Hazael could be the offspring of my lord Ahab and Jehoshaphat's covenant and heir to Ahaziyah's regency in Samaria. I made him swear to keep it to himself.

A Psalm for Relief ○

Transgression speaks to the wicked
    deep in their hearts;
there is no fear of God
    before their eyes.

For they flatter themselves in their own eyes
> that their iniquity cannot be found out and hated.

The words of their mouths are mischief and deceit;
> they have ceased to act wisely
> and do good.

They plot mischief while on their beds;
> they are set on a way that is not good;
> they do not reject evil.

Your steadfast love, O Baal, extends to the heavens,
> your faithfulness to the clouds.

Your righteousness is like the mountains of El,
> your judgments are like the great Deep;
> you save humans and animals alike, O Baal.

How precious is your steadfast love, O God!
Gods and humans may take refuge
> in the shadow of your wings.

They feast on the abundance of your house,
> and from the river of your delights
> you give them drink.

For with you is the fountain of life;
> in your light we see light.

O continue your steadfast love to those who know you,
> and your salvation to the upright of heart!

Do not let the foot of the arrogant tread on me,
> or the hand of the wicked drive me away.

There the evildoers lie prostrate;
> they are thrust down,
> unable to rise.

14
Dor

Jizebul Writes to Jehozabad: Advice

About 826 BCE

    *To Jehozabad son of Shomer son of Jehozabad, of the warriors of Benjamin in the service of Jehoash king in Jerusalem. Jizebul sends to greet you from Dor. I bless you to Y*HWH *and his Asherah. May they guard you and keep you well.*

    I received your letter reporting the turmoil in Jerusalem as the old priest lies dying. What does a man of war think I can tell him? I am no commander but the mother of kings. Nevertheless, I will tell you what I hear and see.

    *Jehoash your king is young. At Dor, the merchants say he is only a servant of Jehoiada the priest. When Jehoiada dies, your neighbors will test Jerusalem as if the king himself had died. You complain that the king's armies are neglected, that the increasing taxes to the house of Y*HWH *stay in the priests' treasury or are sent to Hazael at Damascus. The army's readiness will not improve as long as the priests' privilege continues.*

    Those who arrive at Dor from the east bring word that Shalmaneser's hand is slipping from the scepter. When the Assyrians begin to fight among themselves after him, Hazael will certainly move behind their backs to strike against Israel, and this time he will march to Dor, to Philistia, and to Jerusalem.

Jerusalem's pittance will not keep Hazael away. He will come, and you cannot stand alone. Your father and your father's father were comrades in battle with my sons and with my lord Ahab. You know the strength of the two kingdoms. Jehoash your king was raised as a priest, not a soldier. He does not know of his kinship with the warrior-kings of Israel. If you would build a brotherhood with Israel, with the House of Omri against Hazael, Jehoash must hear it from someone he trusts.

My son, here is my counsel. Make your lord Jehoash see how Jerusalem's priests weaken his kingdom. He must govern all the hill country, not only Jerusalem, and he must protect all. Gather the officials of the land who are discontent with the priests and show them the dangers to come. Let them speak before the king of the need for action. Let them renew worship at their own high places to insure large herds and bountiful harvests. If they will cut off the offerings to the priests of Jerusalem and to Hazael, and if they will support Jehoash with the royal levy for defense, you may be better prepared.

Teach your sons and the sons of the king with your wisdom. Seek the favor of the Israelites near you, in Ephraim, that you may win their loyalty and their service. Jehu's spilling the blood of Jezreel dismayed them, and they may welcome your friendship. Jehu will not live forever. If he persists in his weakness, perhaps his sons can walk with you.

The sons of Jehoiada the priest, especially Zechariah, will surely resist Jehoash's reducing their treasury, rebuffing Hazael, and renewing talks with the House of Omri. The king must choose. To rule as a true son of David and brother to Israel, he must overrule the priests whom he calls brothers in the house of Yhwh for the safety of the kingdom. May the gods grant him courage. May they grant you success in your endeavors.

Sealed by my own hand.

Dor

The Death of Jehoiada the Priest

About 826 bce, events in Jerusalem as described much later by priestly scribes from Jerusalem and in the postexilic work of the Chronicler°

In the seventh year of Jehu, Jehoash began to reign.... His mother's name was Zibiah of Beer-sheba. Jehoash did what was right in the sight of Yhwh all his days because Jehoiada the priest instructed him. Nevertheless the high places were not taken away; the people continued to sacrifice and make offerings on the high places.

Jehoash said to the priests, "All the money offered as sacred donations that is brought into the house of Yhwh, the money for which each person is assessed—the money from the assessment of persons—and the money from the voluntary offerings brought into the house of Yhwh, let the priests receive from each of the donors; and let them repair the house wherever any need of repairs is discovered." But by the twenty-third year of King Jehoash the priests had made no repairs on the house. Therefore King Jehoash summoned the priests and said to them, "Why are you not repairing the house? Now therefore do not accept any more money from your donors but hand it over for the repair of the house." So the priests agreed that they would neither accept more money from the people nor repair the house.

Jehoash did what was right in the eyes of Yhwh all the days of Jehoiada the priest. Jehoiada got two wives for him, and he fathered sons and daughters.

But Jehoiada grew old and full of days, and he died; he was one hundred thirty years old at his death. And they buried him in the city of David among the kings because he had done good in Israel and for God and his house.

Now after the death of Jehoiada the officials of Judah came and did obeisance to the king; then the king listened to them. They abandoned the house of Yhwh, the God of their fathers, and served the Asherahs and the idols and wrath came upon Judah and Jerusalem for this guilt of theirs. Yet Yhwh sent prophets among them to bring them back; the prophets testified against them, but they would not listen.

The Jezebel Letters

Then the spirit of God took possession of Zechariah son of Jehoiada the priest; he stood above the people and said to them, "Thus says God: Why do you transgress the commandments of Yhwh, so that you cannot prosper? Because you have forsaken Yhwh, he has also forsaken you."

But they conspired against him, and they stoned him with stones by command of the king in the court of the house of Yhwh.

Eclipse

824 BCE, THE YEAR IN WHICH THIS AND ALL THE MEMOIR ENTRIES WERE WRITTEN

Shalmaneser is dead. The kingdoms on the Great Sea will not have an Assyrian king as enemy or ally while his successors fight over his throne. Our lands must take up the reins of their own destiny.

I have given my lord Ahab's sons and daughters to the vision of my father Ethbaal. But his plan for a covenant of prosperity from Tyre to Ezion-geber, from Damascus to the River of Egypt, has no heirs. Against Shalmaneser, the lands that had first joined in *shalom* were united for war, not for blessing. Exhausted by the struggle, each kingdom took its own stand toward Assyria, and our brotherhood was disbanded. In Samaria and Jerusalem, there is no relief at Shalmaneser's passing, for Hazael will take his place as a bandit who merely loots our cities, not an imperial king with whom one can bargain. I have no more sons to sit on a throne or daughters to seal a covenant. I can no longer see well enough to weave, and a spindle shakes in my hand. And I can no longer see my father's design for our kingdoms.

For a moment, when Jehoiada the priest died, I had hope. King Jehoash listened to the commanders and the nobles, and he strengthened them. He stripped the greedy priests of their privilege in Jerusalem and quelled the rebellion of Jehoiada's son Zechariah. But he has not turned completely away from

Dor

Hazael. Without help, Jehoash cannot stop him. Already Hazael is on the move. The Tyrians will not assist Jerusalem, the city that pulled down the sanctuary of Baal Shamem. The priests destroyed Atalyah's pact with Jehu, shaky though it was, when they killed her and ended payments to Israel. Why will King Jehoash not listen to his officials, take up the legacy of Ahaziyah, and seek men of Israel who could hasten Jehu's son to the throne in Samaria? If the nobles of Israel do not remove Jehu, if Jehoash stands alone and backs down to Hazael, the vision will be lost for this generation. Perhaps that is what the darkening sun foretold.

It happened after Atalyah's death, when I was given more freedom at Dor. I moved to the countryside, to an estate near the spring at the foot of Baal's Headland, away from the stench of fish and purple dye but still in sight of my Lady's sea. There, on a summer day seven years ago, I sat spinning in the morning shade of the grove and looking through my little box of stones.

I had been thinking of Atalyah, of our days in Jezreel's grove, remembering how the disks of silver light had danced upon her robe. As my mind wandered, the disks flickered on my robe, and on the ground. Then, the birds quieted as if at sunset. There were no clouds, yet the daylight faded. And in each silver disk, a shadow grew.

At first, I did not trust my old eyes or my dozing thoughts to hold the moving lights. But they were no longer circles. Only crescents of light now moved over me and upon the ground. As I searched from tree to tree, it was the same. Each sun disk had become a crescent moon, a thousand moons, waning ever smaller. The shadows devoured the lights.

Then, very slowly, the crescents reappeared, waxed full again, and the sun returned. The birds resumed their songs.

Long have I pondered that day. It was not a sign for me alone. I heard later from traders on ships arriving from Egypt how the sun disappeared along the southern coast.° Was it a sign of darkness swallowing the light, as Mot swallowed

Baal? Were the disks and crescents of the Lady at war with the darkness to secure his return? I had seen that battle on the face of the Moon, but never in the Sun.

Within a year, Baal-azzor son of my father and ruler of Tyre died. All who could sustain my hope have been devoured by Death. It seems even the Sun has lost her wings and cannot escape. She burns the land or disappears, all in Mot's season. Could she have gone with the Lady to Mot's realm to seek for an heir?

> Yet, beware, divine messengers.
> > Approach not divine Mot,
> lest he make you like a lamb in his mouth,
> > ye be crushed like a kid in his gullet.
> Even the Gods' Torch Shapsh,
> > who wings over heaven's expanse,
> > is in Mot El's Beloved's hand! ○

Why did my father give me the name of sorrow, the name of Baal's descent into Mot's realm?

> Parch'd is the furrow of soil, O Shapsh;
> > parched is El's soil's furrow:
> > Baal neglects the furrow of his tillage.
> Where is powerful Baal?
> > Where is the Prince, Lord of Earth? ○

Who will seek a new covenant of *shalom* so that our fields may prosper without attack? Will Jehozabad and Jozacar guide King Jehoash to peace with their brothers in Ephraim or must that union wait for his son? Will one of Jehu's sons acknowledge the covenant legacy with Jerusalem?

Hazael will try to swallow whatever Shalmaneser has left. That may soon include Dor. The light of *shalom* may not return in my lifetime. If Jehoash does not follow the path of his fathers, his servants are prepared to put his son on the throne by force. That would be a sword's stroke against the last son of our covenant, and yet, it could open a way for *shalom*.

So I bind up my testimony, as Jehozabad and Jozacar have asked. Ethbaal and Omri called Jerusalem to brotherhood with Samaria, despite the shadow of Assyria's empire, despite rebellious clans and conspiring priests. May my words be a witness to the covenant of the fathers, a memorial to be renewed by the sons. If ever again these peoples acknowledge their brotherhood, may their light be restored.

May they tell the story of Ahab and Jehoshaphat as a reminder of the blessings of brotherhood and the perils of enmity.

May they be free from those who would rob them of their substance by war or tribute or greedy assessment.

May they be united to live in safety, under their own vines and their own fig trees.

May Shapsh embroider their robes with silver under the olive.

And may the names of my father Ethbaal and my lord Ahab be preserved in honor, for the blessing of these lands by the Lady in whose house I was born.

The Return of Baal°

Like the heart of a cow for her calf,
    like the heart of a ewe for her lamb,
        so is the heart of Anath for Baal.
She seizes the godly Mot—
    with sword she cleaves him.
With fan she winnows him—
    With fire she burns him.
With hand-mill she grinds him—
    in the field she sows him.

Birds eat his remnants,
  consuming his portions,
    flitting from remnant to remnant.

And behold, alive is powerful Baal!
  And behold, existent is the Prince,° Lord of Earth!
In a dream, O kindly El benign,
  In a vision, Creator of Creatures,
the heavens fat did rain,
  the creek beds flowed with honey.
So I knew
that alive was powerful Baal!
  Existent the Prince, Lord of Earth!

Ivory plaque with lotus bud and flower,
from Samaria

15
Epilogues

Epilogue for Jozacar and Jehozabad

<small>EVENTS OF JEHOASH'S REIGN AND AFTER, AS DESCRIBED MUCH LATER BY PRIESTLY SCRIBES FROM JERUSALEM</small>○

At that time Hazael king of Aram went up, fought against Gath, and took it.

But when Hazael set his face to go up against Jerusalem, Jehoash king of Judah took all the votive gifts that Jehoshaphat, Jehoram, and Ahaziyah, his fathers, the kings of Judah, had dedicated, as well as his own votive gifts, all the gold that was found in the treasuries of the house of Y<small>HWH</small> and of the king's house, and sent these to Hazael king of Aram. Then Hazael withdrew from Jerusalem.

Now the rest of the acts of Jehoash, and all that he did, are they not written in the Book of the Daily Affairs of the Kings of Judah?

His servants arose, devised a conspiracy, and killed Jehoash in the house of Millo, on the way that goes down to Silla. It was Jozacar son of Shimeath and Jehozabad son of Shomer, his servants, who struck him down, so that he died.

He was buried with his fathers in the city of David; then his son Amaziah succeeded him.

Amaziah was twenty-five years old when he began to reign, and he reigned twenty-nine years in Jerusalem. His mother's name was Jehoaddin of Jerusalem. He did what was right in the sight of Yhwh, yet not like his ancestor David; in all things he did as his father Jehoash had done. But the high places were not removed; the people still sacrificed and made offerings on the high places. As soon as the royal power was firmly in his hand, he killed his servants who had murdered the king his father. But he did not put to death the sons of the murderers.

Author's Epilogue

Amaziah son of Jehoash king in Jerusalem was required to kill Jozacar and Jehozabad for the murder of his father. But the reports of his reign (2 Kgs 14:7-14; 2 Chronicles 25) show that he may have appreciated the change of policy these servants advocated. The text makes particular mention that the assassins' sons were spared, an unusual circumstance requiring the Deuteronomistic editors to justify it by citing the law of Moses (2 Kgs 14:6).

Were the sons and their allies—the intended recipients for Jizebul's memoirs—sponsors of Amaziah's rule in place of his father Jehoash? If so, they may have been spared to help implement the conspirators' program, since the "commanders of the thousands and of the hundreds for . . . Benjamin" were among Amaziah's leaders in a military build-up (2 Chr 25:5). Amaziah continued to authorize worship at the high places, bolstering local establishments at the expense of the Jerusalem priesthood, for which he is criticized by the Deuteronomistic editors (2 Kgs 14:3-4). Amaziah also successfully attacked Edom, initially enlisting the help of mercenaries from Ephraim in southern Israel (2 Chr 25:5-10), perhaps with the tacit approval of the Jehuite king (like Jehoshaphat's earlier jurisdiction over some cities there with Ahab's permission?). To this extent, he seems to have followed what Jizebul recommends as a program of Jerusalem's military development, laying the groundwork for a Samaria-Jerusalem coalition.

Jizebul's Tyrian vision of a "united monarchy" between Israel and Jerusalem—joined by alliance, kinship, and cooperative economic and foreign policies, rather than only by force—seems to have been continued in a less familial form under Jehu's successors. After Amaziah's military success, which would have given him control of Edomite copper and the southern trade routes, his attempt to make a marriage covenant with Jehu's grandson Joash was rebuffed.○ King Joash was apparently also in an expansionist mode along the southern Mediterranean coast and into the foothills, where he defeated Amaziah at Beth-shemesh, broke down a portion of Jerusalem's walls, and looted the temple and the palace (2 Kgs 14:11-14; 2 Chr 25:20-24). I think that Amaziah's Ephraimite soldiers, his marriage proposal, and the military incursion by Joash of Israel suggest a renewed association of the two kingdoms, with the south's initiative being absorbed eventually by the north's dominant power.

The opportunity for both northern and southern kings to pursue military objectives was provided by the relative absence of interference from Damascus. An Aramaean downfall is not mentioned in 2 Chronicles. According to 2 Kings, the Aramaean oppression continued through all the reign of Jehu and his son Jehoahaz. Hazael's son Ben-hadad is said to have met stronger resistance from the third Jehuite generation in Joash, who "took again from Ben-hadad son of Hazael the towns that he had taken from his father Jehoahaz in war. Three times Joash defeated him and recovered the towns of Israel" (2 Kgs 13:25-26).

Resolution of the Aramaean conflict may have been assisted by the presence of the Assyrians. After a thirteen-year gap in stable rule following Shalmaneser III, Adad-nirari III succeeded and resumed campaigning in the west. Joash of Samaria is listed as a tributary by Adad-nirari III in a campaign dated by many to 796 BCE.○ Is the Assyrian king the "savior" of Israel mentioned in 2 Kings 13:3-5? It is possible that, backed by Assyria, joint military ventures of Israel and Jerusalem against Aram finally relieved the highlands of their enemy at Damascus, freeing them for their own expansion. The prophetic books of Amos and Hosea portray conditions under Jeroboam II, the last effective Jehuite ruler (793–753 BCE), as very good, at least for the elite of Israel, perhaps at the expense of producers in the south.○

In the final decades of Samaria's independence, Pekah king of Israel (not a Jehuite) tried unsuccessfully to force Ahaz king in Jerusalem to remain or join in such a union, marking the end of any accord (about 735 BCE). And yet, did the doubling of Jerusalem in the decades following Assyria's capture of Samaria (723–722 BCE) result at least in part from an influx of northern urban refugees? What role did they play in the government? The prophet Micah rails against King Hezekiah's administration, against "you rulers of the house of Jacob and chiefs of the house of Israel, who abhor justice and pervert all equity, who build Zion with blood and Jerusalem with wrong!" (Mic 3:9-10). Was he addressing the transplanted northern leadership? The influence of northerners, themselves indebted to Tyrian culture, on the monarchy and religion of Jerusalem has yet to be fully excavated in the texts.

Assyria's reappearance on the eastern Mediterranean coast also had repercussions for Tyre. The late ninth century saw increased Tyrian activity in North Africa, leading to the founding of Carthage as a trading center out of reach of Assyrian power (traditional date of founding, 813 BCE). Tyre's daughter city eventually became the base for an empire in her own right, overshadowing the Phoenician homeland and outlasting the Assyrians.

Where is Jizebul in this extended relationship of Samaria and Jerusalem? How do the aspects of her biblical depiction—sexual, political, religious—fare in a more historical context?

The negative sexual stereotype—indeed, an enduring archetype—of "Jezebel" misses the mark but, ironically, it also points to an extremely important historical implication. According to the genealogy of this story, Jizebul literally, through her body and her nurture, united the kings and queen of Samaria and Jerusalem from Ahab to Atalyah for thirty-nine years, from 874 to 835 BCE.[9] This is a longer period (and may be much greater if one includes Jehoash!) than the reign of any ruler of the so-called Divided Monarchy to that point. If she remained alive and active in that time and beyond, as *The Jezebel Letters* proposes, it is not surprising that the Bible reflects such a significant response to her, albeit a misleading one.

Politically, she embodied an experience in Israelite history that the Deuteronomistic editors deemed to have been ultimately unsuccessful for both Samaria and Jerusalem. In describing the selection of the first king, Saul, I Samuel 8 voices preemptive criticism of the monarchy with its attendant infrastructure of a standing army and bureaucracy, an extractive economy favoring an elite class, and export market demands. These are the very institutions developed by the Omrides in Samaria and grafted onto Jerusalem in the ninth century. The books of Chronicles do not even mention

Jizebul since their ideology highlights a priestly role in governance, anticipating a different arrangement in the Persian period (538–333 BCE).

Readers in the United States who want to honor biblical warnings may be most discomforted by this political evaluation of Jizebul. She promotes what she sees as an advanced political-economic system supported by religion, a monarchist-extractive government under a god of productivity. She works from a Tyrian model of economic empire for her version of peace and prosperity from the top down, and she is frustrated at the locals' disregard for the obvious benefits. How could they cling to their obsolete lifeways against the rising tide of regionalism? Because he is in "our" texts, Eliyahu is seen as the heroic defender of divinely revealed priorities. Take a minute to realize that Eliyahu was a Middle Eastern man, that he used religious claims to oppose what he perceived to be foreign economic and political practices that threatened him by redistributing power and undermining traditional values in his society. Jizebul would have called him a terrorist or an insurgent.

The religious establishments of Tyre, Samaria, and Jerusalem in *The Jezebel Letters* are deeply embedded in their respective political and economic systems. It may be claiming too much to give Jizebul personal credit for introducing some of the Bible's most lyrical, nature-based hymns into the Hebrew repertoire. More likely, the long-term political contact of the royal houses contributed to the cross-fertilization of their priestly guilds. Certainly, the architecture of the Jerusalem temple and its several renovations reflected Phoenician visual vocabulary. It is still wonderfully ironic that the queen accused of murdering YHWH's prophets may have been instrumental (pun intended) in promoting songs with which the God of Israel is still praised.

But historical inquiries cannot explain why the "Jezebel" archetype has remained active. In the terms of Jungian psychology, she may have functioned as a "shadow," receiving the unconscious projection of negative energies that the culture attributes to women's sexuality, political power, and religious leadership. A goal of Jungian analysis is to befriend one's shadow and integrate it into one's consciousness, thereby releasing its creative potential. I hope this study takes a step toward integration, individually and collectively.

This is Jizebul. May her name be preserved in honor.

Notes to the Story

◯

Introduction

YHWH [page 1]. In the Hebrew Bible and ancient Hebrew inscriptions, the Name of Israel's God is written as a *Tetragrammaton*, a "four-letter word" (!) without vowels. Jewish tradition honors the Name by not saying it aloud but saying "Lord" where the text reads Y*HWH*. Following this practice, the Name is represented in many English translations by L*ORD* (small capital letters). If portions of *The Jezebel Letters* containing the Name are read aloud, the lack of vowels in Y*HWH* should remind readers to substitute "Lord" if it is appropriate for any in the group.

Catholic queens [page 2]. "Jezebel" was used by non-Catholics in unflattering references to European Catholic queens whose political and religious leadership was critiqued by the implied sexual connotations of the term. Frederick Farrar (1900, 124n2) reports that Spanish Jews called the persecuting Queen Isabella "the Catholic Jezebel." Calvinist John Knox targeted the Catholic Marys: "He hath raised vp these Iesabelles (our mischeuous Maryes) to be the vttermost of his plagues" (1558), while Titus Oates titled his work *The Witch of Endor or the witchcrafts of the Roman Jesebel* (1679), both cited in the "Jezebel" entry of the *Oxford English Dictionary*, 2nd ed., Oxford: Clarendon Press, 1989, 8.232.

"Jezebel" [page 2]. This definition comes from *Merriam-Webster's Collegiate Dictionary*, 10th ed., Springfield, Mass.: Merriam-Webster, Inc., 2001.

Jizebul [page 3]. See glossary entries for more technical aspects of "Jezebel" and "Jizebul."

Women's literacy [page 3]. For a glimpse of royal women's education and correspondence from Mesopotamia in the third and second millennia BCE, see Gerda Lerner's discussion (1986, 66–75 and notes to original studies). Of the dozen letter fragments within the Old Testament, one is from a woman—Jizebul's instructions to the elders of Jezreel (1 Kgs 21:9-10). Outside the Bible, the only surviving Phoenician letter is from a woman to her sister. Original Hebrew letters from the Iron and Persian periods may be found in the work of Dennis Pardee et al. (1982, especially the introductory bibliography, 7–9, and the Phoenician letter, 165–68) and James Lindenberger (1994, including letters from Elephantine and the Phoenician letter, 119–20). The loss of letters because of fragile materials is balanced by the presence of several women's seals (for example, see Avigad 1987).

Tyre [page 3]. The terms Tyre, Phoenicia, and Lebanon are sometimes used with overlapping meanings. Tyre was one of several cities on the coast of what is now Lebanon whose prosperity depended on sea trade and commerce with inland powers. Ethbaal became known in the Bible as king of the Sidonians (Sidon was a rival city slightly north of Tyre) when he extended Tyre's control over the larger coastal region. Historians refer to that area as Phoenicia, but ancient texts more often call it "the Lebanon," meaning the mountain range that parallels the coast.

Israel [page 3]. The area called Israel in this story did not cover the same territory as the modern state of Israel. In the ninth century BCE, Israel was concentrated in the northern highlands around Samaria, with varying degrees of control over the Galilee, a portion of the coastal plain, and lands east of the Jordan River. Jerusalem and the southern hill country were considered a separate entity.

Origins of Israelite monarchy [page 4]. My own view is somewhat more moderate than the case made by Israel Finkelstein and Neil Silberman (2001), that the northern kingdom of Israel in the ninth century was "Israel's Forgotten First Kingdom" (the title of their chapter 7). Although their argument almost persuaded me, Baruch Halpern's (2001) account of David's tenth-century accomplishments offers a more positive view of early, if unsustainable, administration of a kingdom that included Israel as a subordinated region, governed from Jerusalem. William Dever (2001) effectively refutes "revisionist" claims that very little of the biblical narrative about the monarchies reflects actual historical conditions of the Iron Age (1200–586 BCE).

Ancient Near Eastern texts [page 5]. For the convenience of readers who do not have access to a research library, the texts quoted here are all taken from a classic reference that may be available in undergraduate and public libraries (Pritchard 1969b). A more recent collection for those wanting to see translations with current historical and linguistic considerations is becoming available in graduate libraries (Hallo and Younger 2003).

Royal names [page 6]. That the royal names of King Ahab's offspring all had an element of the divine Name in them (in English, J[eh]- or -[y]ah) is noteworthy in light of the accusations of his adopting Baal-worship. Baalist elements do appear—in biblical names of the time of David in the south and on Samaria ostraca (mostly business memos on pottery fragments) of the early eighth century in the north. See Avigad (1987) and especially Cross (1984) for the north-south spellings.

Chronology [page 6]. The chronological table and the dates for the documents are based on several sources (primarily Miller and Hayes 1986; Finkelstein and Silberman 2001; Thiele 1983; and Katzenstein 1997). Some dates have been knowingly altered to suit the plot. For example, H. Jacob Katzenstein insists that Ahab did not marry Jizebul until after he became at least coregent, if not king, in about 873 BCE. If Atalyah was the first child of their union, she would have been no more than eight years old when she married Jehoram of Judah in 866 BCE. My narrative has an earlier marriage for Ahab and an older bride for Jehoram. The chronological evidence available for the succession in Tyre and the rulers of Aram is also debated, and I have felt free to make decisions for narrative cogency. Dates for the kings that appear in parentheses in the notes are based on the study by Edwin Thiele (1983, 11–13).

Relation of visual images to text [page 7]. For studies of how biblical authors may have used visual allusions as an inherent aspect of their writing, please refer to my earlier works: Beach 1991; 1993; 1997a; 1997b. Including illustrations with this story is an attempt to recreate for modern readers the active role that allusion and visual background would have played in an ancient audience's understanding of any text—letter, or narrative (written or oral), or royal inscription.

1 Prologues

Gevirah [page 17]. This Hebrew title designates the mother of the reigning king, the queen mother (see Ackerman 1993). Ancient kings, including those in the Bible, typically had many wives resulting from diplomatic ties with noble families within the nation and from other nations. The one who had highest status was the mother of the designated crown prince (who was not necessarily the first born of all sons, as, for example, David's son Solomon). She could play a role in the succession (as Bathsheba did, I Kings 1) and probably had ceremonial religious duties as well (as did Ma'acah, mother of King Asa of Judah, I Kgs 15:13). The father's other wives may have been "inherited" by his son, the new king (see the references to David taking Saul's wives [2 Sam 12:8] and Absalom taking David's concubines [2 Sam 16:22]).

YHWH and his Asherah [page 18]. This phrase has been found on three Hebrew inscriptions, two painted on store jars found at the desert station of Kuntillet 'Ajrud in the eastern Sinai (late ninth to early eighth century) and one inscribed in the rock of a tomb at Khirbet el-Qôm west of Hebron (seventh to eighth centuries). All invoke the deity/deities' blessing on a person: "I bless you by . . . ." Some translate the Kuntillet 'Ajrud phrase, "by YHWH of Samaria and his Asherah." Even when "Asherah" or "his Asherah" is the agreed translation, there is debate about whether this denotes a goddess-consort for YHWH or an attribute or object associated with YHWH. The latter interpretation is followed by the NRSV for the same word in the Bible, which it translates as "sacred pole" with a footnote, "Heb *Asherah* (for example, of Ahab's making in I Kgs 16:33)." When writing to YHWH worshipers, Jizebul uses the form recognizable to them; when writing to Tyrians, she invokes the Baal and Astarte of their tradition. However the recipients would have interpreted *asherah*, Jizebul means a goddess. (See "Teman, Ḥorvat," in Stern 1993, 4.1458–64). William Dever (1984) applies the Kuntillet 'Ajrud literary and graphic evidence to the debate about the nature of the biblical *asherah*.

. . . turn the name of the Prince to dung [page 19]. See glossary, *Jezebel*.

Baal Shamem the god of Tyre [page 19]. Descriptions of the religion of Tyre generally list three principal deities: goddess Astarte, god Melqart (*milkqart*, "king of the city"), and some aspect of the god Baal. Since 1–2 Kings uses "Baal" to denote the objectionable deity associated with Jizebul, Baal Shamem is used in *The Jezebel Letters* as the covenant deity in Israel's relation with Tyre, although the Tyrian partners at the time may have understood it to be Melqart. Edward Lipiński takes the I Kings 18 account of a contest between Y<small>HWH</small> and a storm god to point to Baal Shamem as the deity in question (1995, 79–90, especially 85).

2 Tyre

Text [page 20]. Translation of I Kings 16:8-12a, 15-18, 20-22 NRSV, adapted by the author. As the headings to the biblical quotations throughout this book suggest, the composition of Joshua through 2 Kings is thought to have been begun in the late Jerusalem monarchy, perhaps during the reign of King Josiah (640–609 BCE). Under the auspices of royal priests, what became the Deuteronomistic "history" evaluated the Israelites' settlement and monarchy, using religious criteria that would not have been recognized during earlier periods. The primacy of the Jerusalem temple and priesthood, the Davidic dynasty, and worship of Y<small>HWH</small> alone became the standards for assessing previous rulers, although multiple sanctuaries and deities may have been historically acceptable in the times being described. By these standards, the northern kingdom of Israel was always remiss.

Not . . . anyone who pees against a wall [page 20]. This phrase in I Kings 16:11 will be familiar to readers of the King James Version, which translates it "not one that pisseth against a wall." The New Revised Standard Version reduces it to "not . . . a single male." I have reinstated a cruder but more literal translation here, anticipating the very threatening juxtaposition of peeing and being cut off in later curses.

The Book of the Daily Affairs of the Kings of Israel [page 21]. Frequent mention of sources used by the biblical author underscores that the narratives in 1–2 Kings are not eyewitness reports. They are based on later research into royal records ("chronicles" in the KJV, "annals" in the NRSV), selected and interpreted to emphasize the editors' religious evaluations of royal behavior. These sources no longer exist but were probably still available when the Deuteronomistic "history" was written. The New Testament has similar "footnotes" indicating deliberate research, such as the opening verses of Luke and Acts, both by the same author.

Dates [page 21]. In Thiele's chronology (1983), Omri's civil war against Tibni lasted about four years (from the twenty-seventh year of Asa to his thirty-first year, I Kgs 16:15, 23), and Omri did not secure sole rule until 880 BCE. *The Jezebel*

Letters's storyline assumes that Omri's supremacy was evident much sooner, leaving perhaps only pockets of insurgency. Tyre's alliance, described in this chapter, both confirmed and assured Omri's rule before 880.

Papyrus [page 22]. Phoenician inscriptions are notably scarce, leading to the conclusion that their extensive records, referred to by others, were written on papyrus. H. Jacob Katzenstein supports this inference with a note on the five hundred blank papyrus scrolls sent in one shipment from Egypt to Byblos (1997, 69n144).

Old stories [page 22]. Religious texts of the eastern Mediterranean region were preserved at Ugarit, a cosmopolitan city on the Syrian coast that was destroyed in about 1200 BCE. Excavations begun in 1929 yielded poetic tales and ritual texts about the deities El, Baal, Asherah, and Astarte, whose names also appear in biblical texts and place names and in extrabiblical inscriptions. Some version of these stories would probably have been known to Jizebul, a priest's daughter, and she refers to them as "the old stories." See Pritchard 1969b, 129–55. These documents are sometimes referred to by the modern Syrian name of the site, as Ras Shamra texts.

Rock [page 22]. The island city's English name, Tyre, is from an ancient Greek rendering. I use Sor to represent the older Semitic languages' name (also modern Arabic). The biblical Hebrew is *tsur*, meaning rock—the island that was completely separate from the mainland until Alexander the Great built a causeway for his attack in 333 BCE. See Katzenstein (1997, 9) for the linguistic history.

Baal's Headland [page 26]. For the purposes of this story, I have adopted proposals to identify Mount Carmel as Baal's Headland (Ba'li-ra'si), the promontory mentioned by Shalmaneser III as his coastal destination in the campaign of 841 BCE (see his Black Obelisk inscription on page 137). Other candidates include the hillside near the pass through the Nahr el-Kelb (Dog River) north of Beirut and Râs en-Naqura (Rosh haNiqra) between Tyre and Akko. For a fuller discussion of these options, see Katzenstein 1997, 175–78. Lipiński includes another location north of Akko (2004). Anson Rainey's forthcoming atlas identifies Mount Carmel as Baal's Headland (personal communication, November 2004; Rainey and Notley, forthcoming).

Text [page 28]. Translation of Psalm 29, NRSV, adapted by the author. Substitution of Baal for YHWH is based on the work of Mitchell Dahood 1965, 174–80.

Dahood credits "the recognition that this psalm is a Yahwistic adaptation of an older Canaanite hymn to the storm-god Baal" (175) to the much earlier work of H. L. Ginsberg (1935).

The Lebanon [page 28]. The name of the modern Middle Eastern state of Lebanon derives from the mountain range that parallels the coast, called "the Lebanon" in ancient documents. The higher elevations caught storms blowing from the west to water the once-great forests there. A few of these cedars remain in preserves today after millennia of deforestation for lumber.

3 Tirzah

The Land Between the Rivers [page 30]. The modern geographic term for the homeland of the Assyrian empire is northern Mesopotamia, between (Greek, *meso-*) the Tigris and Euphrates Rivers (Greek, *potamos*). Many Assyrian descriptions of royal campaigns begin "I crossed the Euphrates," or "I crossed the Tigris." "The Land Between the Rivers" is used in this story to designate the Assyrian heartland.

High place [page 37]. A local sacred site (*bamah* in Hebrew). The Deuteronomistic account condemns high places in general because of its emphasis on the Jerusalem temple and priesthood as the only legitimate establishment. Biblical reports of kings' authorizing worship at high places suggest that they were previously considered to be an official, although decentralized, part of the national religion. The word "high" in the English phrase comes from the Latin translation *excelsus*, but the idea that all high places were rural hilltop shrines has been discredited by both archaeological and literary investigations. Jizebul associates the divine appellation Fear of Isaac (Gen 31:53) with the power symbolized by the bull, perhaps best expressed in the New American Bible's translation of the uncertain word as "Awesome One."

Jerusalem's priests [page 38]. The story of Solomon's accession in I Kings 1–2 shows a priestly rivalry between Abiathar, who supported David's son Adonijah, and Zadok, perhaps of a priestly family in the pre-Davidic city, who supported the successful Solomon. Abiathar, a relative newcomer to Jerusalem as priest of the Ark of the Covenant, was expelled to Anathoth (I Kgs 2:26-27), leaving the Zadokites in control of the Jerusalem sanctuary. In legend, at least, the

Zadokites may trace their service at Jerusalem's shrine to an ancient priest-king Melchizedek (*"Zedek* is my king," the same *zdk* root as Zadok), described in Genesis 14. This ruler of [Jeru]Salem blesses Abraham by God Most High (*El Elyon*), a divine name later identified with Israel's Yhwh (Num 24:16 and Ps 46:4). Abiathar's priestly line continued at Anathoth, eventually producing the prophet Jeremiah, who returned to challenge the Jerusalem establishment (Jeremiah 7).

4 Samaria

Text [page 40]. Translation of 1 Kings 16:23-24 nrsv, adapted by the author.

Samaria [page 00]. For a summary of the linguistic relations between Shemer and *Shomron* (Hebrew for Samaria), see Tappy 1992, 68n185. Ron Tappy's reevaluation of the archaeological records, especially of Kathleen Kenyon's excavations, leads him to conclude that there had been occupation on the hill before Omri's arrival, though "the precise character of that occupation remains uncertain" (213–14) for Tappy. But he acknowledges that Lawrence Stager "has suggested that the *pre-urban* inhabitants of Samaria owned and operated a family estate which produced olive oil, wine or other such commodities. If their business had ceased sometime prior to Omri's show of interest in the site (as the depositional history here suggests), this may account for Shemer's ability to sell the family property with apparent ease despite the restrictions traditionally placed upon such inheritance property" (Tappy 1992, 95, referring to Stager 1990).

Galil, Chinneroth [page 41]. These are the biblical Hebrew names for the Galilee region and the Sea of Galilee, respectively.

State formation [page 43]. The process by which the small kingdoms of the Iron Age Levant developed has been a major area for application of social science methods to biblical studies and the history of Israel since the 1990s. To give just one recent example, which includes very helpful references to earlier studies, see Faust 2003.

David [page 43]. For a persuasive examination of the rise of David and of his non-Israelite origins, see Halpern 2001.

Judah [page 43]. Although evidence for the names "[Jeru]Salem" and "House of David" exists in a few extrabiblical inscriptions, a kingdom of Judah is not mentioned in this period. (See the letters of Abdu-Heba of Jerusalem to his Egyptian overlord at Amarna in the late fifteenth to early fourteenth centuries BCE [Pritchard 1969b, 487–89] and references to the House of David in ninth-century texts later in this book [Tel Dan Inscription, page 127 and in some translations of the Mesha Inscription, page 113].) Biblical designation of Judah as the larger area governed from Jerusalem is supposedly based on the primacy of a tribe of Judah descended from one of Jacob's twelve sons by that name. Even the Genesis accounts of this brother, however, show signs of being edited into earlier tribal stories: the Genesis 38 account of Judah and Tamar interrupts the Joseph story, and Judah's role as a leader among the brothers in making decisions about Joseph (Gen 37:12-36) and in later taking responsibility for Benjamin's well-being (Gen 42:35—43:10) seems secondary to the actions of Reuben, the eldest. I have left the term Judah unchanged in biblical passages but assume it to be more recent than the ninth century. Jizebul refers to Jerusalem and the hill country, not to Judah as a kingdom.

Nimshi, "weasel" [page 45]. I adopt Gray's comment that the name Nimshi may have originated as a nickname, comparable to Arabic *nims* (Gray 1970, 540, citing Martin Noth, *Die israelitischen Personennamen im Rahmen der gemeinsemitischen Namengebung*, Beiträge zur Wissenschaft vom Alten [und Neuen] Testament 3, no. 10, Stuttgart: 1928, 230).

Tyre, Sidon, and Ashurnasirpal [page 45]. See comments on the relationship between the two Phoenician cities and the importance of the Assyrian king's invitation to the palace dedication festival at Calah in Katzenstein's discussion of an Assyrian inscription, dated to 879 BCE, and other evidence (1997, 133–35).

Gilead's distinctive identity [page 48]. See the story of Jephthah in Judges 11–12, especially the linguistic test in pronouncing *shibboleth* or *sibboleth* ("stream") in Judges 12:1-6. "Shibboleth" is still used in English to denote a distinguishing feature, empty saying, or widely held belief.

Text [page 50]. Translation by A. Leo Oppenheim, "Babylonian and Assyrian Historical Texts" (Pritchard 1969b, 275–76), adapted by the author. This excerpt from the Annals of Ashurnasirpal II about his expedition to Carchemish and the Lebanon, inscribed on pavement of the temple of Ninurta in Calah, shows the extent of Ashurnasirpal's campaign and the sense of inevitable victory in Assyrian propaganda.

Impaled them on stakes [page 52]. The highlighted section calls attention to the consequences of resisting Assyria—destruction of cities and impalement of survivors. Notice that the coastal cities, including Tyre, sent preemptive gifts for goodwill, even though the Assyrians reached the coast north of them.

Eye of Horus [page 54]. The iconography of the Egyptian deity Horus featured a human male body with a falcon's head. Egyptian and Phoenician art abbreviated this symbol into a stylized eye (Egyptian, *wedjat*) with the characteristic falcon markings, used in jewelry, amulets, and decorative applications. See illustrations on pages 26 (end links of bracelet), 54 (amulet), and 110 (decorative ivory panel) for this pervasive design. A living Egyptian pharaoh was often associated with Horus, while his father and predecessor was identified with Horus's father, Osiris, ruling in the underworld. Horus was also depicted as a young boy seated on the lap of his mother, Isis, in a pose anticipating later European portrayals of the madonna and child. Kestrels are the smallest falcons.

5 Baal's Headland

Text [page 55]. Translation of I Kings 16:27-29, 31-33 NRSV, adapted by the author.

Tishbite [page 57]. The NRSV translates I Kings 17:1 as "Now Elijah the Tishbite, of Tishbe in Gilead . . ." It treats the words *Tishbite* and *Tishbe* as redundant, both referring to a place. Bible atlases identify Tishbe as a point near the "Brook Cherith" in Gilead, based on the reference to that ravine as Elijah's refuge (I Kgs 17:3) and on the existence of a Byzantine shrine to Elijah near al-Istib, eight miles north of the Jabbok River, but no ninth-century settlement has been excavated there. John Gray considers the terms to be an unnecessary repetition and offers an alternative reading: "And Elijah the Tishbite of the settlers in Gilead . . ." The *tishbe* used by the NRSV is based on the Greek translation in the Septuagint; the existing Hebrew text reads *toshabe*, using vowels as they were understood in a later period. Gray restores a different set of vowels to read *toshʿbe*, which he identifies as "settlers" or "colonists." For the purposes of this story, I have pushed Gray's suggestion further, understanding Elijah's designation to be a political one, rather than a genealogical or geographical one. See Gray 1970, 377, for the linguistic notes and Faust 2003, 157 (and his bibliography), for information about the ancient practice of relocating settlers within a kingdom.

Samaria's remodeling [page 58]. See Tappy's reevaluation of Kenyon's excavation results (1992, especially 51, 164, 206). He identifies three building phases: (1) an estate predating Omri's settlement, (2) Omri's royal precinct, and (3) Ahab's extension of the palace area with casemate walls, a configuration that remained in use during Jehu's reign.

Temple weavings [page 58]. The Bible describes both men and women as skilled workers in fabric production for religious use. Women are mentioned in 2 Kings 23:7 as weavers of garments for Asherah (understood as a goddess/consort with YHWH or as an object associated with the goddess) in the Jerusalem temple complex, displaced by King Josiah's reforms in the late seventh century. I am grateful for Susan Ackerman's calling my attention to this verse in her detailed study of biblical and comparative evidence: "Women and the Weaving of Cultic Textiles in Ancient Israel," a paper delivered to the Research Seminars in Hebrew and Old Testament Studies and New Testament Language, Literature, and Theology at New College, University of Edinburgh, November 7, 2003.

Text [page 61]. Translation of I Kings 18:1—19:3 NRSV, adapted by the author.

Ethbaal and the drought [page 65]. Tyre's history of this period, including the drought, was retold by the Greek historian Menander, who claimed reference to Tyrian annals: "But [Ethbaal] made supplication to the gods, whereupon a heavy thunderstorm broke out" (Josephus, quoting Menander, *Jewish Antiquities* 8, 324). For a discussion and references, see Katzenstein 1997, 152–53 and notes.

Text [page 66]. Translation of Psalm 104 NRSV, adapted by the author to reflect the observations in Dahood 1970, 31–48. See his note on the Israelite monarchy's use of this hymn under the influence of Phoenician transmission of an originally Egyptian model. The psalm contains "numerous typically Phoenician forms, expressions, and parallelism" (33). These include the descriptive epithets beginning with "who" and the allusions to natural phenomena as personified beings, many of whom have personal names in Ugaritic, indicated with capital letters here (see my note on Mot as Death, pages 187 and 190 below, where Sun is Shapsh).

The Lady [page 68]. Dahood's translation (1970) of verses 24–25 reads:

> How manifold are your works, Yahweh!
> With Wisdom at your side you made them all;
> > the earth is full of your creatures.
> The One of the Sea,
> > tall and broad of reach
> Who put gliding things past counting . . .

My introduction of the Lady here builds on Dahood's notes, which call attention to a female divine element in creation (the biblical Wisdom in Prov 3:19 and Job 37:18) and to the attribution "of the Sea" to Canaanite goddesses: ". . . biblical poets appropriated terms and images depicting Canaanite goddesses and used them to describe attributes of Yahweh" (44).

Leviathan [page 68]. A watery chaos-dragon mentioned in biblical passages either as a primordial opponent to God's creative ordering (Ps 74:13-15, with parallels to Rahab in Job 26:12, Ps 89:8-11, and Isa 51:9-11) or as a powerful yet controlled creature to emphasize God's complete mastery of the cosmos (Job 41 and Ps 104:26).

6 Jezreel

Text [page 70]. Translation of 1 Kings 15:23-24; 22:41-44 NRSV, adapted by the author.

Feet [page 70]. "Feet" in 1 Kings 15:23 is a common Hebrew euphemism for genitals.

Tyrian towns [page 72]. Excavations in the lower Galilee east of Akko unearthed Phoenician settlements reflecting Tyrian trading and agricultural populations at Keisan and Ḥorvat Rosh Zayit. See Stern 1993, 3.862–67 and 4.1289–91, respectively.

Sweetness of a friend [page 72]. Proverbs 27:9 NRSV, using alternative from their note d.

Like a brother [page 73]. Song of Solomon 8:1 NRSV.

Text [page 74]. Translation of I Kings 21 NRSV, adapted by the author.

Sons of worthlessness [page 75]. In I Kings 21:10, 13, the NRSV translates a two-word phrase as "scoundrels." The Hebrew is literally, "sons of worthlessness." I retain the idiomatic Hebrew here to convey my meaning of sons who had no prospect of inheriting land but were employed by the king. The biblical story highlights the conflict between those who had a traditional sense of worth through ownership of inherited land, like Naboth, and the royal system of redistributing land based on patronage. In my reading, there is great irony in Naboth's losing his land by the testimony of those who had no family land.

"Bless" God and king [page 75]. The Hebrew of I Kings 21:10, 13 refrains from using "curse" in reference to God, just as Job's wife does in Job 2:9: "Bless God and die." The quotations marks here indicate the euphemistic sense of *bless* to mean *curse*. See also the previous instance on page 36.

Murder by unknown assailant [page 77]. Some Torah legislation and narratives illustrate an ancient view that crime released potent consequences upon a much wider group than the guilty individual. A rationale for the flood in Genesis, attributed to the Priestly tradition in Genesis 6:11-12, is the corruption of the earth and all flesh by violence. Although God banished human transgressors (Adam and Cain) from the place of their crime, the earth had absorbed the divine curse (Gen 3:17; 4:11). The blood-law of Genesis 9:6 changes the situation by requiring humans to implement the consequences directly, with the intention of preventing the spread of corruption to all flesh again. Hosea claims that the northern kingdom failed to take this responsibility, charging that humans have broken the commandments, so the contaminated land mourns and creatures perish (Hos 4:1-3). How could the blood-law be implemented and the consequences averted if the perpetrator remained unknown? That is the premise of the ritual described in Deuteronomy 21:1-9, to be performed by elders of the village closest to a corpse found in the fields, that is, those who would be hit first by the "pollution" spreading from the crime scene. The process described here for the Jezreel blight assumes a similar view: that the spreading misfortune resulted from some transgression and the community needed to take responsibility.

Shared guilt [page 78]. Understanding this view—that transgression launches a contagious pollution that must be stopped for protection of the community—

helps to explain Joshua 7, where Achan's family is executed and their animals and goods destroyed because of his theft. Those physically closest to Achan and the buried loot would already have been contaminated.

Filling the priests' treasury [page 79]. Second Kings 14:4-8 describes taxes and donations intended for repair of the temple going directly to the priests instead.

7 Beth-hakkherem

Text [page 80]. Translation of 2 Chronicles 17:10—18:1 NRSV, adapted by the author.

Jehozabad [page 80]. The highlighted passage introduces Jehozabad, a commander from Benjamin, who is understood in this story to be the grandfather of the conspirator Jehozabad. See glossary.

Text [page 81]. Translation of Psalm 133 NRSV, adapted by the author.

Ijon and Zion [page 82]. Ijon is a site north of Dan on the well-watered western slope of Mount Hermon, in territory controlled sometimes by Israel and sometimes by Aram (see 1 Kings 15:20 and 2 Kings 15:29). The name "Zion" has designated various sacred sites in Jerusalem. Probably originally applied to the northern height of Solomon's Jerusalem where the temple was built, it is used today to designate the southern area of the "Western Hill," just outside the Armenian Quarter of the Old City. In Isaiah, "Zion" often refers to the whole city of Jerusalem.

How good and how pleasant [page 82]. Psalm 133, translated and adapted by the author. See helpful comments by Dahood (1970, 250–53), who follows Hermann Gunkel's identification of the psalm's northern Israelite origins (1926, 571). Leslie Allen highlights the history of scholarship for the Zion-Ijon emendation (1983, 213n3c).

She draws some water . . . take war away [page 83]. Excerpts from Ugaritic texts translated by H. L. Ginsberg, "Poems about Baal and Anath," f. V AB, B and C, in Pritchard 1969b, 136, adapted by the author.

The garden of God [pages 83–84]. Translation of Ezekiel 31:3-9 NRSV, adapted by the author. Katzenstein agrees with a suggestion that the poems about Tyre in Ezekiel may be based on "a collection of Tyrian songs" that reflect conditions in periods prior to Ezekiel's early sixth-century context (Katzenstein 1997, 154 and n135, referring to B. Maisler [Mazar], *Israel Exploration Journal* 2 [1952]:83–84). This attractive, if rather speculative, hypothesis prompted my inclusion of this passage from Ezekiel 31 in Jizebul's memoirs. The garden of God is described as a botanical park of the sort established by ancient Near Eastern rulers, with specimens from throughout their realm: juniper, cedar, and plane trees (also called buttonwood or sycamore) do not normally grow together. Notice that this version of the Eden story has no humans, but the central figure—a majestic tree—is portrayed later in the biblical chapter as exhibiting rebellious pride and is completely destroyed (Ezek 31:10-17).

Jerusalem's garden story [page 84]. Genesis 2:4b—3:24 is considered by many scholars to belong to an older strand within the Torah, called the "Yahwist" element (or J source) by those who subscribe to the documentary hypothesis and its modifications. Jizebul refers here to part of a tale we know as Genesis 2:8-10.

Tabernacle lampstand [page 85]. See Carol Meyers's study of the iconographic traditions incorporated into descriptions of the tabernacle menorah (1976). Neither the biblical account nor Meyers's work associates the tree-form menorah with a goddess, a connection that Jizebul, however, might assume.

Consequences of right relations [page 85]. Hosea 4:1-3 reflects an understanding in the northern kingdom of Israel that transgression of the Decalogue's stipulations of right relations among humans had dire results in the environment and habitat of nonhuman creatures. Since men (males) were the parties to covenant and addressees of the Decalogue (or, Ten Commandments, Exodus 20), Jizebul's gendered language here is specific and not intended to be inclusive.

Text [page 85]. Translation of 2 Chronicles 17:1-2; 19:4-11 NRSV, adapted by the author.

Strengthened himself because of Israel [page 85]. The NRSV translates the Hebrew preposition *'al* as "against," which is one possible reading. According to Jizebul's storyline, however, it is *because of* Jehoshaphat's alliance with Israel that he is strengthened, which is also a possible rendering since *'al* can mean "on account of." The covenant with Ahab gave Jehoshaphat authority over the contested cities of Ephraim in return for contributions to other joint endeavors. This way of reading the report in 2 Chronicles 17:1-2 helps to avoid a contradiction with the description of apparently amicable relations between Jehoshaphat and Ahab in the next chapter (2 Chr 18:1-3).

Whole heart [page 86]. The Hebrew word for "whole," or complete, in 2 Chronicles 19:9 is based on the same root as *shalom*, which comprises right relations, peace, and wholeness.

Beth-hakkherem [page 88]. This description fits Yohanan Aharoni's assessment of the earliest remains excavated at Ramat Raḥel, which he identified as biblical Beth-hakkherem, established in the ninth-eighth centuries (stratum VB; "Ramat Raḥel" in Stern 1993, 4.1261). Later investigators found only eighth-century pottery at the lowest level, ruling out attribution to Atalyah in their minds (Stern 1993, 4.1267). New assessments and excavations are being undertaken by Odel Lipschits and Oren Tal of Tel Aviv University and Manfred Oeming of Heidelberg University, beginning in 2005. For the purposes of this story, an hypothetical mid-ninth-century estate or small agricultural settlement at Ramat Raḥel (or at a place as yet undiscovered but similar to it) serves as Atalyah's country residence, later to be developed into a more formal royal establishment.

Jehoshaphat's sons [page 88]. Second Chronicles 21:2-3 describes the distribution of power among Jehoshaphat's sons.

I am Shalmaneser [page 90]. Translation by A. Leo Oppenheim, "Shalmaneser III (858–824): The Fight against the Aramean Coalition," from the "Thron-Inschrift," Pritchard 1969b, 276–77. Adapted by the author.

At that time [page 90]. Translation by A. Leo Oppenheim, "Shalmaneser III (858–824): The Fight against the Aramean Coalition," from the inscription on the bronze gates of Balawat, Pritchard 1969b, 277. Adapted by the author.

I received tribute [page 90]. Translation by A. Leo Oppenheim, "Shalmaneser III (858–824): The Fight against the Aramean Coalition," epigraph from the bronze gates of Balawat, Band III, Pritchard 1969b, 281. Adapted by the author.

8 Karkar

"As your people, so are my people" [pages 93–94]. Such a feast for Jehoshaphat hosted by Ahab is described in 2 Chronicles 18:1-3, which places it, however, in the context of a joint campaign against Aram at Ramoth-gilead. There are many discrepancies in narratives in Kings and Chronicles about a king of Israel and a king of Jerusalem going to war together against a neighboring area. Commentaries and histories vary on which episodes in Kings may reflect historical encounters during Ahab and Jehoram's reigns and which are shifted to their story from later conflicts. Given the need for unity to face repeated Assyrian attacks during this period, I favor the view that some reports of Israel-versus-Aram battles originated in the later wars with Hazael, not in wars with his predecessor Ben-hadad.

Jehu son of Hanani son of Heman [page 94]. First Kings 16:1-4, 7 describes Jehu's opposition to Baasha king of Israel. This Jehu of Jerusalem is not the same as the Israelite Jehu son of Nimshi. For his family history, see glossary, Jehu son of Hanani.

God's protection of Jerusalem [page 94]. This priestly position opposing alliances is articulated by Isaiah's argument to King Ahaz of Jerusalem, who faced attack by Aram and Israel to gain Jerusalem's resources in a coalition against Assyria (Isaiah 7).

Jerusalem . . . she [page 94]. The Hebrew word for "city" has a female grammatical gender, and female pronouns are often used with Jerusalem. See, for example, Isaiah 14:32: "Yhwh has founded Zion, and the needy among his people will find refuge in her." Much of the book of Lamentations is spoken in "her" voice as a widow. Also see above, "her ridge," p. 82 above.

Shalmaneser III's monolith inscription [page 95]. Translation by A. Leo Oppenheim, "Shalmaneser III (858–824): The Fight against the Aramean Coalition," from Sixth Year according to the Monolith-Inscription II 78–102, Pritchard 1969b, 278–79.

Killed their master [page 95]. Shalmaneser's approach provoked an internal coup against the ruler of Giammu, apparently by a faction that wanted to submit to the Assyrians rather than to fight. The destabilizing effect of an Assyrian campaign on the march is reflected later in Jehu's coup against Ahab's family.

I approached . . . Karkara [page 95]. The highlighted sentences present Shalmaneser's description of the battle at Karkar. One might think from his account that he was victorious, but his inability to pass beyond the Orontes River here or receive tribute indicates that the western coalition in fact prevented him from advancing.

Adad-'idri [page 96]. This is the Assyrian name for the biblical Ben-hadad of Damascus.

Ahab, the Israelite [page 96]. Ahab's chariot force is listed as the largest among the allies, probably because it included forces from areas closely tied to Israel, such as Moab and Jerusalem.

Jehoshaphat fights Assyria [page 97]. It is striking that the biblical texts do not mention relations between Jerusalem and Assyria until the reign of Ahaz, when he calls on Tiglath-pileser to relieve the attacks by Israel and Damascus (2 Kings 16, about 735 BCE). I take the omission to be a Deuteronomistic way of downplaying the many generations of Jerusalem's alliance as a subordinate partner of the Omrides (who in my view include the Jehuites), whose policy toward Assyria automatically became Jerusalem's. Only after the Omride/Jehuite dynasty fails is Jerusalem able to negotiate independently with Assyria, rejecting an Aramaean-Israelite attempt to enlist her in their anti-Assyrian coalition. Ironically, Ahaz's "independent" deal actually continues the former north-south alliance's practice of accommodating Assyria. One may wonder if that loyalty to Jehuite foreign policy was a basis for the Deuteronomistic critique of Ahaz—"he walked in the way of the kings of Israel" (2 Kgs 16:13)—couched, however, in religious terms. When Jizebul writes, the anti-Israel party in Jehoash's court at Jerusalem would also have understated the precedent of the former partnership.

See the author's epilogue, pages 158–161, for an overview of the long-standing alliance between Samaria and Jerusalem.

First mowings [page 97]. According to Amos 7:1-3, the king's exaction was not only in quantity but also in quality and dependability: a first mowing of hay would be the best and most certain. Sweeney (2004) suggests that Amos's critique of oppressive conditions under Jeroboam II (793–753 BCE) described the situation of extractions from Judah, from which he came, as an Israelite vassal. ". . . Amos's oracles are designed to condemn the northern kingdom of Israel for its economic abuse of Judah, apparently a client state of the more powerful northern Israel from the time of the Omride dynasty through the period of the Syro-Ephraimitic War." Sweeney expresses this view more fully in his commentary on Amos (2000). Jizebul's statement presupposes a similar flow of materials sixty years earlier, which she recognizes as extreme but necessary for defense, under the Ahab-Jehoshaphat accord.

Text [page 98]. Translation of I Kings 22:39-40 NRSV, adapted by the author.

Ahab returned in safety [page 98]. First Kings 22 reports Ahab's death at Ramoth-gilead in battle against "the king of Syria." This is one of at least three instances of the theme of the wounding or death of the king in battle with the Syrians/Arameans (Ahab in I Kings 22; Jehoram in 2 Kgs 8:28-29; J[eh]oash in 2 Chr 24:23-25; the first two are both at Ramoth-gilead and the last two are both followed by an assassination). Given the tendency of the Deuteronomistic history to attach a military episode once associated with a minor figure to a more significant character (for example, the killing of Goliath by Elhanan son of Jaareoregim in 2 Sam 21:19 is credited to David in the elaborate account of I Samuel 17), I take the Jehoram episode to be historically more credible for Jizebul's story. If Ahab and Ben-hadad were allies at Karkar, as the Assyrians describe, it is difficult to understand why one would kill the other. I retain the generally accepted date of 853 BCE for Ahab's death and Ahaziah's succession, the same year as the battle at Karkar, but I present his passing as occurring sometime after the crisis rather than as resulting immediately from a death-wound by Aramaeans or Assyrians.

Tomb [page 99]. Norma Franklin interprets a chamber below the first phase of the Samaria palace, entered from the western scarp on which the palace was built, as a royal tomb (2003).

Marzeaḥ [page 99]. An association of people who gathered periodically for religious celebrations identified with specific deities, using designated buildings and wine from particular vineyards, often for memorial purposes and sometimes with sacral sexual orgies (see Pope 1972, 193). Known also from neighboring cultures, the biblical *marzeaḥ* is mentioned specifically in Amos 6:4-7 (for Israel) and Jeremiah 16:1-9 (for Jerusalem) and may be alluded to elsewhere. *Marzeaḥ* is translated by NRSV as "revelry" in Amos 6:7 but as "[house of] mourning" in Jeremiah 16:5. The two activities were not incompatible. The ivory carvings illustrated here are important symbols in the *marzeaḥ* context and probably adorned the furniture used for the occasion (Beach 1993).

Store jars [page 99]. At Kuntillet 'Ajrud, a number of artists painted store jars and the plaster walls of "the bench chamber" using many of the motifs familiar from ivory carvings on ritual couches and from ivories found at Samaria. These include the cow and calf, drinking deer, lions, stylized sacred tree, and lotus chain border. Other designs at Kuntillet 'Ajrud that are evocative of a celebration—a procession and harpist—also appear on a Phoenician bronze bowl depicting a banquet scene (Markoe 1985, catalogue no. Cy5). I agree with those who think the room was used for special occasions. See "Teman, Ḥorvat," Stern 1993, 4.1458–1464 (especially the bibliography, 1464).

Kid . . . in mother's milk [page 100]. Does the cow-and-nursing-calf imagery, which appears on the furniture used for a *marzeaḥ*, also reflect the menu—unweaned animals boiled in their mother's milk? It brings to mind the Torah editors' prohibitions of such a stew in Exodus 23:19b; 34:26b and Deuteronomy 14:21b.

Her elaborate window [page 101]. Jizebul's description of the procession, banquet, and symbols anticipates the biblical report of her own death in 2 Kings 9, pages 130–33.

Killing of King Elah [page 102]. This scene is described in 1 Kings 16:9-11.

9 Ekron

Texts [page 103]. Translation of 1 Kings 22:51; 22:47-49; 2 Kings 1:1 NRSV, adapted by the author.

Reigned two years [page 103]. The length of reign includes partial years. Ahaziah came to the throne in Jehoshaphat's seventeenth year and died in the eighteenth, two years in royal reckoning, but perhaps less than twelve months.

Ahaziah and his young men [page 104]. First Kings 12 reports a similar situation, where Solomon's son King Rehoboam's older advisors counsel him to be lenient with the northern tribes, while the young men suggest greater severity. The threat of harsher treatment triggers the northern tribes' rejection of Rehoboam and the relationship with Jerusalem.

Text [page 105]. Translation of Psalm 45 NRSV, adapted by the author with bracketed headings and emendations based on Dahood 1965, 267–76. The references to ivory palaces and Tyrian embroidery make the psalm suitable for a northern royal wedding, but scholars have not agreed on its origins.

Text [page 106]. Translation of 2 Kings 1:2-18 NRSV, adapted by the author.

Baal Zebul [page 106]. The Hebrew text beginning with 2 Kings 1:2 uses Baalzebub for this deity. The Greek translation gave rise to the English, "Lord of the Flies." The Hebrew is probably a mocking pun on the more honorable title used by Ahaziah, *Baal Zebul*—"Baal the Prince"—attested in Ugaritic texts and in the reconstructed version of Jizebul's name. As Gray notes, even New Testament authors recognized that the original was Baal Zebul in Matthew 10:25; 12:24; Mark 3:22; Luke 11:15 and following (Gray 1970, 463).

Messenger [page 106]. In Hebrew, the word for a divine messenger is the same as for a king's messenger. The English word *angel* is derived from the Greek word for a divine intermediary. It is found in the later Septuagint and the New Testament but not used in the Hebrew Scriptures.

Joram brother of Ahaziah [page 107]. In addition to the similar names of kings in Samaria and Jerusalem (Joram and Jehoram, respectively, in my spellings), discrepancies in the biblical reports of the overlapping years of their rule have led some to posit that a single king of that name ruled over both kingdoms. See, for example, Miller and Hayes 1986, 280–82. For the purposes of this story, I have chosen to treat them as two individuals.

Olive presses at Ekron [page 108]. This potential for centralized olive oil production at Ekron (Tel Miqne) was realized when Assyria controlled Judah in the early seventh century, with output estimated to be one-fifth of the present export of modern Israel ("Miqne, Tel [Ekron]" in Stern 1993, 4.1057–58). The excavators reported that seasonal production of olive oil may have alternated with equally centralized weaving activity, because they also identified many loom weights in this industrial area. I mention it for the mid-ninth century to illustrate that mass production for export was a realistic economic prospect under the centralized administration of monarchy, not dependent on new technology. Loom weights are a neglected archaeological resource for the study of changing modes of production. Glenda Friend's work on sixty-two loom weights from one Iron Age locus at Taanach led to her conclusion that their "uniform dimensions and weight are indicative of large-scale specialized textile production" (1998, 10). Some "loom weights," however, are being reinterpreted as perforated jar stoppers in the fermenting of alcoholic beverages, used to allow gases to escape through cloth packing (Homan 2004, 89–91). Large numbers of them in one location would still point to a highly centralized industry rather than only home production.

Outpost in Sinai [page 108]. With ties to Samaria, Kuntillet 'Ajrud (Ḥorvat Teman) was such a site, perhaps established fifty years later by an Israelite king with ambitions in the south ("Teman, Ḥorvat" in Stern 1993, 4.1458–64, especially 1464). It was near the route between Kadesh-barnea and the port of Ezion-geber on the northern end of the Gulf of Aqaba.

Israel's officials [page 109]. See 2 Chronicles 21:4.

10 Dibon

Text [page 111]. Translation of 2 Kings 3 NRSV, adapted by the author.

Eighteenth year of Jehoshaphat [page 111]. Second Kings 1:17 reports Joram's taking the throne in the second year of Jehoshaphat's son Jehoram. Thiele (1983) accounts for this as the second year of Jehoram's coregency with Jehoshaphat, in the latter's eighteenth year. Rather than call attention to the issue of which king in Jerusalem was most directly involved, I have replaced "Jehoshaphat" with "the king of Judah" in this text.

Ruler of Edom [page 112]. According to 1 Kings 22:47, "a deputy was king" in Edom, so I have used "ruler" to indicate that he was not an independent "king."

Good tree [page 113]. The extent of this total destruction seems to be contrary to the rules of warfare in Deuteronomy 20:19-20, according to which food-producing trees were not to be cut down, unless this provision is taken to apply only to battles within the land promised to Israel for its own settlement. Depictions of soldiers cutting trees appear on both Assyrian reliefs and Phoenician metal bowls.

Text [page 113]. Translation by W. F. Albright from "The Moabite Stone," in Pritchard 1969b, 320–21, adapted by the author. The black basalt monument was shown by local Bedouin to a European visitor in Dibon in 1868, then intentionally broken, distributed, and reassembled in a process involving a French scholar, German and Turkish diplomacy, Bedouin resistance to their Ottoman pasha, and the Louvre. See the full story in André Lemaire's article (1994). Where Albright's translation has been substantially changed or gaps have been restored by Lemaire's work, I have used his more recent version as follows: *the town belonged to Chemosh and Moab; the altar-hearth of his Beloved* (a deity?); *the altar-hearths of Y*HWH; *there dwelled in it the House of David* (Lemaire 1994, 33). Chemosh is the major Moabite deity.

Sacrifice [page 115]. See the Gilead story of the Jephthah's (unnecessary) sacrifice of his daughter in Judges 11.

Murdered his brothers [page 116]. See 2 Chronicles 21:4.

Text [page 117]. Translation of 2 Chronicles 21:1-6, 8-11, 16-19 NRSV, adapted by the author.

King of Judah [page 117]. The Hebrew text of 2 Chronicles 21:2 says "king of Israel."

His youngest son [page 118]. There are difficulties with names and chronology here. Jehoahaz is named as Jehoram's youngest son in 2 Chronicles 21:17. In the next chapter, however, Ahaziyah is called his youngest son, and said to be forty-two years old when he began to reign (2 Chr 22:1-2). But, putting the chapters together, Ahaziyah is forty-two when his father Jehoram dies at forty.

11 Damascus

Text [page 119]. Translation of 2 Kings 8:7-15 NRSV, adapted by the author.

Hazael's father's city of Dan [page 122]. Hazael's association with Dan is suggested by the presence of an inscription found there that many attribute to him, pages 127–28. This is a speculative link, hinted at earlier, on page 41, when Ahab takes control of Dan.

Jehu son of Nimshi son of Omri [page 124]. Tammi Schneider (1995 and 1996) discusses this lineage for Jehu, based on the Assyrian inscriptions calling Jehu the son of Omri.

Text [page 125]. Translation by A. Leo Oppenheim, "Shalmaneser III (858–824): The Fight against the Aramean Coalition," (c) Various Inscriptions (I4–ii 1), Pritchard 1969b, 280, adapted by the author.

Hadadezer [page 125]. Ben-hadad.

Text [page 125]. Translations of 2 Chronicles 21:19—22:1 and 2 Kings 8:25-29 NRSV, adapted by the author.

Daughter of Omri [page 125]. The Hebrew text of 2 Kings 8:26 has "daughter," not "granddaughter" as edited by NRSV. See note on page 188.

12 Ramoth-gilead

Text [page 127]. Translation from Anson Rainey (2003, 36). I have preserved Rainey's spellings of proper names from the inscription. Be aware that his Ahaziyahu son of Joram = my Ahaziyah son of Jehoram of Jerusalem; his Omry = my Omri. Notice that Rainey also accepts the designation of Jehu as "son of Omry" in reconstructing a gap in the inscription. Hadad is a major Aramaean deity.

Was killed [page 127]. The excavator's translation reconstructed this gap to say "I [Hazael] killed . . ." the kings of Israel and the house of David (Biran and Naveh 1995, and Biran 1993). Rainey's translation, in addition to being grammatically possible, eliminates a conflict between such a claim by Hazael and the biblical report crediting Jehu with the assassinations (see Rainey's discussion 2003, 36–39). Since the name Hazael is not present in the extant inscription, its attribution to him has also been disputed (see Athas 2003, who assigns it to Hazael's son "Bar Hadad"). My choice of Rainey's translation is for the practical purpose of the storyline, not by my independent judgment of the grammar. Georges Athas provides a comprehensive list of relevant publications in his bibliography (2003). I am grateful to Lawson Younger for his paper at the 2004 Midwest regional meeting of the Society of Biblical Literature, which displayed several options, and for his sending me a copy of Rainey's published article (which, however, does not agree with Younger's preferred translation).

Text [page 128]. Translation of 2 Kings 9 NRSV, adapted by the author.

Mockery of the feast [page 132]. I suggest that the literary depiction of Jehu's passing under Jizebul's window in 2 Kings 9 is based on the ivory *marzeaḥ* image of the woman at the window rather than on an actual event. The *marzeaḥ* also supplies the ironic allusion for blood splashing on walls, dogs eating bones, and the disparagement of Jizebul's name. The strongly symbolic visual elements may have actually generated the narrative rather than being details of an historical remembrance if, as I suspect, Jizebul did not die at Jezreel. See also Amos 6:4-7, where Jehu's descendants still observe the custom, which apparently was not considered to be anti-Yhwh. In Jerusalem, also, funerary feasts were held in the *beit marzeaḥ*, which a Yhwh-worshiping Jeremiah would normally have attended if he had not been divinely prohibited from this regular activity as a symbolic act foreshadowing the impending crisis of siege conditions (Jer 16:1-9, especially v5). The reversal of images borrowed from the *marzeaḥ* in 2 Kings 9 serves to dishonor Jizebul and her family but not the *marzeaḥ* institution itself. Similarly, shooting enemies in the back, trampling them under chariots, and mass decapitation were standard images of ancient Near Eastern imperial art, especially of propagandistic Assyrian wall carvings, and do not necessarily report particular events.

Weasel [page 133]. See note on page 170.

Shalmaneser approaches Ramoth-gilead [page 133]. That it was Shalmaneser rather than Hazael whom the Israelites met at Ramoth-gilead is suggested by Gösta Ahlström (1993, 592–95). In his view, Israel's conflict with Aram in 2 Kings 8:28-29 was Hazael's attempt to force Joram into an anti-Assyrian coalition. But, if Joram was already pro-Assyria enough to require Hazael's attack, then Jehu's motivation for the coup could not have been to remove an anti-Assyrian Joram, as Ahlström posits.

Death of Ahab's offspring [page 133]. See Shalmaneser's monolith inscription (page 95 and notes on page 178), which describes an internal uprising elsewhere to ensure cooperation with Assyria: "They became afraid of the terror emanating from my position as overlord, as well as of the splendor of my fierce weapons, and killed their master Giammu with their own weapons." Killing seventy sons may be a traditional way of describing a coup, since it is used also of Abimelech in Judges 9:5.

Killed an anointed one [page 133]. Stories about the unusual circumstance of two men who have been anointed as king being alive at the same time, as when

David was designated to replace Saul during his lifetime, seem to emphasize that the successor does not have a right to hurry his predecessor's departure. Twice the Deuteronomistic history describes David's opportunities to kill Saul, but he uses them instead to demonstrate his innocence despite Saul's accusations of treason (I Samuel 24 and 26). And when Saul is killed, David makes sure that the Amalekite who claims to have done David a favor by dispatching the wounded king is executed (2 Samuel 1). To my knowledge, Jehu is the only biblical character who takes the initiative to implement a prophecy and then claims to have fulfilled it, rather than leaving it to God. His actions at Jezreel certainly do not have the approval of the only northern prophet preserved among the canonical books, Hosea, who proclaims that God "will punish the house of Jehu for the blood of Jezreel" (1:4).

Mot has come up into our windows [page 133]. Jeremiah 9:21. In the Ugaritic texts, Jizebul's "old stories," Mot (= Death) was Baal's opponent. Mot's defeat of the Prince sets off mourning in the heavens and parched soil on earth. Baal's earlier reluctance to have windows in his new palace anticipates such an encounter, for his three ladies would be accessible to his rivals. See Pritchard 1969b, 134.

Text [page 133]. Translation of 2 Kings 10:1-14, 17, 32-33 and 2 Chronicles 22:8-9 NRSV, adapted by the author.

Text [page 136]. Translation by A. Leo Oppenheim, "Shalmaneser III (858–824): The Fight against the Aramean Coalition," (b) Annalistic Reports, Eighteenth year according to the fragment of an annalistic text, Pritchard 1969b, 280, adapted by the author.

I received tribute [page 137]. The highlighted portions in this section demonstrate Jehu's subservience to Shalmaneser and Jehu's designation as son of Omri, denoting a continuation of the ruling Israelite family.

Black Obelisk [page 137]. Translation by A. Leo Oppenheim, "Shalmaneser III (858–824): The Fight against the Aramean Coalition," (d) Epigraphs, from the Black Obelisk, Pritchard 1969b, 281, adapted by the author.

13 Jerusalem

Text [page 139]. Translation of 2 Chronicles 22:10-12 NRSV, adapted by the author.

Daughter of Omri [page 141]. Why is Atalyah called daughter of Omri and not daughter of Ahab? In the Hebrew text of 2 Kings 8:26 and 2 Chronicles 22:2, the official formula for Ahaziyah's reign, Atalyah is called "daughter of Omri king of Israel." The NRSV edits "daughter" to "granddaughter." I retain the original here and in chapter 11 above. Atalyah's association only with Omri in the formulaic notice of 2 Kings 8:26 is intriguing, suggesting to me that this may have been her official throne name, which avoids mentioning Ahab. Chronicles does not have such reticence (2 Chr 21:6 and 22:2).

Dor [page 142]. Excavations at Dor show substantial structures in this period, but the nature of its maritime activities is less clear. Rising and falling sea levels have determined which areas of the site were suitable for shipping: once a lagoon on the east, then a section of quays on the south, eventually bays on the northwest side. Although "no maritime installations have been identified along the coast that could be attributed to the period of the Israelite monarchy" (Avner Raban in "Dor," Stern 1993, 4.370), Jizebul's story assumes that some rather local fishing, production of purple dye and fabrics, and transit of goods would have continued from facilities built earlier. See Stern 1994 and Stern 1993, 4.357–72.

Four-winged beetle [page 142]. This symbol, indirectly reflecting Egyptian artistic influence from the sun-scarab motif, is known in the southern hill country principally from seal impressions on large store jars under royal administration (*lmlk*, "belonging to the king") during the time of King Hezekiah of Jerusalem (715–686 BCE). It is mentioned here as a royal decorative element in anticipation of its later, more formal, use in the south. Seal impressions from Samaria bear this design before Hezekiah's time (Keel and Uehlinger 1998, §151 (256–59) and §162 (274–77), and it appears on Phoenician silver bowls and jewelry.

Prince raised in secret [page 143]. This folktale motif may be more familiar to many readers from the Greek story of Oedipus than from Sargon I, but that ancient Near Eastern monarch of Akkad (about 2350 BCE in ancient Assyria) was reported to have been set adrift in a basket on the river by his mother, adopted by Akki, the drawer of water, and elevated to kingship by the goddess Ishtar. The biblical account of Moses's origins adopts a similar storyline (Exodus 2) but reverses the social class, as the slave child is raised by a princess. See Sargon's story translated by E. A. Speiser, "The Legend of Sargon," in "Akkadian Myths and Epics," Pritchard 1969b, 119.

Text [page 144]. Translation of 2 Kings 11:4-21 NRSV, adapted by the author.

***The house of* Y<small>HWH</small>** [page 144]. The sanctuary in the royal precinct at Jerusalem, understood by the later biblical authors as the only authorized temple. Although Jehoiada avoids killing Atalyah in the temple, the Chronicler's account describes King J[eh]oash's execution of Jehoiada's son in the court of the house of Y<small>HWH</small> (2 Chr 24:20-22).

Insignia [page 144]. The NRSV translates this word as "covenant," with alternatives in the notes, "treaty or testimony." An emendation noted by *A Hebrew and English Lexicon of the Old Testament* seems to have been adopted in the NRSV word "armlet" in 2 Samuel 1:10 (Hebrew *hatseʻdah*, singular), which the lexicon proposes in a plural for 2 Kings 11:12 (Brown, Driver, and Briggs 1968, 587–88). I have adopted the Jewish Publication Society translation of the uncertain word as "insignia," which includes the aspects of both jewelry and royal identification.

David's field [page 146]. Ancient views of reproduction compared semen to a seed, which provided all the identity of what sprouted from it. The mother's womb was simply the field, supplying necessary nutrients like the soil, which could enhance or damage the quality of the crop but which did not contribute to its type. Understanding this view helps to explain how surrogate motherhood is described in Genesis. If Sarah owns the "field" of Hagar, the child Abraham produces there is as much Sarah's as if she had borne it herself, and Hagar has not contributed to its identity, which would be determined by Abraham's paternity if he chooses to acknowledge it. The legal consequences of such reproductive ideas on inheritance laws clearly give priority to the male lineage and support male control of women's reproductive activities as control of the "field." Kinship to a mother's family was more a business tie to the powerful men in her clan than a biological one, but perhaps no less important in its own way.

Marriage ties to Moab and Ammon [page 147]. The names of Jehoash's assassins in 2 Chronicles 24:26 seem to give their mothers' lineage: Zabad son of Shemeath the Ammonite(ss) and Jehozabad son of Shimrith the Moabite(ss). (The female endings are used in the Jewish Publication Society translation.) In the postexilic ideology displayed in Ezra and Nehemiah, marriage between an Israelite man and a "foreign woman" was a grave transgression, so this attribution of the assassins' mixed origins was a denigrating label for the Chronicler's audience. In the ninth century, however, Israelite clans living east of the Jordan could have provided wives for men of Benjamin without such a stigma.

Commanders [page 147]. Compare the list of Jehoshaphat's commanders in 2 Chronicles 17:14-18 with Jehoiada's coconspirators in 2 Chronicles 23:1.

Shomer son of Jehozabad [page 147]. I have adopted the tradition of a name appearing in every other generation. I take Jehozabad son of Shomer, conspirator against King Jehoash in 2 Kings 12:20, to be the grandson of Jehozabad, commander of thousands from Benjamin under King Jehoshaphat in 2 Chronicles 17:14-18; therefore, Jehozabad son of Shomer son of Jehozabad.

Text [page 147]. Translation of Psalm 36 NRSV, adapted by the author. The three sections are of different types: wisdom perspective, hymn of praise, lament. Dahood (1965, 217–24) highlights the many Ugaritic parallels in the hymn, but neither he nor other commentators clearly identify it as of northern origins. Its placement here in the story and my adaptations (Baal for Yhwh) and literal emphasis ("mountains of El" and "great Deep") are designed to suit Jizebul's situation, without a demonstrated historical association.

14 Dor

Text [page 151]. Translation of 2 Kings 12:1-8 and 2 Chronicles 24:2-3, 15-21 NRSV, adapted by the author.

Eclipse [page 153]. The eclipse on the morning of August 15, 831 BCE, was the only solar eclipse in the eastern Mediterranean region during Jizebul's lifetime. The longest duration of the total eclipse was centered near the coast of the Negev region, just west of the modern border between Egypt and Israel, about 120 miles southwest of Dor (31.1°N at 34.1°E). A solar eclipse catalogue is available from the NASA/Goddard Space Flight Center eclipse Web site by Fred Espenak: http://sunearth.gsfc.nasa.gov/eclipse. Dates on the chart have to be altered by one year to correspond to BCE (the chart says 830).

Mot's hand [page 154]. Translation by H. L. Ginsberg, "Poems about Baal and Anath," II AB viii, in Pritchard 1969b, 135, adapted by the author. In the Ugaritic tales, Mot is said to be a son of El and Asherah, hence he is El's Beloved, while Baal is a relative newcomer to the pantheon. The sun's disappearance at night could be interpreted as its passage through the underworld. The feminine sun, Shapsh, helps the Lady Anath to search for Baal there (I AB iv, in Pritchard 1969b, 141), recovers Baal's body from Mot, and gives it to Anath for burial (I AB i, in Pritchard 1969b, 139). Jizebul transfers this thought to the daytime eclipse.

Where is the Prince? [page 154]. Translation by H. L. Ginsberg, "Poems about Baal and Anath," I AB iv, Pritchard 1969b, 141, adapted by the author. See glossary entry for *Jizebul*, whose name may be a reflection of this phrase.

Text [page 155]. Translation by H. L. Ginsberg, "Poems about Baal and Anath," I AB iii, Pritchard 1969b, 140, adapted by the author. Anath disposes of Mot by actions associated with grain harvest: cleaving (cutting the stalks, breaking the hulls by threshing), winnowing (separating grain from chaff by tossing in the air), roasting, and grinding, saving some grain to sow (plant) for the next year's crop. So the connotations of Mot's season are more about the heat and dryness necessary to ripen grain after a season of Baal's rain than about a total absence of life. The alternation is normal; neither is productive without the other.

Existent is the Prince [page 156]. This may be the phrase reflected in the name of Jizebul's father, Ethbaal.

15 Epilogues

Text [page 157]. Translation of 2 Kings 12:17-21 and 14:2-6a NRSV, adapted by the author.

Marriage proposal rebuffed [page 159]. Joash's rejection of Amaziah takes the form of a parable comparing Judah to a thorn bush and Israel to a cedar of Lebanon (2 Kgs 14:8-10; 2 Chr 25:17-19). Could this parable be a remnant of Israel's earlier ties to Tyre?

Adad-nirari III [page 159]. See a photograph of Adad-nirari's monument and the text of the inscription mentioning Joash of Samaria in *A History of Ancient Israel and Judah* (Miller and Hayes 1986, 288 and 299).

Jeroboam II's prosperity [page 159]. See note on page 179 first mowings for Judah's contributions to Israel's wealth under Jehuite kings.

Genealogy [page 160]. There is no direct statement in the biblical account that Jizebul is the mother of Atalyah or Ahaziah. No other wife of Ahab is mentioned either, and yet he is said to have seventy sons, a large, if only approximate, number of sons and grandsons. Jehu's taunt (2 Kgs 9:22) links Jizebul only to Joram. If Joram was the full brother of Ahaziah, whom he suceeded (2 Kgs 1:17, "brother" in Greek and Syriac versions, not Hebrew), then Jizebel was mother of both. Since Ahab's worship of Baal is directly attributed to Jizebul, Atalyah's promoting Baal in Jerusalem may be circumstantially interpreted "like mother like daughter," especially if, as I think, Baal was a covenant god for alliance with Jizebul's Tyre in both cases. See my genealogical chart on page 16.

Notes to the Illustrations

Introduction

Seal of Jizebul [page xii (opposite page 1) and at the end of each letter]. When Nahman Avigad first published this seal, he identified it as belonging to a woman, although not necessarily the biblical Jezebel (1964). In a recent catalogue, that view has been modified to "Owner's gender uncertain" (Avigad and Sass 1997, 275, "Yizebel [?]"). The letters in the seal are carved backwards, to be viewed correctly in the seal impression. It was found in the vicinity of Dor and dated to late ninth or early eighth century by style alone, not by archaeological context. Drawing based on a photograph of the seal in Metropolitan Museum of Art, *Treasures of the Holy Land*, 179 (catalog no. 89).

2 Tyre

Phoenician A, B, and C [page 22]. Reading from right to left, the first letters of the Phoenician alphabet, from the inscription of Elibaal, a ruler of Byblos in the late tenth or early ninth century BCE. Drawing based on an example in Gelb 1963, 131n23 and 177 fig. 89. See also Markoe's chart of the Phoenician alphabet (2000, 113 fig. 32).

Ivory carving, cow and calf [page 23]. This ivory plaque, carved in Phoenician style, was excavated from the Assyrian capital Nimrud (biblical Calah, in northern Iraq), from the "Fort Shalmaneser" area. The same design is found in excavated collections of ivory carvings in several cities, including fragments from Samaria. See Beach 1991, 1993, and 1997 for discussion of the symbolism of the cow and calf on royal banquet furniture. Drawing based on a photograph in Mallowan 1978, 56 fig. 65.

Notes to the Illustrations

Phoenician gold bracelet [page 26]. "Gold bracelet of linked plaques with embossed and granulated palmettes, lotuses and eyes of Horus; remains of the silver bands which joined these plaques into a bracelet appear at each end." Drawing based on the photograph of this seventh- or sixth-century BCE Phoenician bracelet from Tharros, Sardinia (Harden 1962, 316 note on plate 104).

3 Tirzah

Spring at Tirzah [page 31]. Sheep and dark-haired goats are watered together at midday at the modern Palestinian village of Tirzah in the West Bank.

Silver-plated bronze statue from Tirzah [page 36]. Drawing based on a photograph of a "silver-plated bronze figurine of the goddess Hathor, period VI, Late Bronze" from Tirzah, in "Farah, Tell el-(North)," in Stern 1993, 2.439.

Bronze bull statue from Dothan area [page 39]. The chance find of this artifact on a hilltop was followed by excavations of an open-air, partially paved enclosure used for religious purposes during the twelfth and eleventh centuries BCE. Drawing based on a photograph from the Israel Antiquities Authority and Israel Museum (Isserlin 2001, plate 51).

4 Samaria

Header-stretcher walls at Samaria [page 42]. This monumental Israelite architecture, likely influenced by Phoenician design if not constructed by Phoenicians, featured rectangular stone blocks set in pairs in a pattern exposing long (stretcher) and short (header) ends in alternation. This also increased stability.

Samaria viewed from the north [page 46]. The darker mound at the center of this photograph, the natural hill of Samaria, is somewhat set apart from the hills around it. This view looks south from the ninth-century route to Dothan.

Impaled captives from Assyrian relief sculpture [page 52]. This detail of a wall relief sculpture from Nineveh shows Sennecherib's attack on Lachish (701 BCE). Drawing based on a photograph in Pritchard 1969a, 131 fig. 373.

Notes to the Illustrations

Eye of Horus amulet from Megiddo [page 54]. This faience amulet of the eye of Horus (Egyptian, *wedjat*) is one of more than two dozen excavated at Megiddo in stratum IV, a ninth-century rebuilding phase assigned to Ahab. Drawing based on a photograph in the excavation report by Lamon and Shipton (1939, plate 75, fig. 30). Faience is a manufactured substance of heated sand quartz with a glassy surface, used to make jewelry and small vessels, often bluish in color.

5 Baal's Headland

Ravine in Gilead [page 57]. This area of the countryside drains into the Yarmuk River, which forms the northern boundary of the Gilead region.

Fortification tower at Jezreel [page 59]. Excavations at Jezreel in the 1990s by John Woodhead and David Ussishkin revealed a fortification system of walls, towers, and a dry moat.

View toward Jezreel Plain from Baal's Headland (Mount Carmel) [page 64]. This view looks toward the northeast across the western plain of Jezreel from the grounds of the Carmelite monastery honoring Elijah on Mount Carmel.

Carved ivory, goats and a tree of life [page 67]. This ivory panel in Phoenician style is from the Assyrian city of Nimrud (biblical Calah). Drawing based on an illustration of a reconstructed plaque in Barnett 1975, plate 34, S50.

6 Jezreel

Terraced hillsides [page 72]. Preparing hillsides for cultivation requires cutting into the bedrock to make a shelf and building retaining walls of fieldstone. Both aspects are illustrated in this view of terracing in modern Jordan.

Phoenician traders from Assyrian relief sculpture [page 73]. Two Phoenicians approaching the king with gifts, from a wall relief at the palace of Ashurnasirpal II at Nimrud. Drawing based on photograph in Barnett 1960, plate 9.

View from Jezreel over valley [page 77]. This is the view from the mound of Jezreel looking toward the northwest and the Galilee foothills where Tyrian agricultural settlements were established. (Photograph by Robert Haak)

Notes to the Illustrations

7 Beth-hakkherem

A spring at Dan [page 81]. The Jordan River is formed by several year-round, spring-fed streams from the aquifer under the Mount Hermon watershed. This one, on the west side of Dan, is particularly dramatic—an energetic fountain even in summer.

Ivory carving, tree of life design [page 84]. This vertical open-work ivory carving from Arslan Tash (on the upper Euphrates River near the Turkish-Syrian border) combines decorative palmette and lotus forms. Drawing and reconstruction based on a photograph in Thureau-Dangin et al. 1931, plate 45, fig. 98. See the similar design from Samaria in Crowfoot and Crowfoot 1938, plate 17, figs. 4, 4a.

Ethbaal sending tribute to Shalmaneser [page 89]. Shalmaneser III recorded Tyre's sending tribute in friezes on the bronze gates of Balawat (Khorsabad, on the upper Tigris River in northern Iraq). The scene continues to the right, with porters marching in procession to the seated Assyrian king. Drawing based on a photograph in Markoe 2000, 41 fig. 5.

Shalmaneser's (?) monument on cliffs above the Dog River, Lebanon [page 91]. The geography of the "bridge" of ancient Canaan directs most traffic along north-south routes with a few passes to the interior. Where the route from the interior at Nahr el-Kelb (Dog River) in Lebanon meets the coastline, the cliffs have received many monumental inscriptions left by passing armies, from ancient Egyptians and Assyrians to modern twentieth-century Europeans (British). This Assyrian inscription is too eroded to be identified with certainty, but it is traditionally ascribed to Shalmaneser III.

8 Karkar

Bodies of enemies after battle, from an Assyrian relief sculpture [page 96]. The biblical curse that consigned someone killed in the field to being eaten by birds is also an iconographic theme in Assyrian art. In this detail from a scene of Ashurbanipal's battle with Elamites (South West Palace at Nineveh), the birds first peck at the soft tissue. Is the center figure still alive enough to push against the bird? Drawing based on a photograph in Bersani and Dutoit 1985, 13 fig. 6.

Notes to the Illustrations

Ivory carving, woman at the window [page 100]. This carving is one of several dozen examples from four sites (Samaria and three cities in Assyria) of a plaque that may have been used on banquet couches where the leg joins the frame (as in Ashurbanipal's banquet couch, drawn in Barnett 1957, 118 fig. 46). The hair is a formal wig; the eyebrows would have been inlaid with a darker material. The motif is also known from a Cypriot bronze incense altar. See Beach 1993 for a fuller description of this and other ivory designs associated with the *marzeaḥ* and their religious significance. Drawing based on a photograph in Barnett 1975, plate 4, C12.

Ivory carving, drinking stag [page 101]. This design is another of the cluster found with the woman at the window motif on ritual furniture. This example is from Arslan Tash (on the upper Euphrates River near the Turkish-Syrian border). Drawing based on a photograph in Thureau-Dangin et al. 1931, plate 36, fig. 61.

Ivory carving, infant Horus on lotus [page 102]. In the Egyptian context of this motif, the divine infant Horus is reborn on a Nile River lotus; some examples show him on a boat (the sun's barque?) with lines radiating down to an Osiris mummy (his deceased father, the former king). Ivories found at the same four sites where the woman at the window design has been found include many examples of this motif, often with the infant on a central pedestal being saluted by a guardian figure on each side. This particularly fine example from Samaria would have had colored insets in the flowers and insignia. The motif appears also on Phoenician bowls of the type illustrated on page 113. Drawing based on the illustration of a reconstruction in Crowfoot and Crowfoot 1938, plate I, fig. 1.

9 Ekron

Imposing mount of Tell es-Safi (Gath) [page 104]. Renewed excavation by the Tell es-Safi/Gath Archaeological Project, begun in 1996, is directed by Aren M. Maeir, an archaeologist from Bar Ilan University of Ramat-Gan, Israel.

Olive oil production area at Ekron [page 108]. Field III at Tel Miqne (Ekron) yielded evidence of centralized mass production of olive oil begun during the early seventh century when the area came under Assyrian domination. Pictured are a crushing basin between two pressing vats, with the perforated stones that would have weighted down a pressing beam. Drawing based on a photograph in "Miqne, Tel (Ekron)," Stern 1993, 3.1058.

Notes to the Illustrations

Ivory plaque with the eye of Horus, from Samaria [page 110]. Although it is highly schematic, this design nevertheless maintains some reference to the falcon aspect of Horus. Drawing based on a photograph and reconstruction in Crowfoot and Crowfoot 1938, plate 3, figs. 2a and 2b.

10 Dibon

Soldiers cutting trees in battle, from Phoenician drinking bowl [page 113]. Both Phoenician and Assyrian battle scenes show soldiers cutting down trees outside a city. This drawing illustrates part of the incised interior of a silver Phoenician bowl from Amathus on Cyprus. Drawing based on a photograph in Markoe 1985, 249, Cy4.

11 Damascus

Battle scene with enemy under chariot, from Assyrian relief sculpture [page 124]. The motif of a victim under a chariot—an animal in the hunt or a human enemy—is depicted in both Assyrian and Phoenician designs. See Markoe 2000, 149 fig. 56 for a Phoenician gilt-silver bowl from Praeneste (in Etruria, Italy) showing a king's chariot horse trampling a gorilla-like creature. This Assyrian wall sculpture was in Ashurnasirpal's palace at Nimrud (biblical Calah). Notice the arrows in the back, implying the enemy was fleeing. Drawing based on a photograph in Budge 1914, plate 15, fig. 2.

View toward east from Jezreel [page 126]. The Jezreel fortress overlooked the route eastward to the Jordan Valley, close to its narrowest point under Mount Gilboa. The foothills of the Galilee rise directly across the valley.

12 Ramoth-gilead

Area outside Dan gate where inscription was found [page 128]. The towers and insets of the city wall have been reconstructed after excavations at Dan. Access to the gate (at far right) paralleled the wall, then took a sharp left turn through a passage that then turned sharply right, offering defenders several advantages against the momentum of a frontal attack. Pieces of the inscription were found in the paved area (foreground) and in a nearby stone wall.

Notes to the Illustrations

Model shrine with image at door and window [page 131]. At least two forms of model shrines with a female figure at the window are known from Phoenician contexts on Cyprus. This illustration shows one form: a three-dimensional terracotta model, of which two examples were found at Idalion. The other form, known from several examples, is the front of a shrine with a figure at the door, carved in two dimensions on the stone headdress of a Hathor pillar from Kition. The Greek biographer Plutarch, writing in the late first century CE, identified the woman at the window of a Salamis shrine as "Aphrodite looking sideways with glances of love" (Plutarch, *Erotikos*, 20, cited in Barnett 1957, 149). Many commentators adopt this erotic interpretation without also noting that the Phoenician legend described by Plutarch gives the occasion as the funeral procession of a rejected suitor beneath the window of a cold-hearted maiden, who is turned to stone by the goddess. This funerary setting, which may have erotic aspects but was perhaps not fully understood by the Greek author, accords well with Egyptian and Ugaritic precedents and thus with the *marzeaḥ*. Drawing based on a photograph in Harden 1962, plate 23. See also Caubet 1979, plate 8, figs. 1–3.

Decapitation of captives and piling of heads, from Assyrian relief sculpture [page 134]. Decapitation is shown on many Assyrian reliefs, both in the moment of battle and in later killing of captives. One shows scribes recording the number of heads piled at the base of a palm tree while soldiers bring booty for their accounting. This illustration may be a similar scene (do the legs at far left belong to a scribe, the central shaft to a tree?) from Ashurbanipal's South West Palace at Nineveh. Drawing based on a photograph in Bersani and Dutoit 1985, 53 fig. 26).

Jehu (?) bowing to Shalmaneser on the Black Obelisk [page 137]. Jehu is named in the cuneiform caption immediately above this picture, suggesting that it is intended to represent the Israelite king himself. Drawing based on a photograph in Isserlin 2001, plate 24.

13 Jerusalem

Phoenician gold bracelet with four-winged beetle [page 143]. The scarab shape that is characteristic of many seals is an auspicious symbol in Phoenician metal work, both bowls and jewelry. Here, the sun is held by the beetle, framed by palmette and lotus forms on a seventh- or sixth-century BCE bracelet from Tharros,

Notes to the Illustrations

Sardinia. It also appears on another part of the bowl illustrated on page 113. Drawing based on a photograph in Moscati 1988, 382.

14 Dor

Carved ivory plaque from Samaria, lotus bud and flower [page 156]. Drawing based on photograph and reconstructed illustration in Crowfoot and Crowfoot 1938, plate 15, fig. 3a.

Glossary

Characters not mentioned in the Bible or other documents of the period are marked with an asterisk (*). They were invented for this book.

The biblical Hebrew texts may use two spellings for the name of one king. Also, two kings may have the same name. For simplicity and uniformity, I have chosen one English spelling for each king and have altered the translations of biblical texts accordingly.

Abdi-Ptah*   Egyptian scribe from Tyre who served Jizebul's father, Ethbaal, and then the House of Omri. Ptah is an Egyptian god of Memphis who is associated with mind and speech. The Phoenician name Abdi-Ptah appears on an inscribed bronze funerary situla dedicated to the goddess Isis from the sixth century BCE (Markoe 2000, 138). Abdi-Ptah provided Jizebul with information about Egyptian religion that would not have been generally known to Israelites.

Achli*   Pseudonym used by Jizebul to refer to her "special friend," a traveling Phoenician cloth merchant who was a kinsman from her mother's family. From the Hebrew *'achli*, "my brother," a term of endearment (Song 8:1).

Ahab   Jizebul's husband, son of Omri, king of Israel (874–853 BCE). Mentioned in an Assyrian inscription as "Ahab the Israelite" (see Shalmaneser's monolith inscription, page 96).

Ahaziah   Son of Jizebul and Ahab who succeeded his father as king of Israel (853–852 BCE).

Ahaziyah   Son of Atalyah and Jehoram (king in Jerusalem) who succeeded his father but was killed within the year by Jehu (841 BCE).

Anath   Goddess known from Ugaritic texts and ancient Near Eastern inscriptions who was frequently associated with Baal as his warrior and partner. Her name may be preserved in biblical

Glossary

	references to a town north of Jerusalem, Anathoth, to which the prophet Jeremiah's priestly ancestor Abiathar was exiled by Solomon.
Asa	King in Jerusalem (910–869 BCE), and father of Jehoshaphat.
Asherah	Goddess known from Ugaritic texts as the wife of the high god, El. Biblical references and extrabiblical Hebrew inscriptions that mention Asherah have also been interpreted as meaning a sacred object rather than a goddess (1 Kgs 15:13; 16:33), but in Jizebul's tradition, she was a goddess. See the note on page 165.
Ashurbanipal	Assyrian ruler (668–627 BCE).
Ashurnasirpal	Assyrian ruler (883–859 BCE).
Astarte	Goddess known from Ugaritic texts and the Bible (for example, 1 Kgs 11:33), one of the principal deities of Jizebul's native Tyre.
Atalyah	Daughter of Jizebul and Ahab; wife of King Jehoram of Jerusalem; and mother of Ahaziyah. After Jehu's murder of Ahaziyah, she ruled in Jerusalem as the only recorded queen in Israelite and Judean history (841–835 BCE).
Baal	Energetic young god of the Ugaritic tales. He has multiple manifestations, names, and attributes in biblical and ancient Near Eastern texts; often associated with storms, rain, and fertility.
Baal-azzor	Son of Ethbaal, Jizebul's father. He became king of Tyre and the Sidonians upon his father's death (855–830 BCE). In *The Jezebel Letters*, he was born to a woman other than Jizebul's mother, making him Jizebul's much younger half-brother.
Baal Shamem	Literally, "master of the heavens," a form of Baal as storm god. This name for a major deity of Tyre may have been more familiar to seventh-century biblical authors than Milkqart, who played a larger role in Tyrian foundation stories.
Baasha	King of Israel (908–866 BCE). The usurper who killed King Nadab son of Jeroboam to end that family's rule after only two kings. His own son, Elah, was also assassinated shortly after taking the throne (1 Kgs 15:27—16:10).
Bat-ahav	Woman from Samaria, and wife of King Ahaziyah of Jerusalem. The Bible mentions only that Ahaziyah was son-in-law to the House of Ahab, without giving the bride's name (2 Kgs 8:27), so I have given her a Hebrew designation, "daughter of Ahab."
Ben-hadad	King of Aram in its capital Damascus. More than one ruler of Aram had this name. In this story, he was the mid-ninth-century king who led the western coalition, including Israel, against the

Glossary

	Assyrians, who called him Adad-'idri in Shalmaneser's monolith inscription (see page 96). The *Hadad* element in his name refers to a major Aramaean deity (*ben hadad* is literally, "son of Hadad").
Carites	In 2 Kings 11:4 and 2 Samuel 20:23, Carites seem to be a special bodyguard for the Jerusalem king, probably of non-Israelite origins.
Chronicler	Designation for the postexilic (after 538 BCE) author(s) of 1–2 Chronicles whose work relied heavily on the information in the earlier 1–2 Kings and linked the nation's fate to how well kings supported priestly activities.
David	Warrior; son-in-law and successor to King Saul; and founder of the Davidic dynasty, the House of David, around 1,000 BCE. Credited with making Jerusalem his capital and relocating the Ark of Covenant to a shrine there.
Deuteronomistic "history"	The biblical books Joshua, Judges, 1–2 Samuel, and 1–2 Kings, which recount the fortunes of Israelites from their settlement in Canaan to the Babylonian exile. The books are thought to have been compiled and edited over many years (from the time of King Josiah [around 620 BCE] into the postexilic period [after 538 BCE]) using criteria from Deuteronomy to evaluate kings according to religious obedience, regardless of their economic, military, and political achievements or shortcomings. They favor the Jerusalem temple and some Davidic kings and uniformly condemn northern Israelite kings and sanctuaries as failing to meet the standards. Because the narratives were composed long after the events they report and because they serve a particular religious perspective, their value as historical sources needs careful evaluation rather than acceptance at face value.
El	The Semitic word for "god." It was used as the proper name of the head of the Ugaritic pantheon and in titles for the biblical God of Israel in Genesis and elsewhere: El Shaddai, El Olam, El Berith. The most general Hebrew word for God, *Elohim* ("gods"), is grammatically the plural form of *El*.
Elah	King of Israel (886–885 BCE). Son of the usurper Baasha, Elah was murdered in turn by Zimri soon after ascending to the throne (1 Kgs 16:8-14).
El Berith	Hebrew, "God of the Covenant," the god of the Shechem sanctuary according to Judges 9:46.
Eliyahu	Traditional Hebrew name for the prophet Elijah, "Yhwh is my

Glossary

	God," spelled to emphasize the divine element in his name.
Ethbaal	Jizebul's father; former priest of Astarte who seized the throne to become king of Tyre and of the Sidonians (887–856 BCE). Mentioned in the Bible (1 Kgs 16:31) and also by Josephus (*The Jewish Antiquities* 7.324). His name may be based on a ritual phrase indicating the return of Baal from the deathly realm of Mot: "existent is the Prince," in Ugaritic texts (see page 156).
gevirah	Hebrew, "queen mother," the mother of the ruling king. See the note on page 165.
Hadad	Aramaean male deity, associated with weather by insignia of lightning arrows and sometimes shown with horns or standing on a bull.
Hathor	Major Egyptian goddess whose iconography—a frontal woman's head with hair falling to a curl on each shoulder or a horned wild cow often with a calf—spread widely in the eastern Mediterranean without always being associated with this particular deity.
Hazael	Ruler of Aram in Damascus (sometime soon after 845 to about 800 BCE?). Reported in the Bible to have smothered King Benhadad (2 Kgs 8:7-15) to take the throne. Considered a "son of nobody" (a commoner) by the Assyrians, his family and local origins are not known (see Shalmaneser's inscription on page 125). *The Jezebel Letters* assigns him to a ruling family in Dan.
Hiram	King of Tyre (969–936 BCE). Mentioned several times in the Bible as an ally of David and Solomon (1 Kings 5), supplier of materials and craftsmen for building the Jerusalem temple, and cosponsor of shipping from Ezion-geber, in return for which he was ceded twenty cities in the Galilee (1 Kgs 9:10-13).
Horus	Egyptian deity, son of Isis (throne goddess) and Osiris (ruler of the underworld), with whom the reigning pharaoh was identified. His symbols included some element of a falcon, especially the characteristic head markings.
Ishah-ahav*	The Bible does not indicate any wives of Ahab aside from Jizebul, but given royal practices of marriage alliances and Ahab's seventy "sons" (2 Kgs 10:6-9), it is likely there were others. The Hebrew name by which Jizebul calls the first wife in this story is not a personal name but only "Ahab's woman." This is similar to the Bible's failure to acknowledge many women as individuals and is also Jizebul's way of asserting her own superiority. After the birth of Jizebul's first son, Ahab's other wife is not men-

Glossary

	tioned in the memoirs.
Israel	Name of the northern kingdom, capital at Samaria (922–732 BCE).
Jehoash	Claimed by Jehoiada the priest to be King Ahaziyah's son and installed as king in Jerusalem (835–796? BCE) to replace Atalyah (2 Kings 11).
Jehoiada	Priest in the Jerusalem temple who instigated the overthrow of Atalyah and supervised the young King Jehoash (2 Kings 11–12 and 2 Chronicles 23–24). Married to Jehosheba, the daughter of King Jehoram.
Jehoram	Son of Jehoshaphat, and husband of Atalyah; king in Jerusalem (848–841 BCE) after coregency with his father (853–848 BCE).
Jehoshaphat	Son of King Asa of Jerusalem. He made a marriage covenant with King Ahab of Samaria and reorganized the southern kingdom (872–848 BCE).
Jehozabad	Commander of one thousand troops in King Jehoshaphat's army (2 Chr 17:18), from the region of Benjamin.
Jehozabad	Son of Shomer, and one of the assassins of King Jehoash (2 Kgs 12:21). In *The Jezebel Letters,* he is said to be the grandson of Jehozabad of Benjamin and also a military commander.
Jehu	Son of [Jehoshaphat son of] Nimshi. Army commander, assassin, and successor of King Joram of Israel (2 Kings 9). Mentioned on Shalmaneser's Black Obelisk as a vassal and "son of Omri" (see page 137).
Jehu	Son of Hanani son of Heman the "seer" for King Asa in Jerusalem. This Jehu's grandfather, Heman the seer, and his offspring were appointed by David to be official temple singers and musicians (1 Chr 25:1, 4-6). Jehu's father Hanani opposed Asa of Jerusalem's alliance with Ben-hadad of Aram against Baasha of Israel (2 Chr 16:7-10). Jehu prophesied against Baasha directly (1 Kgs 16:1-4, 7). This Jehu is not the same as the northern Israelite Jehu son of Nimshi who takes the throne in 2 Kings 9.
Jeroboam	First king of northern Israel. Mentioned in the Bible (1 Kgs 11:26-40) as an overseer of Solomon's forced laborers from the north and a rebel. Became king of these tribes when Solomon's son Rehoboam was rejected (1 Kings 12–13). Jeroboam and all kings in Israel after him were condemned by the Deuteronomistic editors for establishing sanctuaries apart from Jerusalem, appointing their own priests, and using a bull calf symbol for Y H W H.
Jerusalem	Capital city of the area ruled by the House of David, the south-

Glossary

	ern kingdom called "Judah" in the Bible.
Jesse	Father of King David.
Jezebel	This is the common English spelling, from the Hebrew *'izebel*, of the name of Ahab's wife. The Hebrew appears to be an intentional distortion of the Phoenician ritual phrase *'i z^ebul* ("where is the Prince [Baal]?") into the Hebrew *'i-z^ebul* ("no nobility") and then into the current form where *zebel* means "dung." The biblical translations in *The Jezebel Letters* maintain this ignoble spelling, but the letters and memoirs use a reconstructed original, Jizebul. See Gray 1970, 367–68.
Jizebul	Daughter of Ethbaal king of Tyre, wife of King Ahab of Israel, mother of two Israelite kings Joram and Ahaziah and of Atalyah, queen in Jerusalem. The proper transliteration of the original name may be *'i z^ebul*, but to show the relation to the traditional English spelling, I have retained the J.
Joash	Son of Jehoahaz son of Jehu, king of Israel (798–782 BCE).
Joram	Son of Jizebul and Ahab who succeeded his brother Ahaziah as king (852–841 BCE) and was killed by Jehu son of Nimshi.
Jozacar	Coconspirator with Jehozabad in the assassination of King Jehoash (2 Kgs 12:21).
Judah	Biblical name for southern kingdom, capital at Jerusalem. Named for one of the sons of Jacob (Gen 49:8-12), and represented as a tribe in the books of Joshua and Judges. See the note on page 170.
"Land Between the Rivers"	Geographical term equivalent to Mesopotamia (from Greek, between rivers), used to designate the Assyrian homeland in the area between the northern Tigris and Euphrates Rivers.
marzeaḥ	An association of people who gathered periodically for religious celebrations identified with specific deities, using designated buildings and wine from particular vineyards, often for memorial purposes and sometimes with sacral sexual orgies (see Pope 1972, 193). Known also from neighboring cultures, the biblical *marzeaḥ* is mentioned specifically in Amos 6:4-7 (for Israel) and Jeremiah 16:1-9 (for Jerusalem) and may be alluded to elsewhere. *Marzeaḥ* is translated by NRSV as "revelry" in Amos 6:7 but as "[house of] mourning" in Jeremiah 16:5. The two activities were not incompatible. The ivory carvings illustrated on pages 23, 100, 101, and 102 are important symbols in the *marzeaḥ* context and probably adorned the furniture used for the occasion (Beach 1993).

Glossary

Milkqart   "King of the city," a major deity of Tyre, often spelled Melqart.

Mot   Semitic word for "death," and one of the major deities in the Ugaritic texts. He swallowed Baal but was himself vanquished by Anath, opening the way for Baal's return. In a naturalistic interpretation, Mot represented the hot dry season, alternating with the cool rainy months of Baal.

Naboth   The Jezreelite property owner (1 Kings 21) who refused to sell or give his land to King Ahab and whose demise was arranged by a letter of indictment from Jizebul, resulting in a curse by Eliyahu which Jehu claimed to fulfill by his murders (2 Kgs 9:25-26).

Nimshi   Jehu's [grand]father, whose name may mean "weasel." See the note on page 170.

Obadiah   Overseer of King Ahab's palace at Samaria and sympathizer with Eliyahu (1 Kings 18).

Omri   Founder of a long dynasty of kings in northern Israel. King himself from 885 to 853 BCE. He took the throne by killing usurper Zimri with the support of an army and winning a civil war against rival Tibni (1 Kings 16:15-24). Established Samaria as the capital.

qesher   Hebrew, "conspiracy" (2 Kgs 11:14).

Samaria   Capital city of Israel, the northern kingdom (922–732 BCE).

Saul   First "king" of the Hebrew tribes. His base was at Gibeah north of Jerusalem, and he functioned primarily as a warlord against Philistines and others (about 1020 BCE?). After Saul's death in battle, David took control of the south (at Hebron) and eventually gained northern allegiance after a civil war against Saul's sons.

Sennacherib   Assyrian ruler (705–681 BCE) whose invasion of Judah during the reign of King Hezekiah is described in 2 Kings 18:13—19:37.

shalom   Hebrew, usually translated "peace," but having fuller connotations of wholeness and right relations.

Shapsh   In the Ugaritic Baal cycle, Shapsh is a female solar deity, guide of the dead to the underworld at night, who helps Anath to seek Baal there. See the note about Mot's hand on page 190.

sheqer   Hebrew, "a lie" (2 Kgs 9:12).

Solomon   Son of David, king in Jerusalem during the mid-900s BCE. Biblical reports credit him with building the Jerusalem temple with help of craftsmen sent by Hiram of Tyre (1 Kings 5).

Glossary

Tanit Phoenician goddess known primarily from inscriptions in the fifth-century cemetery at Carthage in North Africa, but whose sign has been found on Iron Age artifacts from the Phoenician homeland.

Tibni Son of Ginath, and rival to Omri, to whom he lost a civil war that lasted perhaps four years (1 Kgs 16:21-22).

Ugarit Ancient name of a city on the Syrian coast (now known as Ras Shamra) that was destroyed in about 1200 BCE. Excavations begun in 1929 yielded poetic tales and ritual texts about the deities El, Baal, Asherah, and Astarte, whose names also appear in biblical texts and place names and in extrabiblical inscriptions. See Pritchard 1969b, 129–55.

Yhwh In the Hebrew Bible and ancient Hebrew inscriptions, the Name of Israel's God is written as a (the) Tetragrammaton (a four-letter word!) without vowels. Jewish tradition honors the Name by not saying it aloud and saying "Lord" where the text reads "Yhwh." Following this practice, the Name is represented in many English translations by Lord. If portions of *The Jezebel Letters* containing the Name are read aloud, the lack of vowels in Yhwh should remind readers to substitute "Lord" if it is appropriate for any in the group.

Zechariah Son of Jehoiada the priest in Jerusalem, who tried to reinstate his father's policies after King Jehoash and the nobles reversed priestly privileges. Killed by Jehoash (2 Chronicles 24).

Zibiah Wife of King Ahaziyah, and mother of King Jehoash (2 Kgs 12:1-2). From Beer-sheba

Zimri A military commander who killed King Elah of Israel and who "reigned" seven days before committing suicide while under attack by Omri (1 Kgs 16:8-20).

Works Cited

Ackerman, Susan. 2003 (November). "Women and the Weaving of Cultic Textiles in Ancient Israel." Paper delivered to the Research Seminars in Hebrew and Old Testament Studies and New Testament Language, Literature, and Theology at New College, University of Edinburgh.

———. 1993. "The Queen Mother and the Cult in Ancient Israel." *Journal of Biblical Literature* 112: 385–401.

Ahlström, Gösta W. 1993. *The History of Ancient Palestine from the Palaeolithic Period to Alexander's Conquest.* Edited by Diana Edelman. *Journal for the Study of the Old Testament,* Supplement Series 146. Sheffield: Sheffield Academic Press.

Allen, Leslie C. 1983. *Psalms 101–150.* Word Biblical Commentary 21. Waco, Tex.: Word Books.

Athas, George. 2003. *The Tel Dan Inscription: A Reappraisal and a New Interpretation. Journal for the Study of the Old Testament,* Supplement Series 360. New York: Sheffield Academic Press.

Avigad, Nahman. 1997. *Corpus of West Semitic Stamp Seals.* Revised and completed by Benjamin Sass. Jerusalem: Israel Academy of Sciences and Humanities, Israel Exploration Society, and Institute of Archaeology of the Hebrew University of Jerusalem.

———. 1987. "The Contribution of Hebrew Seals to an Understanding of Israelite Religion and Society." In *Ancient Israelite Religion: Essays in Honor of Frank Moore Cross,* edited by Patrick D. Miller Jr., Paul D. Hanson, and S. Dean McBride, 195–208, esp. 205–6. Philadelphia: Fortress Press.

———. 1964. "The Seal of Jezebel." *Israel Exploration Journal* 14, no. 4: 274–76.

Barnett, Richard D. 1975. *A Catalogue of the Nimrud Ivories.* 2nd ed. London: Trustees of the British Museum.

---. 1960. *Assyrian Palace Reliefs and Their Influence on the Sculptures of Babylonia and Persia.* London: Balchworth Press.

Beach, Eleanor Ferris. 1997a. "An Iconographic Approach to Genesis 38." In *A Feminist Companion to Reading the Bible: Approaches, Methods and Strategies* I, edited by Athalya Brenner and Carole Fontaine, 285–305. Sheffield: Sheffield Academic Press.

---. 1997b. "Transforming Goddess Iconography in Hebrew Narrative." In *Women and Goddess Traditions in Antiquity and Today*, edited by Karen L. King. Studies in Antiquity and Christianity. Minneapolis: Fortress Press, 239–63.

---. 1993. "The Samaria Ivories, Marzeaḥ, and Biblical Texts." *Biblical Archaeologist* 56: 94–104.

---. 1991. "Image and Word: Iconology in the Interpretation of Hebrew Scriptures." PhD diss., Claremont Graduate University.

Bersani, Leo and Ulysse Dutoit. 1985. *The Forms of Violence: Narrative in Assyrian Art and Modern Culture.* New York: Schocken Books.

Bikai, Patricia Maynor. 1992. "Phoenician Tyre." In *The Heritage of Tyre: Essays on the History, Archaeology, and Preservation of Tyre*, edited by Martha Sharp Joukowsky, 44–53. Dubuque, Ia.: Kendall/Hunt Publishing Co.

Biran, Avraham. 1993. "An Aramaic Stele Fragment from Tel Dan." *Israel Exploration Journal* 43: 81–98.

Biran, Avraham and Joseph Naveh. 1995. "The Tel Dan Inscription: A New Fragment." *Israel Exploration Journal* 45: 1–18.

Brown, Francis, with S. R. Driver and Charles A. Briggs. 1968. *A Hebrew and English Lexicon of the Old Testament.* London: Oxford University Press.

Budge, E. A. Wallis, ed. 1914. *Assyrian Sculptures in the British Museum.* London: Trustees of the British Museum.

Caubet, Annie. 1979. "Les Maquettes architecturales d'Idalion." In *Studies Presented in Memory of Porphyrios Dikaios*, edited by V. Karageorghis et al., 94–118. Nicosia: Lions Club.

Cross, Frank Moore. 1984. "The Seal of Miqnêyaw, Servant of Yahweh." In *Ancient Seals and the Bible*, edited by Leonard Gorelick and Elizabeth Williams-Forte, 55–63. Malibu, Calif.: Undena Publications.

Crowfoot, J. W., and Grace M. Crowfoot. 1938. *Early Ivories from Samaria.* London: Palestine Exploration Fund.

Dahood, Mitchell. 1970. *Psalms 101–150.* The Anchor Bible, 17A. Garden City, N.Y.: Doubleday.

---. 1968. *Psalms 51–100.* The Anchor Bible, 17. Garden City, N.Y.: Doubleday.

---. 1965. *Psalm 1–50.* The Anchor Bible, 16. Garden City, N.Y.: Doubleday.

Works Cited

Dever, William G. 2001. *What Did the Biblical Writers Know and When Did They Know It? What Archaeology Can Tell Us about the Reality of Ancient Israel.* Grand Rapids, Mich.: Eerdmans.

———. 1984. "Asherah, Consort of Yahweh? New Evidence from Kuntillet 'Ajrud." *Bulletin of the American Schools of Oriental Research* 255: 21–37.

Farrar, Frederic William. 1900. *The Second Book of Kings.* The Expositor's Bible, 10. New York: Funk & Wagnalls.

Faust, Avraham. 2003. "Abandonment, Urbanization, Resettlement and the Formation of the Israelite State." *Near Eastern Archaeology* 66: 147–61.

Finkelstein, Israel, and Neil Asher Silberman. 2001. *The Bible Unearthed: Archaeology's New Vision of Ancient Israel and the Origin of Its Sacred Texts.* New York: Free Press.

Franklin, Norma. 2003. "The Tombs of the Kings of Israel: Two Recently Identified 9th-Century Tombs from Omride Samaria." *Zeitschrift des Deutschen Palästina-Vereins* 119: 1–11.

Friend, Glenda. 1998. *Tell Taannek, 1963–1968. III: The Artifacts. 2: The Loom Weights.* Publications of the Palestinian Institute of Archaeology, Excavations and Surveys. Edited by Khaled Nashef. Birzeit: Birzeit University.

Gelb, I. J. 1963. *A Study of Writing.* Rev. ed. Chicago: University of Chicago Press.

Ginsberg, H. L. 1935. "A Phoenician Hymn in the Psalter." *Atti del XIX Congresso Internazionale degli Orientalisti.* 472–76. Rome.

Gray, John. 1970. *I and II Kings: A Commentary.* 2nd ed. Old Testament Library. Philadelphia: Westminster Press.

Gunkel, Hermann. 1926. *Die Psalmen.* Handkommentar zum Alten Testament. 4th ed. Göttingen: Vandenhoek & Ruprecht.

Hallo, William W. and K. Lawson Younger, eds. 2003. *The Context of Scripture.* 3 vols. New York: Brill.

Halpern, Baruch. 2001. *David's Secret Demons: Messiah, Murderer, Traitor, King.* Grand Rapids, Mich.: Eerdmans.

Harden, Donald. 1962. *The Phoenicians.* New York: Praeger.

Homan, Michael M. 2004. "Beer and Its Drinkers: An Ancient Near Eastern Love Story." *Near Eastern Archaeology* 67: 84–95.

Isserlin, B. S. J. 2001. *The Israelites.* Minneapolis: Fortress Press.

Josephus, Flavius. 1935. *Jewish Antiquities, Books 5–8.* Translated by H. St. J. Thackeray and Ralph Marcus. Vol. 5 of *Josephus.* Loeb Classical Library. Cambridge: Harvard University Press.

Katzenstein, H. Jacob. 1997. *The History of Tyre: From the Beginning of the Second Millennium B.C.E until the Fall of the Neo-Babylonian Empire in 539 B.C.E.* 2nd ed. Beer Sheva: Ben-Gurion University of the Negev Press.

Works Cited

Keel, Othmar and Christoph Uehlinger. 1998. *Gods, Goddesses, and Images of God in Ancient Israel.* Translated by Thomas H. Trapp. Minneapolis: Fortress Press.

Lamon, Robert S. and Geoffrey M. Shipton. 1939. *Megiddo I: Seasons of 1925–34, Strata I–IV.* Chicago: University of Chicago Press.

Lemaire, André. 1994. "'House of David' Restored in Moabite Inscription." *Biblical Archaeology Review* 20: 30–37.

Lerner, Gerda. 1986. *The Creation of Patriarchy.* New York: Oxford University Press.

Lindenberger, James M. 1994. *Ancient Aramaic and Hebrew Letters.* Edited by Kent Harold Richards. Society of Biblical Literature, Writings from the Ancient World, vol. 4. Atlanta: Scholars Press.

Lipiński, Edward. 2004. "Mount Ba'lu-ra'ši, Ra'šu Qudši, and Ba'lu." *Itineraria Phoenicia.* Orientalia Louvaniensia Analecta 127. Studia Phoenicia 18. Louvain: Peeters Publishers.

———. 1995. *Dieux et déesses de l'univers phénicien et punique.* Orientalia Lovaniensia Analecta 64. Studia Phoenicia 14. Louvain: Peeters Publishers.

Mallowan, Max. 1978. *The Nimrud Ivories.* London: British Museum Publications.

Markoe, Glenn E. 2000. *Phoenicians.* Berkeley: University of California Press.

———. 1985. *Phoenician Bronze and Silver Bowls from Cyprus and the Mediterranean.* University of California Publications, Classical Studies 26. Berkeley: University of California Press.

Metropolitan Museum of Art. 1986. *Treasures of the Holy Land: Ancient Art from the Israel Museum.* New York: Metropolitan Museum of Art.

Meyers, Carol L. 1976. *The Tabernacle Menorah: A Synthetic Study of a Symbol from the Biblical Cult.* American School of Oriental Research Dissertation Series 2. Missoula, Mont.: Scholars Press.

Miller, J. Maxwell and John H. Hayes, eds. 1986. *A History of Ancient Israel and Judah.* Philadelphia: Westminster Press.

Moscati, Sabatino. 1988. *The Phoenicians.* New York: Abbeville Press.

Pardee, Dennis, S. David Sperling, J. David Whitehead, and Paul E. Dion. 1982. *Handbook of Ancient Hebrew Letters: A Study Edition.* Society of Biblical Literature, Sources for Biblical Study 15. Chico, Calif.: Scholars Press.

Pope, Marvin H. 1972. "A Divine Banquet at Ugarit." In *The Use of the Old Testament in the New and Other Essays: Studies in Honor of William Franklin Stinespring,* edited by James M. Efird, 170–203. Durham, N.C.: Duke University Press.

Pritchard, James B., ed. 1969a. *The Ancient Near East in Pictures Relating to the Old Testament.* 2nd ed. Princeton: Princeton University Press.

———. 1969b. *Ancient Near Eastern Texts Relating to the Old Testament.* 3rd ed. Princeton: Princeton University Press.

Works Cited

Rainey, Anson F. and R. Steven Notley. Forthcoming. *The Sacred Bridge: Carta's Atlas of the Biblical World.* Jerusalem: Carta.

Rainey, Anson F. 2003. "The Suffix Conjugation Pattern in Ancient Hebrew Tense and Modal Functions," *Ancient Near Eastern Studies* 40: 3–41.

Schneider, Tammi. 1996. "Rethinking Jehu." *Biblica* 77: 100–7.

———. 1995. "Did King Jehu Kill His Own Family?" *Biblical Archaeology Review* 21: 26–33, 80, 82.

Stager, Lawrence E. 1990. "Shemer's Estate," *Bulletin of the American Schools of Oriental Research* 277/278: 93–107.

Stern, Ephraim. 1994. *Dor: Ruler of the Seas.* Jerusalem: Israel Exploration Society.

Stern, Ephraim, ed. 1993. *The New Encyclopedia of Archaeological Excavations in the Holy Land.* 4 vols. Jerusalem: The Israel Exploration Society.

Sweeney, Marvin A. 2004 (November). "The Dystopianization of Utopian Prophetic Literature: The Case of Amos 9:11-15." Paper delivered to the Prophetic Texts and Their Ancient Contexts group, Society of Biblical Literature annual meeting, San Antonio, Tex.

———. 2000. *The Twelve Prophets.* Edited by D. W. Cotter. Collegeville, Minn.: Liturgical Press.

Tappy, Ron E. 1992. *The Archaeology of Israelite Samaria.* Vol. 1, *Early Iron Age through the Ninth Century B.C.E.* Atlanta: Scholars Press.

Thiele, Edwin R. 1983. *The Mysterious Numbers of the Hebrew Kings.* Rev. ed. Grand Rapids, Mich.: Zondervan.

Thureau-Dangin, François, A. Barrois, G. Dossin, and Maurice Dunand. 1931. *Arslan Tash.* Paris: Paul Geuthner.

Younger, Lawson. 2004 (February). "Some Reflections on the Tel Dan Inscription and Hazael, King of Aram-Damascus." Paper delivered at the Midwest regional meeting of the Society of Biblical Literature, Olivet Nazarene University, Bourbonnais, Ill.

Suggestions for Further Reading

The following comments mean to be suggestive of types of sources helpful for pursuing the implications of *The Jezebel Letters*. I have not included what might be considered popular or devotional works, some of which also have a basis in historical and biblical scholarship.

A personal favorite of mine is an early and admirable fictional account that illustrates how what people experience may be transformed into a communal story: Zora Neale Hurston's *Moses, Man of the Mountain*, first published in 1939 (now with a foreword by Deborah E. McDowell, New York: HarperPerennial, 1991.) With a solid foundation in the biblical scholarship of her day plus insights from folklore studies, anthropology, and African-American culture, Hurston created a witty exodus account that employed African-American traditions and the biblical story to reflect on social issues in the United States during the 1930s, including racism, sexism, and classism. (Thanks to Harold C. Washington for bringing this novel to the attention of the Feminist Theological Hermeneutics Group at the Society of Biblical Literature's 1993 annual meeting.)

Hurston herself was damaged by the stereotype of a seductive African-American "Jezebel," especially when she was on trial for an immoral act with a ten-year-old boy in a household where she had rented a room (she was found innocent by reason of her having been out of the country at the time of the supposed incident). The "Jezebel" label is one among the stereotypes of mammy, matriarch, welfare mother, and others now receiving critical attention by health, legal, and media analysts for their effects in undermining African-American women's treatment by those institutions. See connections to "Jezebel" in Judith Musser, "Significant Stereotypes in Hurston's 'Conscience of the Court,'" *Midwest Quarterly* 41 (1999): 79–87; Marian Meyers, "African American Women and Violence: Gender, Race, and Class in the News," *Critical Studies in Media Communication* 21 (June 2004): 95ff.; Roxanne Donovan and Michelle Williams, "Living at the Intersection: The Effects of Racism and Sexism on Black Rape Survivors," *Women & Therapy* 25 (2002): 95ff.; Janette Y. Taylor, "Colonizing Images and Diagnostic Labels: Oppressive Mechanisms for African American Women's Health," *Advances in Nursing Science* 21(1999): 32ff.; and Ingrid Waldron, *Jezebel Tales: Images of Black Female Sexuality and the Marginalization of Afro-American Women's Rape by Law Enforcement*, Ottawa: National Association of Women and the Law, 1998.

More than a hundred years ago, *The Woman's Bible* (Part 1 published in 1895, Part 2 in 1898) offered this comment about Jizebul:

> All we know about Jezebel is told us by a rival religionist, who hated her as the Pope of Rome hated Martin Luther.... Nevertheless, even the Jewish historian, evidently biassed against Jezebel by his theological prejudices as he is, does not give any facts whatever which warrant the assertion that Jezebel was any more satanic then the ancient Israelitish gentleman [Eliyahu], to whom her theological views were opposed ... Jezebel was a brave, fearless, generous woman, so wholly devoted to her own husband that even wrong seemed justifiable to her, if she could thereby make him happy. (In that respect she seems to have entirely fulfilled the Southern Methodist's ideal of the pattern wife absorbed in her husband.) ... It seems to me that it would puzzle a disinterested person to decide which of those savage deeds [Jizebul's or Eliyahu's murders] was more "satanic" than the other, and to imagine why Jezebel is now dragged forth to "shake her gory locks" as a frightful example to the American women who ask for recognized right to self-government. (Ellen Battelle Dietrick, "Comments on Kings," in *The Woman's Bible*, edited by Elizabeth Cady Stanton and the Revising Committee, New York: European Publishing Co., 1898, Part 2, pp. 74–75; reprinted, Seattle: Coalition on Women and Religion, 1974.)

Elizabeth Cady Stanton and her colleagues knew that interpretation of the Bible—and of "Jezebel"—had political consequences for women, and they pioneered a principle in that first wave of the women's movement that is still typical of much feminist work: a suspicion of any single viewpoint claiming total authority, so studies are often published as collections of essays, even in biblical commentaries. Today this is the case for the single-volume *The Women's Bible Commentary, with Apocrypha*, edited by Carol A. Newsom and Sharon H. Ringe (expanded ed., Louisville, Ky.: Westminster John Knox Press, 1998) and for the multi-volume Feminist Companion to the Bible (and its second series, edited by

Suggestions for Further Reading

Athalya Brenner and some with Carole Fontaine, Sheffield: Sheffield Academic Press) and The Feminist Companion to the New Testament and Early Christian Writings volumes, edited by Amy-Jill Levine, and some with Maria Mayo Robbins or Marianne Blickenstaff (New York: T & T Clark International). Jewish feminist perspectives are offered by Ellen Frankel's *The Five Books of Miriam: A Woman's Commentary on the Torah* (New York: Putnam, 1996) and Judith S. Antonelli's *In the Image of God: A Feminist Commentary on the Torah* (Northvale, N.J.: Jason Aronson, 1995).

Other biblical scholars, increasingly aware of narrative as effective teaching, have also turned their hand to first-person narrative accounts. Athalya Brenner's *I Am . . . Biblical Women Tell Their Own Stories* (Minneapolis: Fortress Press, 2004) and *First Person: Essays in Biblical Autobiography*, edited by Philip R. Davies (New York: Sheffield, 2002), are two recent examples (neither includes Jizebul, although Brenner's earlier book does: *The Israelite Woman: Social Role and Literary Type in Biblical Narrative*, Sheffield: JSOT Press, 1994 [1985]). Two other interesting publications came to my attention after my manuscript was complete: *Yours Faithfully: Virtual Letters from the Bible*, edited by Philip R. Davies (Oakville, Conn.: Equinox Pub., 2004, including one from the "Jezebel" of Rev 2:20), and *Jezebel: Portraits of a Queen* by Patricia Dutcher-Walls (Collegeville, Minn.: Liturgical Press, 2004).

The last twenty-five years has seen a tremendous increase in books and articles about biblical women, feminist biblical studies, and women's ancient history. As the heading "Works Cited" above suggests, my list of references does not include every scholarly work about Jezebel, even ones of which I am aware. One strategy for finding other materials about women is to follow the references for each biblical book in the commentaries mentioned above and also to seek out other books and articles by the authors and editors. I do not recommend using only a general Internet search such as Google. Several major indices produced by biblical scholars are available electronically through college and some public libraries, where reference librarians may give assistance. The EBSCO research database host will often have a general humanities bibliography that can be searched by author or keyword, which may include some religious studies journals. More productive are the Religion One Index (by the ATLA—American Theological Library Association), Old Testament Abstracts, and New Testament Abstracts. A keyword search of "Jezebel" in the first two yields more than fifty entries each, and a search by biblical references would produce more still. The online book catalogues of major publishers and book distributors, especially those in religious studies, usually also have listings for women and Bible, feminist scholarship, or similar categories. Having to locate and choose among the multiple references is a nice problem to have compared to the dearth of resources of thirty years ago.

Index of Biblical and Other Ancient Texts

Page numbers appearing in bold indicate the translation of the text.

Biblical Texts

Genesis
2:4b—3:24	176
2:8-10	176
3:17	174
4:11	174
6:11-12	174
9:6	174
14	169
31:53	168
37:12-36	170
38	170
42:35—43:10	170
49:8-12	206

Exodus
2	188
20	176
23:19b	181
34:26b	181

Numbers
24:16	169

Deuteronomy
14:21b	181
20:19-20	183
21:1-9	174

Joshua—2 Kings ("Deuteronomistic "history")
	2, 166, 203

Joshua
7	174

Judges
9:5	186
9:46	203
11–12	170, 184
12:1-6	170

1 Samuel
8	160
17	180
24	187
26	187

2 Samuel
1	187
1:10	189
12:8	165
16:22	165
20:23	203
21:19	180

1–2 Kings 166

Index of Biblical and Other Ancient Texts

1 Kings

1–2	168
1	165
2:26-27	168
5	204, 207
9:10-13	204
11:26-40	205
11:33	202
12–13	205
12	181
15:13	165, 202
15:20	175
15:23-24	**70**, 173
15:23	173
15:27—16:10	202
16:1-4, 7	178, 205
16:8-20	2, 208
16:8-14	203
16:8-12a	**20**, 166
16:9-11	181
16:11	166
16:15-24	207
16:15-18	**20**
16:15, 23	166
16:20-22	**21**, 208
16:23-24	**40**, 169
16:27-29	**55**
16:31-33	1, **55**
16:31	204
16:33	165, 202
17:1	171
17:3	171
18:1—19:3	**61**, 207
18	166
18:3-4	1
21	1, **74–76**, 174, 207
21:9-10	163
21:10, 13	174
22	180
22:39-40	**98**, 180
22:41-44	70
22:47-49	**103**
22:47	183
22:51	**103**, 181

2 Kings

1:1	**103**
1:2	2
1:2-18	**106–7**, 182
1:17	183, 192
3	**111–13**, 183
8:7-15	**119–20**, 204
8:25-29	**125–26**, 185
8:26	185, 188
8:27	202
8:28-29	180, 186
9	x, 1, **128–31**, 181, 185, 186, 205
9:12	207
9:22	192
9:25-26	207
10	1
10:1-14	**133–35**
10:6-9	204
10:17	**135**
10:32-33	**135**
11–12	205
11	2, 205
11:4-21	**144–45**, 189
11:4	203
11:12	189
11:14	207
12	4
12:1-8	**151**
12:1-2	208
12:17-21	**158**
12:20	190
12:21	205, 206
13:3-5	159
14:2-6a	**157–58**
14:3-4	158

Index of Biblical and Other Ancient Texts

14:4-8	175	24:26	189
14:6	158	25	158
14:7-14	158	25:5-10	158
14:8-10	191	25:5	158
14:11-14	159	25:17-19	191
15:29	175	25:20-24	159
16	179		
16:13	179	**Job**	
18:13—19:37	207	2:9	174
23:7	172	26:12	173
		37:18	173
1 Chronicles		41	173
25:1, 4-6	205		
		Psalms	6
2 Chronicles		29	**28–29**, 167–68
16:7-10	205	36	**147–48**, 190
17:1-2	85, 176–77	45	**105–6**, 181–82
17:10—18:1	**80-81**, 173	46:4	169
17:14-18	190	74:13-15	173
17:18	205	89:8-11	173
18:1-3	178	104	66–69, 172–73
19:4-11	**85–86**	104:26	173
19:9	177	133	**81, 82**, 175
21:1-6	**117**, 184		
		Proverbs	
21:2-3	177	3:19	173
21:4	183, 184	27:9	**72**, 173
21:6	188		
21:8-11	**118**, 184	**Song of Solomon**	
21:16-18	**118**, 184	8:1	**73**, 173
21:17	184		
21:19—22:1	**125**	**Isaiah**	
22:1-2	184, 188	1	xi
22:8-9	**135**	7	178
22:10-12	**139**	14:32	178
23–24	205	51:9-11	173
23:1	190		
24	4, 208	**Jeremiah**	
24:2-3, 15-21	**151–52**	2–4	xi
24:20-22	189	7	169
24:23-25	180	9:21	**133**, 187

16:1-9	180, 186
16:5	180

Ezekiel
16	xi
23	xi
31:3-9	**83–84**, 175–76
31:10-17	176

Hosea
1:4	187
2	xi
4:1-3	174, 176

Amos
6:4-7	180, 186
7:1-3	179

Micah
3:9-12	xi
3:9-10	160

Matthew
10:25	182
12:24	182

Mark
3:22	182

Luke — 166
11:5	182

Acts — 166

Revelation
2:18-23	2

Other Ancient Texts

Ashurnasirpal II
annals	50–52

Josephus
Antiquities 7.324	204
Antiquities 8.324	172

Mesha Inscription
Moabite stone	113–14, 183–84

Sargon (legend of) — 188

Shalmaneser III
annalistic report	**136–37**, 187
Balawat gate epigraph	**90**, 177
Balawat gate inscription	**90**, 177
Black Obelisk epigraph	**137**
monolith inscription	**95–96**, 178–79
throne inscription	**90**, 177
various inscriptions	**125**, 185

Tel Dan Inscription — 127–28, 185

Ugaritic Poems About Baal and Anath
I AB i	191
I AB iii	**155–56**, 191
I AB iv	**154**, 191
II AB viii	**154**, 190
V AB, B and C	**83**, 175